“You shouldn't allow [illegible] should marry.”

He drew a deep bre[illegible] time—why the hell w[illegible]

She went white. “You [illegible] nothing about what happened before!”

Jay winced.

He hated, *hated* to see her hurting. Guilt ate like hot acid at his gut. He truly deserved to writhe in hell. He couldn't keep silent...not anymore. “Georgia—”

“I don't want to talk about it—and certainly not to you. It's none of your business, Jay.”

The words were a punch in his chest.

His breath caught in his throat at the haze of hurt in her eyes. He wanted to look away before she could see into his soul and read the truth that blazed there in ten-foot-tall letters of gold fire.

If he told her the truth now, he'd drive her straight into Fordyce's arms—she was halfway there already.

Then he'd lose all chance to win her back. Forever.

* * *

A Tangled Engagement is the first book in the Takeover Tycoons series.

Dear Reader,

Did you love fairy tales growing up? Or myths and legends? I did.

I'm sure—just like me—you sometimes read several versions of a similar story told in different ways. I adore this! When I was seven or eight years old I discovered "Cap-o'-Rushes," a magical English fairy tale about a wealthy father and his three daughters... the youngest of whom taught him a lesson he would never forget.

So how could I resist dreaming up a series of tales about three sisters and their autocratic father, who is determined to marry them off to men of his choosing? He's intent on securing the legacy of the luxury fashion house he's spent his lifetime building. Of course, they respond as the modern independent women that they are...

A Tangled Engagement is Georgia's story. The eldest daughter, she's accustomed to being the organized and responsible one. Until Jay Black, the luxe brand's numbers man, threatens her position and becomes her main rival in the battle to be her father's successor.

Please sign up to my newsletter at www.tessaradley.com to find out more about how the series is developing.

I'd love you to find me on Facebook at AuthorTessaRadley or follow me on Twitter, @tessaradley. And don't forget to check out my previous Desire books at www.tessaradley.com.

Happy reading!

Tessa

TESSA RADLEY

A TANGLED ENGAGEMENT

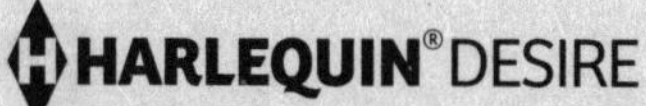

Recycling programs for this product may not exist in your area.

ISBN-13: 978-1-335-60378-4

A Tangled Engagement

This edition published by arrangement with Harlequin Books S.A.

For questions and comments about the quality of this book, please contact us at CustomerService@Harlequin.com.

Printed in U.S.A.

USA TODAY bestselling author **Tessa Radley** has always loved reading. It started with fairy tales, and it never stopped. Tessa keeps a towering TBR pile of books on her desk, another on her nightstand... there's even one on the dining table. During Tessa's writing day, Cleo-of-the-China-blue-eyes is her constant (and constantly complaining!) feline companion. Regular beach walks with her darling dog, Ruby, are a favorite form of exercise—you can catch pictures on Tessa's Twitter feed, @tessaradley. To find out more about what she's reading and writing, join Tessa's newsletter at www.tessaradley.com.

Books by Tessa Radley

Harlequin Desire

Millionaire Under the Mistletoe
Falling for His Proper Mistress
Saved by the Sheikh!
The Boss's Baby Affair
Reclaiming His Pregnant Widow
One Dance with the Sheikh
Staking His Claim

Takeover Tycoons

A Tangled Engagement

Visit her Author Profile page at Harlequin.com, or tessaradley.com, for more titles.

You can find Tessa Radley on Facebook, along with other Harlequin Desire authors, at Facebook.com/harlequindesireauthors!

For all my wonderfully wild writer friends.
You're all simply awesome!

One

Georgia Kinnear could barely contain her excitement.

Her father commanded the head of the long oval table that dominated the Kingdom International boardroom, a position that granted him an unobstructed view of all present for the Managing Committee's weekly meeting.

Norman Newman and Jimmy Browne had been her father's yes-men for almost three decades—more than Georgia's entire lifetime. Both men served as directors on the board of the luxury goods company, but gossip had it that they'd decided to retire and would not be re-appointed at the annual general meeting later today. Not that her father had breathed a word. Showing his hand had never been Kingston Kinnear's style.

If the rumors that had been swirling around Kingdom's cutting rooms and stores all week were true, the annual general meeting due to start in an hour was going to change her life forever…

It was about time!

Her father glared down at his watch. “Where’s Jay?”

Jay Black was the original corporate crusader—never late, always prepared, always dangerously well-informed. A rival to respect. Georgia was thankful that no one appeared to have noticed the tension and constant skirmishes she had with him. By unspoken agreement, they both preferred to keep it that way. Their private war. Yet, despite her wariness toward him, taking the opportunity to put the knife in behind his back didn’t feel right.

“The copier jammed—he’ll be here any moment,” she told her father, and tried not to think about how good Jay had smelled when she’d crouched beside him, trying to fix the troublesome machine. Like Central Park on a sunny spring day—all green and woody.

Her father puffed, and Georgia tensed, steeling herself for an outburst.

“That thing has been giving problems all day. I’ll get a technician to check it,” Marcia Hall said calmly, and her father stopped huffing.

“Thank you.” Georgia smiled across at her father’s PA of more than two decades. The woman was a saint. Marcia knew exactly how to placate her irascible father, a skill Georgia had never acquired—despite growing up with him and working alongside him since leaving school.

Georgia wished Jay would hurry up.

In an attempt to steady herself, she focused on the larger-than-life photos of celebrities along the wood-paneled walls. Each wore—or carried—Kingdom goods. Totes. Clutches. Coats. Scarves. Gloves. Umbrellas. And, of course, the epochal luggage Kingdom was famous for. Each image was emblazoned with the legendary advertising slogan: "My Kingdom. Anytime. Anywhere."

Her father cleared his throat, and the room fell silent. "We'll start without Jay."

Switching her attention to her father, Georgia said, "Uh, no, let's wait—"

He quelled her interruption with a sharp sideways cutting gesture of his right hand, leaned back in the padded high-backed leather chair and rested his elbows on the armrests.

Her father took his time studying his audience, and Georgia's nerves stretched tighter than a pair of too-short garters. Her left hand trembled a little, and to occupy herself, she smoothed the yellow legal pad on the table in front of her and picked up her Montblanc pen, one of her most treasured possessions.

Norman Newman, the soon-to-be-gone Chief Operating Officer, was seated on Georgia's left, sandwiched between her and her father.

Chief Operating Officer…

She savored the sound of his title. By the end of today, it would be hers.

Together with her sisters, Roberta and Charis, Georgia already sat on the Managing Committee that was responsible for the day-to-day management of the company. An appointment to the Board of Directors would launch her career into the stratosphere. And then she'd join the inner sanctum of the Financial Committee—the ultra-secret FinCo—where all Kingdom International's real decision-making happened.

It was impossible to sit still.

She couldn't wait for her and Roberta to be appointed to the board, couldn't wait to implement the ideas they'd been talking about for years. New stores. New design directions. New global markets. Ideas their father—backed up by his pair of yes-men—had resisted. But that would change now...with the end of Jimmy and Norman's reign.

Kingston would finally have to listen to his two daughters...

Surreptitiously, she stuck her hands under the edge of the table and wiped her suddenly sticky palms down her skirt.

Where *was* Jay? The fashion house's financial analyst had already been appointed to the secret FinCo by her father, which had caused Georgia many sleepless nights. It was time for him to witness her triumph.

The boardroom door opened.

At last!

Even her father turned his head to watch him enter. Tall. Perfectly proportioned and elegant in a dark business suit, Jay moved with easy grace.

Georgia flashed him a wide smile. With his arrival, her over-stretched nerves eased a little. But instead of his customary taunting grin, Jay didn't spare her a glance; his dark head remained bent, his attention fixed on the sheaf of papers in his hand.

"You all know that I am not getting any younger," her father was saying, "but I've always been determined to give Methuselah a run for his money."

A ripple of laughter echoed around the table.

What was this? Georgia went still. Did her father also plan to announce his own retirement today? It was her dream to follow in her father's footsteps, her plan to one day be President and Chief Executive Officer of Kingdom International. But she'd never expected the opportunity to come so soon.

Too soon.

Even she knew that. He couldn't retire. Not today. She'd never be appointed…

She rapidly speculated about who he'd lined up to take his place.

Jay had seated himself in the empty chair to her father's left. She shot him a questioning look across the expanse of polished cherry wood. As the luxury fashion house's financial analyst, Jay was in prime position to have the best insight into her father's convoluted thought process—something that constantly raised disquieting emotions in her.

But Jay's attention was fixed on the stack of papers he'd set down on the table in front of him. Somewhere in that pile were documents that were about to transform her life forever. Yet, suddenly Georgia couldn't stop wondering what else might be in there.

One of her father's infamous surprises?

Did Roberta know something she didn't?

Meeting Georgia's questioning gaze across the boardroom table, Roberta rolled her green eyes—glamorously defined with black-eyeliner—toward the ceiling while her perfectly manicured nails toyed with a pink cell phone. Clearly Roberta thought the comment nothing more than Kingston's idea of a joke.

"I have no plans to retire yet." Her father smiled,

and Georgia's pulse steadied a little. "The corner office is far more comfortable than any in my home. My daughters will have to someday carry me out in a box."

There was more laughter. This time, Georgia joined in, the sound high-pitched to her own ears. Of course, her father had been joking. He wouldn't give up his position so easily…

Georgia's attention switched back to Jay, but from this angle, all she could see was the top of his head.

A rapid glance along the length of the boardroom table revealed the mood amongst the other members of the Managing Committee. Since the start of the rumors, Georgia had quietly set up one-on-one meetings with each of them to smooth the coming transition. She was satisfied she had them all on her side. Yet, right now, they all appeared mesmerized by her father.

With one exception…

At the foot of the table, her youngest sister doodled in a sketchbook, locked in a secret world of Kingdom's nascent designs. Charis didn't look like she'd registered a single one of their father's jokes. No surprise there. Meetings were her idea of hell.

Georgia knew her youngest sister would not be interested in an appointment to the board…or whether their father planned to retire. As long as Charis had a pencil and paper, she was in her element.

Again, Georgia tried—in vain—to catch Jay's attention. She willed him to look up so she could figure out what was going on inside that maddening, quicksilver mind.

But he remained stubbornly hunched over the documents in front of him, his espresso-dark hair falling over his forehead.

A wild thought swept into her head.

Was it possible…?

Had her father lined *Jay* up for *her* job?

Old insecurities swamped her. But she weighed the evidence. Only minutes ago, she and Jay had been engaged in a teasing exchange by the copier. Jay had even joked about buying her a cup of coffee when she got the appointment—

No, not *when*, but *if*—

Her breath caught.

He'd definitely said *if* she got the appointment…

Had Jay been trying to warn her?

She replayed that silly exchange. Despite the teasing, he'd seemed a little terse. She'd attributed it to his battle with the monstrous machine. But had it been guilt?

He'd said there was something he had to talk to her about. He must've already known he was getting the appointment she craved.

She stared blindly at the pen between her damp fingers as her thoughts whirled chaotically. *She* was the ideal candidate to replace Norman. She knew it, and so did her father. She'd proven she could do the job over and over in the past couple of years.

The pen slipped under the pressure of her fingertips. Her father couldn't possibly have decided to give *her* job to Jay.

Could he?

The faster Jay read, the more the words on the page in front of him blurred together. He shook his head, fighting to make sense of the cumbersome legalese.

What kind of prick had drafted this nonsense?

He speared one hand into his hair to push it off his brow. It needed a cut. But he hadn't had time. The past two weeks had flashed past as he'd fought to clear his desk of never-ending fires. And he still hadn't gotten to the bottom of the quiet niggling rumors about Kingdom on Wall Street.

He suppressed a groan as his focus on the black print sharpened. Kingston Kinnear had lost his damned mind. And he couldn't have picked a worse time to go nuts.

In three days' time, Jay was going on leave—his first visit home in years. And he'd made a vow to come clean with Georgia before he left. If he weren't such a goddamned coward he would've done it a long time ago.

Today was already too late…

He hadn't expected his orderly work existence to rapidly turn to crap.

Kingston's retention of a new firm of attorneys to handle "a special project" had seemed harmless enough. If Jay hadn't been so focused on fixing every last crisis before going on leave he might have suspected something clandestine was happening. And maybe talked Kingston out of this insane course of action.

Too late now.

He shuffled the papers back together into an orderly pile, then linked his hands together on top of it as though holding them down would stop the mayhem from escaping. Then he looked up—straight into the pair of Colorado-sky blue eyes he'd been avoiding.

Georgia was smiling at him. She lifted an eyebrow in question and his gut sank into the Italian loafers he wore.

Jay looked toward the head of the table where the

cause of all the trouble sat. Kingston placed his palms on the armrests of the chair and pushed himself slowly and deliberately to his feet. It was the only chair with armrests, giving it the appearance of a throne, which, no doubt, was exactly the impression he intended to convey. Finally, he straightened the lapels of his hand-tailored suit jacket with a dramatic touch of showmanship.

The boardroom went so silent that Jay could hear the whir of the state-of-the-art air-conditioning. At last, Kingston spoke. “While public stockholders own forty-nine percent of Kingdom, I have always enjoyed the comfort of holding a majority interest and I have been considering the future of the company for a while now.”

Georgia sat straighter. Jay knew she was expecting an appointment to the board today…

On top of the tower of documents, his hands curled into fists.

A frisson of electricity zapped around the boardroom. Even Charis had stopped her frenetic sketching and was watching her father intently.

For the first time, Jay wondered whether Kingston had already secretly begun selling off his private stock—it would explain the recent, unexpected movements in the stock market.

The old bastard was stringing them all along…

Or did the youngest Kinnear daughter have any idea of what her father planned? Charis was, after all, the apple of her father’s eye. Jay still hadn’t worked out what Kingston had planned for his youngest daughter. So far, nothing in the documents he’d speed-read had dealt with her fate. But Jay had no doubt that Kingston had control of his youngest daughter’s life finely outlined. He rather suspected that this time even Charis had been kept in the dark.

The tension in the boardroom had become palpable.

Georgia chose that moment to speak. "Roberta, Charis and I have always been deeply involved in every facet of the company—we are all heavily invested in Kingdom's future."

What a miserable understatement! Kingston expected his daughters to live and breathe the company. And Georgia, even more than her sisters, had made Kingdom her life. There had been moments when her blinkered commitment to Kingdom had caused Jay to despair.

It was Charis who put what everyone was thinking into words. "The obvious thing, Daddy, would be to divide your fifty-one percent share equally among the three of us."

"That would be the obvious solution," drawled Roberta.

Jay braced himself for the firestorm to come.

Finally, Kingston spoke into the silence. "To do so would fragment the company. If I transferred seventeen percent to each of you, it would leave Kingdom extremely vulnerable to takeover."

So Kingston had heard the same rumors he'd been hearing—and hadn't mentioned a word. The first rumblings had surfaced a couple of months ago, but Jay's own investigations hadn't turned anything up. The market had settled down. Then this past week, the stocks had fluctuated, and yesterday the share price had been especially erratic.

"Not if we stood together—we'd still hold the controlling interest." Georgia's knuckles were white as she clutched the pen like a lifeline. Jay discovered that his own hands were clenched just as tightly.

"When have the three of you ever stood together?" scoffed her father.

At the other end of the table, Charis dropped her pencil, and the sound was loud in the large boardroom. "Daddy—"

"So what do you intend to do?" Roberta challenged the old tyrant, talking straight over her sister. "Give everything to Charis?"

"I have three daughters—I must take care of each," Kingston said with breathtaking sanctimony. Jay knew the wily old codger had never done anything that didn't serve Kingdom—and himself—best. "But naturally, I will reward my most loyal daughter."

"Don't you mean your favorite daughter?" The edge to Roberta's voice was diamond-hard.

Across the table, the gold pen fell from Georgia's fingers with a thud. "My loyalty to you is beyond doubt." The glitter of hurt in her eyes caused Jay to freeze. "I put in eighty-hour work weeks—heck, I don't have a life outside of these walls. I haven't had a vacation in over two years."

"That's your choice." Kingston shrugged away her plea.

Georgia's lips parted, but she must've thought better of what she'd intended to say. Eyes downcast, she picked up the pen and capped it, and then set it down on the legal pad in front of her.

"You have been unusually silent, Charis. What do

you have to say, honey?" Kingston's chilly eyes defrosted as they rested on his youngest daughter.

Charis raised her chin and faced her father down across the length of the table. "Nothing."

"Nothing?" A freeze returned to the blue eyes so disconcertingly like Georgia's in color. "You will be more enthusiastic shortly, my daughter."

Jay felt the hairs on the back of his neck prickle as, taking his time, Kingston's gaze rested on each of his three daughters in turn. "The incentive will be straightforward," he announced. "Whoever proves their loyalty to me first will receive twenty-six percent of the total Kingdom stock—over half my share—and that should be a big enough block to give real power. The other two of you will split the remaining twenty-five percent."

Murmurs broke out around the table. But the three sisters sat like stone.

Jay couldn't bring himself to confront the bruised hurt in Georgia's eyes. And he knew Kingston had barely gotten started…

Kingston should not have been permitted to torment his daughters in such a cat-and-mouse fashion. Jay forced his hands to relax, smoothing over the stack of papers that contained untold chaos.

"Before you ask, your father has devised a way for each of you to prove your loyalty." He spoke without inflection, not allowing his fury to boil over. "He has a plan."

Two

Georgia's throat closed. Murmurs of surprise swept through the boardroom and then subsided. Across the boardroom table, Jay watched her father through narrowed eyes.

"Jay is correct—but then I always have a plan." Satisfaction oozed from her father's measured tone. "That's how I grew Kingdom from the business my great-grandfather started in a back room into the billion-dollar brand it is today."

"What kind of plan?" Georgia finally found her voice.

Her father didn't even glance her way. "I'm concerned my daughters will be taken advantage of by the unscrupulous money-grubbing sharks that hunt the fashion waters. So I have prepared a shortlist of men able to protect—"

Georgia's breath caught. "A list of men?"

"Protect? Who? Us? *Why?*"

Their father ignored Georgia's and Roberta's squawks of outrage. "The first of my daughters to marry the candidate I have chosen for her will be deemed the most loyal and will be awarded the twenty-six percent holding in Kingdom."

"What?" Georgia and Roberta burst out in tandem.

He was talking as if they weren't even present.

What was going on?

Then it dawned on her. The answer must lie in the documents neatly stacked in front of Jay. He'd still barely spared her a glance.

Georgia had had enough.

Rising in her seat, she pushed aside the clutter of pad, pen, phone and empty take-out coffee cup, and reached across the width of the table. Her feet left the plush carpet and her skirt tickled the back of her thighs as it rode up against her pantyhose. No matter. Modesty was not a priority.

"Georgia!" her father thundered.

So he'd finally noticed her…

She blocked out the familiar angry voice and, with a final heave forward, snatched the block of papers in front of Jay and then slithered back into her seat clutching her prize, her heart pounding in her ears.

Commotion had broken out. But Georgia didn't allow herself to be distracted; she was too busy skimming the pages.

"What the hell is this?" Her eyes lifted to lock with Jay's in silent challenge. He flinched. So he should!

"The shares are to be transferred to me and my husband on the day of my marriage…?"

"Marriage?" Roberta was beside her. "Let me see that! I didn't even know you were dating, you secret sister."

Not for the first time, Georgia wished she shared her sister's irreverent sense of humor. "I'm not dating anyone—and I have no intention of getting married." Ever. Georgia's knuckles clenched white around the pages. Not after Ridley. As always, she expertly blocked what she remembered of that disaster out of her consciousness while she did a rapid scan of the thunderstruck faces around the table. Jay's expression was flat, closed off in a way she'd never seen.

Then she appealed for a return to normality. "Jay, what on earth is going on?"

Before Jay could respond, Kingston said loudly, "Georgia, I have chosen a man for you who will do a fine job running the company when I retire."

Panic filled her. "But—"

He held up a hand. "I'm familiar with your dream, and the man I have chosen will match you perfectly."

As Georgia shook her head to clear the confusion, Roberta spoke softly into her ear. "He's about to graft his own vision onto your dream, and then he'll sell it back to you."

"What do you mean?" Georgia whispered.

"Just watch and listen, sister. The master is at work." Roberta sounded more cynical than usual. "Let me see those documents."

Georgia eased her death grip on the papers.

"He will mentor you," her father was saying. "Teach you what it takes."

"You think I need a mentor?" Georgia said faintly. "After all these years? I know the business backward. I know the products, and more importantly, I know the people. I'll head up Kingdom when you step down one day—it's my birthright. And that journey starts today—with the announcement of my appointment to the board."

But her father was shaking his head. "You may be my daughter, but you're not getting a free ride."

A free ride? How could he even think that? But she'd already read the answer in his eyes. He was going to make her jump through hoops—because he didn't believe she could do it. It wasn't just that she was a woman, that she wasn't the first-born son he'd wanted. He would never believe she wouldn't let him down again…

She'd hoped he'd forgotten. Shame suffused her. She should've known… Unlike her, he never forgot a thing!

Nor did he ever forgive.

He blamed her for both the humiliating breakup with Ridley, of which she remembered enough patchy detail to make her swear off dating for life…*and* the horrific car crash that had followed, of which she remembered nothing at all.

"Oh, my God! It even says who you're going to be marrying…" Roberta's voice broke into Georgia's desperate thoughts.

"What?" Her head whipped around.

"Look!" Roberta shoved the papers back at Georgia. "You're going to marry Adam Fordyce."

"Adam Fordyce?" Charis echoed from across the room. "You can't marry Adam Fordyce!"

"That's what it says here, in black-and-white." Roberta's perfectly manicured red nails jabbed at the paper. "That's who Kingston has picked out as your marriage mentor—or perhaps I should say merger mentor? Because that's what this is starting to sound like. I didn't even know you knew him."

This was crazy…

The splintering light from the giant chandelier overhead was suddenly too bright. Georgia touched her fingertips to her temples. Had she gone crazy, too?

A swift glance around the boardroom table revealed that only Jay hadn't reacted. He sat silent and watchful, the familiar gleam of laughter absent from his eyes.

It struck Georgia with the force of a lightning bolt.

He'd known of her father's plan all along…

The betrayal stung. She and Jay clashed often. He infuriated her. He taunted her. The close working relationship he shared with her father concerned her. But despite the rivalry and never-ending mockery, he'd always been honest with her—sometimes brutally so.

Jay had known…and he hadn't mentioned a word about it.

Georgia sucked in a deep breath. She'd deal with Jay—and the unexpected ache of his treachery—later. For now, she had to derail her father's plan. "Of course, I can't marry Adam Fordyce. I don't know him from Santa Claus."

"Unfortunately, he doesn't reside at the North Pole. He lives in Manhattan and he heads up Prometheus," murmured Roberta. "*Forbes* named him one of the top ten—"

"Oh, I know all that! But I've never met the man."

"And trust me—" Roberta was shaking her head "—Adam Fordyce is nothing like Santa Claus. He's the coldest-hearted bastard you'll never want to know."

Charis banged her sketchbook on the table. "That's not true."

Georgia suppressed the urge to scream. "I'm not marrying anyone, and when I do get married, you won't learn about it from a bunch of documents I had no part in drawing up." She shot a killing glare across the table at Jay. "Now, Kingston, why don't you take a few minutes to tell us all what you've been cooking up?"

Her father didn't hesitate. "Adam and I agree it's—"

"'Adam and I agree'?" Georgia repeated, staring at him in horrified dismay. "You've actually discussed this with Adam Fordyce?"

"Oh, yes, we've come to an understanding."

Of course, he had. Otherwise, it wouldn't already be reduced to black-and-white on paper. Jay had known all about it. Adam knew about it. Norman and Jimmy were probably in on it, too. Half the world had known what her father planned for her future…but no one had bothered to fill her in.

Hurt erupted into a blaze of fury she could no longer suppress; it flamed outward, until her skin prickled all over with white-hot heat.

She couldn't bring herself to look at Jay. So she focused her anger on the one man who she'd worked to impress her whole life. Her father.

"How could you have arranged all this behind my back?"

"Easily!" Kingston's gaze sliced into the heat of her anger like an arctic blast. "You will marry Adam Fordyce."

But, for once, he didn't freeze her into silence. Georgia had had enough. "I told you—I haven't met this man, much less even been on a date with him."

"I've already fixed that." Kingston smirked with satisfaction. "Fordyce will escort you to the Bachelors for a Better Future Benefit on Friday night."

"You're joking!"

"I never joke about business. I've arranged the most important alliance you will ever be part of, Georgia."

He sounded so proud…so confident that she would go along with it.

Why should she be surprised? He'd pulled this kind of stunt before. Except that time, she'd fallen head-over-heels into his manipulative scheme.

Never again.

Even as Georgia reeled from emotions she couldn't find words to express, her youngest sister waded into the fray. "When did you and Adam get so cozy, Dad?"

Georgia finally found her voice. "Let me handle this, Charis. I'm the one he's trying to marry off."

"Not only you." Kingston gave Charis a fond smile. "I've found suitable husbands for all three of you."

A stunned hush followed his pronouncement.

"That's preposterous!" Charis was on her feet.

Her father's face softened. "Charis, the man I've chosen for you is the man I've come to regard as a son over the past two years."

Shock filled Georgia and her attention snapped back to Jay. "You...*you* are going to marry Charis?"

Jay's face was frozen.

Jay and...Charis?

Her sometimes ally, full-time rival...was marrying her sister?

Georgia's stomach churned.

Since Jay had come to work at Kingdom, they'd sparred and argued—or at least she'd argued, while more often than not, he'd simply needled her, provoked her...then laughed at her irritation. He'd unerringly turn up at her office with the take-out coffees she craved, arriving just in time for her to bounce strategies off him. He might excel at pushing her buttons, but Jay was insightful and very, very clever, and all too often his opinions were right on the mark. Despite her distrust, she'd come to rely on his cool level-headedness.

And he'd betrayed her.

Stupid!

She should've known better than to trust one of her father's sidekicks. At least this time, she wasn't infatuated with Jay—or engaged to marry him. Like with Ridley.

Everyone was talking at once. Roberta had drawn herself up to her full height. She looked like some lush goddess. "There's only one thing I want to know. To whom have you dared to barter me?"

But Kingston didn't spare her or Georgia a glance.

Charis's face was pale. She was saying something, but Georgia couldn't concentrate. The sound of her heart pounded fast and furious in her ears and she felt completely incapable of the clear, analytic thought that usually came easily.

All she could think about was that today was supposed to be the best day of her life.

"Father—" Her voice sounded high and thin. Alien. Like someone else's.

She hardly ever called him *Father*—and certainly never at work. It never helped to become emotional. Kingston detested tears, and she'd displayed enough weakness two years ago to last a lifetime.

And her father still held that against her.

She concentrated on the celebrity photos on the wall. Charis had designed most of those carefully crafted products. Roberta had dreamed up the advertising campaigns. And she herself knew the production process from start to finish—how to make sure they made millions from every product launch.

Did her father not understand how indispensable she was to the Kingdom brand? Did he never wonder why he and Norm could find time to play golf so often?

The only way to appeal to his sense of logic was to find a strategic or monetary angle that would make him pay attention.

She drew a breath. "Kingston—"

That sounded better. Stronger. But he didn't even turn his head; all his attention was focused on Charis.

"So, let me get this totally clear. Adam Fordyce is going along with this?" Charis demanded.

As Jay had already gone along with it…

"Oh, yes." Her father actually smiled. "Fordyce is a powerful man and he needs the right kind of wife. And Georgia will be perfect."

Georgia couldn't believe what she was hearing. That's what her father thought of all the years…her whole life…that she'd put into Kingdom? It qualified her to be…what?

The perfect wife?

It was the kind of label Jay, at his most provocative, might have used to needle her…but, tragically, her father was serious.

"And what if we're not prepared to go along with this…madness?" Charis picked up her sketchpad and held it like a shield against her chest.

"If any of you refuses to put Kingdom first—and fails to show loyalty to me—you'll forfeit the right to stock in Kingdom and immediately have to clear out your desk and be escorted off the premises by security." Kingston's eyes were colder than the ice that covered the Hudson River in mid-winter. "You will no longer be welcome in my business, in my home…or in my life. You will cease to exist."

The air whooshed out of Georgia's lungs, as terror blinded her.

"I'm not going to be a part of this insane scheme, Father." Charis's eyes burned great dark holes in her pale face.

Georgia was startled by the sudden urge to give her sister a hug. Neither of them had ever been the touchy-feely type.

"You can split your stocks between Roberta and Georgia however you choose." Charis stormed past them to the door. "Because…I quit."

Georgia was aware of a ghastly hollow feeling of rejection in the pit of her stomach.

Nothing would ever be enough to make her father proud of her.

Even if she hadn't lost her mind, along with a chunk of her memory, on that disastrous night a little over two years ago when she'd discovered Ridley in bed with another woman.

Even if she'd been perfect.

Unable to help herself, she blurted out, "You don't believe I can run and manage the Kingdom brand, do you, Kingston?"

Roberta leaned forward to murmur, "He doesn't think any woman can run his precious Kingdom!"

But Georgia couldn't summon up a smile. There was only a deep, aching hurt—and endless bewilderment.

What about Jay's role in this? They spent all their working hours arguing, negotiating, talking about every single facet of Kingdom's business, but he hadn't been watching her back. He'd been in on her father's plan… and he hadn't tipped her off.

How could she have allowed him to render her so vulnerable? She'd grown lax and complacent. She hadn't even seen this ambush coming.

"What does Kingston think we've been doing all these years?" she said softly, for her sister's ears alone.

Roberta shrugged. "Who knows? He's always thought women are nothing but pretty decorations."

"That's not true!"

Roberta gave her a long look, and then shrugged again. "At least I had a break from working with him every day while I was in Europe. But you and Charis…" She flipped back her strawberry-red hair with her hand. "I don't know why the hell I ever came back to New York."

Georgia's gaze flickered to her father. But he wasn't paying them any attention. Already on his feet, his face scarlet, he headed toward the exit, chasing after their younger sister with Marcia tottering in his wake.

"Charis!" he bellowed through the open set of double doors. "Get Charis, Marcia. Fetch her back!"

Her father's PA scuttled to do his bidding, and he swung around. Georgia fell back at the ugly fury on his face. "After everything I've done for her!"

It hurt to acknowledge that Charis had always been her father's favorite…

A strange croak sounded.

Georgia stared at her father. Where his face had been red moments before, now it had turned ashen. He clutched at his chest.

Her breath caught. "Father…?"

As she watched, his knees crumpled.

"Jay, help him!" Georgia shoved back her seat and rushed around the table.

Jay got there first, grasping Kingston beneath his shoulders as he sank to his knees on the carpet.

"The resolutions…" her father gasped.

"Stop worrying about the company," Georgia said.

"Who's going to look after Kingdom if—"

"Don't. Don't say it." Fear caused her voice to crack. "Don't even think it."

Kingston Kinnear was immortal—a living legend. He couldn't die.

Her father was struggling to say something.

"Please. Don't talk."

"I'm not going to die." A groan. "I'm more worried about…a takeover."

Georgia bit back her response. She should've guessed he considered himself immortal. "There'll be no takeover. We'll take care of—"

His next moan struck terror into her heart.

"Oh, no!" She dropped down next to him, panic making her breathless. His pasty skin had broken into a sweat.

Then Roberta was beside her.

Their father lay on the carpet. Jay had helped him onto his side and was pushing his jacket open, ripping his tie undone.

"Oh, God, he's having a heart attack!"

Roberta's gasp rooted Georgia to the ground. Her brain stopped working. All she could think was that she hadn't done the first aid course she'd sent the rest of the administrative staff on—because she hadn't had time. She should've done it…then she'd have known what to do—instead of kneeling on the sidelines like some kind of lost soul.

"Roberta, can you get his cuff buttons undone and check his pulse?" Jay instructed her sister.

Jay looked as coolly competent as ever—which only made Georgia feel more inadequate. She was falling apart at the seams, and he was as steady as a rock.

She looked around wildly. "Can anyone help with CPR?"

"He doesn't need it yet—he's breathing." Jay's fingers had moved from her father's wrist to hover over his mouth.

“Oh.” She hadn’t even known that. Her sense of helplessness increased.

“Call an ambulance,” Jay instructed, his hand still over her father’s mouth.

Frozen, she couldn’t take her eyes off Jay’s fingers. Was he *still* breathing? Georgia didn’t dare ask.

“Call now,” Jay ordered.

Adrenaline surged through her. She shot to her feet and hurried over to where her cell phone still lay on the boardroom table beside the Montblanc pen her father had given her for her twenty-first birthday.

Daddy.

It was a silent scream. The shaking was worse than before, and her fingers fumbled as she attempted to grasp the phone. He hadn’t been *Daddy* for decades. *Kingston* at work—which was most of the time. Occasionally *Father.* But never *Daddy.*

The glass face of her phone swam before her. She was crying. Dammit! A tear dripped onto the screen. Her hands were shaking so badly she could barely punch the emergency dial button.

She couldn’t fall apart. Not now.

Not when Kingston—the only real parent she’d ever known—was about to die.

Three

Jay paused in the hospital lobby as he spied Georgia's unmistakable silver-blond hair. She was tucked up in the farthest corner of a space that doubled as a coffee shop and gift shop.

If he hadn't been so concerned about her, he might have chuckled. He'd known he would find Georgia in the coffee shop, driven by her craving for the mule-kick of caffeine. *Black gold,* she called it.

He took his time studying her. She'd pulled a short black blazer over that sexy saint-and-sinner vintage YSL blouse. The stark color made her hair look like sunlit-silver in contrast. A coffee mug sat less than three inches away from her right hand. It appeared empty. In front of her, her laptop stood open, and she was hunched down behind the dull silver lid.

Working…even in this time of crisis.

Then his gaze took in her motionless fingers against the keyboard.

No. Georgia wasn't working.

She was hiding, Jay realized. Using her computer to block out the world.

Pity filled him.

She hadn't spotted him yet, so he detoured to the counter laden with bunches of flowers to order a couple of double-espresso shots. He suspected it was going to be a long night.

She looked up as he wound his way through occupied tables, her normally clear sky blue eyes clouded by worry.

The unexpected air of fragility that clung to her tugged at Jay's heart. "May I join you?"

A range of complex emotions flickered in her eyes, including the animosity that often sparkled there. "Would it make any difference if I said no?"

Their intermittent sparring had been going on since the day she'd returned from sick leave after her car accident to find him ensconced in the office beside hers—the office that had belonged to Good-riddance Ridley. His predecessor had done him no favors. It had taken Jay less than a day to realize that she considered him the latest in a series of yes-men hired by her father to usurp the place she one day expected to accede to. A competitor. A threat. He should've handed in his notice and quit then and there, and let her legendary father hire someone else to drive her crazy.

But he'd never been a quitter.

"Tell me to leave, if you'd rather be alone."

She hesitated, and then let out a sigh. “Actually, I’m not sure that I want to be alone.” Georgia shut the lid of her laptop and slid it into the black patent leather Kingdom tote perched on the seat beside her. “Roberta’s taken Marcia home. And I haven’t been able to reach Charis to let her know Kingston…um, father…has had a heart attack.”

“We don’t know for certain that it was a heart attack.” Jay pulled out a chair, sat down and placed the two cups on the table between them, while he searched frantically for appropriate words of comfort. “The EKG looked good. And the first round of blood tests indicated that his enzyme levels were normal—let’s wait for the next set of tests before we jump to conclusions.”

“There’s definitely something wrong.” Her expression was bleak. “He collapsed.”

Jay wanted to let her drop her head against his shoulder and pull her close into his embrace, until her face hid in the junction between his collar and his ear. There, he knew, she would find sanctuary. She would tremble, and the tears would come…as they had once before… and no one would ever know of her pain.

Except for him.

He’d held her during a night she’d never remembered, during a night he’d never told anyone else about—not even Georgia. On Jay’s first day at Kingdom International, he’d promised himself he would never touch her…not until she remembered that night. But she never had. Jay had known he had to tell her about that night, but it had gotten harder to come clean with each passing day he spent working with her.

There was a permanent entry in his monthly task

list: *Buy Coffee & Tell Georgia the Truth Today*. Yet, every month he moved that sole uncompleted task forward to the next month. He just couldn't bring himself to do it. Because he was a coward. So this last month, he'd added a second drawn-in-sand deadline to the daily deadline he'd avoided for too long: to tell her the truth before he went on leave. And now that deadline was almost upon him.

But how the hell was he supposed to burden her with the truth now? With her father's life still in danger?

Maybe tomorrow...*if* Kingston's prognosis was good.

Finally, he said, "He's going to be okay."

She glanced around and, apparently reassured that no one at the nearby tables could overhear, she responded, "We don't know that."

Jay nodded, acknowledging the emptiness of his clumsy platitude. "We'll have a better idea once the chest X-rays are done."

She let out a breathy sigh, despair darkening her eyes. She reached for the nearest cup and took a long sip of the richly aromatic liquid before setting it down. "Back in the boardroom, I thought he was dying."

He could tell that soft heartfelt admission to him had cost her.

"Your father is as tough as boot leather."

Jay couldn't bear to see her like this...hurting. She always took care to appear capable and in control. "He's a fighter. He's not going anywhere—and especially not until the annual general meeting has been held."

Georgia choked. "I hadn't even thought about that. When will—"

"Don't worry. Your father has." Back at the office,

as the gurney had been wheeled past, Kingston had reached out from under his blanket to grab Jay by the jacket. “I’ve been tasked with making sure Jimmy and Norman are back at work tomorrow.”

The smile he’d half hoped for didn’t appear.

“Roberta and I—”

Jay halted her with the shake of his head.

“You’re both under enough strain at this time.” He thought better of telling Georgia to let up on being the control freak for once in her life. The mocking humor he normally employed to make her examine her decisions—and make sure he kept his distance—would be out of line. “Take whatever help you can get.”

Her chin lifted, and she pushed back a silver strand of hair. “Kingston wouldn’t.”

“You’re not your father.”

Georgia gave him a narrow-eyed look. She prided herself on being a chip off the old block. It made Jay want to shake her. She was worth ten of the icy man who rarely noticed her—and who certainly never listened to her. She could be so goddamned blind!

Her father could learn a thing or two from her.

“I keep getting nightmarish flashes of what happened. He was ranting one moment, furious as only he can get. The next, he was on his knees. I’ve never felt so helpless.” Georgia dropped her face into her hands. “I can’t imagine going to work at Kingdom without him there.”

Again, Jay ached to put his arms around her, draw her close. But he knew she’d hate that he’d seen her so vulnerable. So, he did what he knew worked best: he leaned back…and waited.

At last, her hands fell away from her face, and she straightened. Jay could see her silently lambasting herself for showing any weakness.

"Jay, what if he needs surgery?" The words came out in a rush.

"Whatever he needs, he's in the right place to get it." He forced a grin. "His recovery is going to be hell. He's going to be a first-class pain-in-the-ass patient."

"Oh, God." Georgia looked appalled. "You're no help."

"I'm a great help—you couldn't do without me." He winked at her.

That look of haunting helplessness faded to be replaced with a glint of irritation.

Much better. He could tolerate blue sparks of annoyance…anything was better than that desolate little-girl-lost look.

"If you wanted to help, you'd offer to take care of him yourself." She took another gulp of coffee.

"No, thanks. Kingdom couldn't afford the danger pay I'd demand."

She choked.

"But you could hire someone else to do it," he suggested.

She set the cup down. "Then they'd need danger pay!" A flush of shame slid across her face, dousing the spark of amusement that had lit her eyes for an instant. "I shouldn't be joking. Surgery always carries risks. What if…" Her voice trailed away.

Jay instantly stopped grinning. "We don't even know that he's going to need surgery. They're still running tests."

"I know. I know. I shouldn't be jumping ahead. But it's awful being so powerless. All that chaos and then… nothing. I detest this waiting."

Georgia was used to dealing with crises on a daily basis—and solving them. Sitting around like this would be driving her nuts.

"I know this is hard for you," he said softly.

Her eyes flooded with emotion. Jay glimpsed fury… and fear. For a brief moment, her bottom lip quivered. Then she squared her shoulders.

"I've just remembered." Her tone was brisk, the chink of vulnerability vanquished. "You wanted to meet after the annual general meeting. We could do that now. What did you want to discuss?"

He'd planned to tell her about the night that they'd first met.

Placing one hand on top of hers, Jay discovered her silken smooth skin was unexpectedly cold to his touch. Was she in shock?

"Georgia, it can wait." No way was he about to dump that on her now.

Beneath his hand, her knuckles grew rigid. "But—"

He laced his fingers through hers, and cupped his free hand over the top of their intertwined fingers. He'd just broken his promise to himself not to touch her. There was a tightness in his chest.

He gave her fingers a gentle squeeze. "Everything can wait until we have more definitive word on your father's condition."

"You're right." Her hand convulsed under his. "You've been a rock, Jay. Thank you for coming—for asking the doctors all the questions Roberta and I were too scared to voice. And thanks for the coffee."

Her eyes, naked and exposed, sought his; Jay felt the jolt of impact right to his toes. Her thanks made him feel like the worst kind of fraud. But he couldn't bring himself to lighten the mood, to joke about watering down her coffee. He was too hyper-aware of her hand cradled within his larger hand, of the silkiness of her skin, of her unexpected vulnerability—and the shame of his own deceit.

On a soft exhalation of breath, she said, "Most of all, thank you—thank you!—for saving my father's life. I can never repay that."

He didn't want her gratitude. He was a jerk. An utter jerk.

He looked at their hands, linked together. He should never have touched her. Not until she had all the facts. God! What would happen then? After that, who knew if she'd ever let him this close again?

And who would blame her?

Shutting that miserable thought out of his mind, Jay did what he always did—sought escape from a wretched situation in humor.

"I never thought I'd be using Kingston as a dummy model for my first aid refresher course." He cocked an eyebrow at her. "Another coffee?" But he didn't really want to get up, because then he'd have to let go of her hand.

Beep. Shaking her hand free of his, Georgia leaped for her phone, her eyes frantically scanning the text message. When she looked up, the wild panic had returned to her eyes. "He's back from X-rays. I have to go."

That too-brief moment of shared—Jay didn't know what to call it—intimacy? Hell on earth?—was over.

He pushed his unfinished coffee aside. "I'll come with you."

The following morning, Georgia discovered that Jay had already beaten her back to the hospital coffee shop. Wary, she idled at the entrance, wrinkling her nose at the sharp tang of antiseptic that she encountered everywhere in the hospital, even here.

Toughen up!

Georgia took a breath and approached Jay's table.

Yesterday, he'd betrayed her. *So what!* It wasn't the first time she'd been betrayed; it wouldn't be the last. Today, after seeing the cardiologist, they had business to take care of. Her father would expect nothing less. She was strong. Pure steel. That's how he had forged her.

"I knew you'd turn up here sometime."

Jay gave her an easy smile as he rocked back in the chair and folded his arms behind his head. His light blue business shirt pulled tight across his chest, revealing ridges of muscle Georgia had no business noticing.

"Is your father out yet?" he asked.

She unglued her gaze from his chest and shook her head.

In the bright light of morning, fear still tasted bitter at the back of her throat. The second round of blood tests had been reassuring. It hadn't been a heart attack. Though further tests were being performed right now as a precaution.

"Has Charis been in touch?"

She shook her head again, her stomach winding

tighter than a spring. She'd left messages everywhere for her sister. On her cell phone. Her home phone. Her social media pages. At the beach house in the Hamptons. Nothing. And when she'd called Lissa—Charis's best friend—she'd learned Lissa hadn't heard much from Charis lately. Her sister had been too busy with preparing Kingdom's next collection.

All the pressure was getting to Georgia. Normally, she thrived under pressure. The challenge. The cut and thrust of deals and deadlines. But it was nothing like this gut-wrenching emotional tumult she was contending with now.

"She'll come," Jay said.

"I don't know. When she quit, it sounded pretty final to me." Then she realized Jay wasn't talking about Charis coming back to work at Kingdom, but about visiting their father. Perhaps he already knew her sister better than she did. He was going to marry her after all. That caused a maddening twinge in her chest, and made her to snap, "I hope she calls soon—we need her to finalize the spring collection." And Kingston must be missing her…

What if Charis never got the chance to say goodbye?

God. Her father had been so pale…

Georgia had been so angry with him…at his arrogant assumption that he could run her life…force her to marry a man of his choosing. And then he'd collapsed, and her world had fallen apart.

Distractedly, Georgia combed the fingers of her left hand through her hair, and the tiny diamonds on her Cartier watch glittered like dewdrops caught in the sun's first rays. Kingston had recently been talking about getting into watches. She and Roberta had argued against it…

How she wished she could have that time over. She would have been more cooperative.

She looked up to catch Jay studying her. His hazel eyes had taken on the watchful green glint that always meant his brain was working at full tilt. And this time, she was the focus.

"What?" she demanded, instantly on the defensive. She'd never liked feeling like a bug under a microscope. Any way, she wasn't the traitor here.

"Let me get you a coffee."

"Because coffee solves everything?" Despite the under-eye concealer she'd applied, she suspected last night's lack of sleep showed. "Sit—you already have one." She extracted her wallet from her Kingdom Traveler tote and headed for the counter.

She felt antsy this morning, hot and bothered as though her clothes were too tight. They weren't.

Less than two hours ago, she'd finally gone home for a change of clothes. For once, she'd given no thought to what she'd flung on. Clad in the boyfriend blazer she'd worn yesterday, a pair of black wool trousers bought in Paris and her favorite black suede boots, she might appear dismally funereal, but there was nothing wrong with her clothes.

The problem lay with her.

She could feel Jay's eyes boring into her as she waited in line. It made her uncomfortable. Despite his concern, she didn't trust his motives for one moment.

Deep down—or maybe not so deep down—she was mad at him.

Murderously mad.

She accepted that much of Jay's work was highly confidential—he was the in-house finance guru after all—but yesterday it had been her personal life…her future…that he'd colluded with her father about. Maneuvering so that he could marry Charis—to secure himself a major chunk of Kingdom stock. And under the weight of the eternal debt she owed Jay, she was hurt and disappointed and very, very angry with him—the cocktail of emotions was confusing and exhausting. How was she supposed to pretend nothing had happened? Business as usual? Pah! She didn't know how she and Jay were going to be able to work together.

Even though he'd saved her father's life, she was far from ready to forgive him.

It was an impossible situation.

Once back at the table, Georgia set the mug of coffee down and bent forward to slide her wallet into her patent leather tote. Kingdom, of course, but last season's stock, Jay noted as he rocked back in his chair.

Sitting down, she said, "You and I need to talk."

There was a cool edge to her voice and her eyes had an uncanny resemblance to her father's. Yet, something more human, something close to reproach lurked in the blue depths.

Jay winced.

How had she found out? His chest contracted. He was never going to be ready for this confrontation—that's why he'd kept putting it off.

Coward.

"Okay, give it to me with both barrels." He braced himself.

"Your involvement in my father's scheme—" Her voice broke.

For a moment, he failed to absorb the meaning of her words. Then the blood rushed out of his head. She didn't know! He'd been granted a reprieve.

"You should've warned me!"

"Wait—" he demanded.

She warded him off with both hands. "Don't, Jay. No excuses."

He leaned back in the chair, light-headed, his heart jolting inside his chest. "I never make excuses."

No, he only lied to her every damned day.

"I expected better of you, Jay." Her lashes fluttered down, veiling the flash of whatever emotion—anger? Frustration? Both?—that had flickered within, and her silver hair fell forward to hide her face. But Jay was too desperate to allow her to shut him out.

"Georgia!"

She lifted her head and swung her hair back. "What?"

To his horror, Jay saw that her eyes glistened. *Tears*. That was why she'd looked away. Georgia hadn't wanted him to see how much she was hurting.

"I thought—" She broke off.

The bewilderment that clouded those beautiful eyes almost ripped his heart out. He suppressed the urge to reach for her hand. To touch her. To offer the comfort she didn't want from him.

"Look at me," he demanded.

The look she turned on him was scorching; the tears

had been seared away. Jay infinitely preferred her anger to her tears.

Then with a jerky movement, Georgia lifted the mug and took a hasty sip, sputtered and started to cough. Black liquid splashed everywhere as the mug tilted precariously. He reached out and steadied the cup.

When he looked up, Georgia's eyes were streaming.

She glanced around frantically. "Oh, damn!"

Jay pulled a white linen handkerchief out of his pocket. "Here, take this."

"It will stain."

"It doesn't matter."

"Thank you." She took it, her hand brushing his for an instant. She appeared oblivious to his sudden stillness. She wiped her eyes. Quickly. Surreptitiously. As though she feared people might see her crying. When all trace of tears had been wiped away, she turned her attention to the table and dabbed furiously at the spreading pool of spilled coffee.

Head bent, she murmured, "Damn you! I thought there was some degree of respect between us."

The words ripped into his heart. He deserved them—but not for this.

"I didn't expect you to stoop to conspiring with my father to marry me off to Adam Fordyce. Under our rivalry, I thought—"

Jay didn't want to hear more.

He couldn't claim their competition was all in her mind. Hell, he'd provoked her often enough. It had offered great camouflage for his real feelings after all. But he'd *never* colluded against her.

He scooted the chair closer, leaned forward and lowered his voice. “Here’s the truth. I couldn’t have warned you about his plan involving Fordyce—because I didn’t know anything about it myself.”

She stopped blotting the tabletop and looked up. He’d never seen her eyes so endlessly blue.

“That’s not possible. How could you not have known? He gets you to vet everything that might come back to bite him—”

“—in the ass,” Jay finished for her.

Her mascara was smudged, and there was a spark of disbelief in her eyes. His heart clenched. She’d never looked more fragile. Or madder at him.

“I’m not lying to you. The first inkling I had was when I started reading those damned documents after they jammed the copier. I didn’t get to see what your father was up to until the Managing Committee meeting was about to start.” Jay paused. It was crucial that she believed him. “Your father outsourced his ‘special project’ to an external law firm he hired because he knew I wouldn’t have the time. Because I’ve spent the past week clearing my desk.” And fighting to gather the courage to confess his labyrinth of lies to Georgia. “I’m going on leave, remember?”

“Oh, God. After everything that happened yesterday…” She sighed. “I forgot about that.”

Jay could see the wheels spinning in her brain.

“Trust me, had I known about his plan, I would’ve told your father it was a dumb-ass idea.”

She made a choking sound. It was less than a laugh, but the tightness around her eyes eased a little.

“I’d have liked to have been a fly on the wall for that

conversation," she said. "Or maybe not. He hates being challenged. You'd probably have been out of a job."

Not likely. But Jay didn't argue the point. He was too relieved that she was still talking to him. It felt like the sun and the stars had come out...at the same time.

But the spell of brightness would be all too brief. Once he told her—

"Although when you marry Charis, your job will be secure."

His teeth snapped shut so hard at her words that his jaw hurt. "I'm not going to marry your sister."

Georgia took her time examining his every feature. Finally, she appeared satisfied. "And Kingston knows that?"

"We've never discussed it."

Now he wasn't being entirely truthful, though there had never been an explicit conversation. For months, the old codger had implied that Jay's advancement within Kingdom might be fast-tracked if he obeyed certain instructions. And for months, Jay had stubbornly ignored the not-so-subtle nudges to date his boss's youngest daughter. His long-term interest did not lie with the Kingdom, but with something—or rather, someone—else.

Clearly, he should've taken Kingston's ham-handed attempts at matchmaking more seriously—or at least found a way to mention them to Georgia over one of the pitiful cups of take-out coffee he brought her most days—but he'd had no desire to bad-mouth the most important man in Georgia's life. Besides, he'd already stumbled so far down the unholy path of silence that it had become a habit to say nothing at all.

So, here he was—once again—trapped in the quagmire of his own silent stupidity.

"Well, I'm glad to hear that you didn't know."

Like magic the shadow that had hung over him evaporated. "You believe me?"

"Why on earth wouldn't I?" She studied him as though she were trying to read his mind. "You have plenty of faults, but dishonesty has never been one of them."

Jay shut his eyes. All at once, the shadows closed back in, darker than ever. There were so many things he needed to confess. But Georgia was hardly in the right frame of mind to learn about his deception. She had enough on her plate. He'd had the best of intentions to tell her the truth. How he'd met her at a fashion trade show. How he'd comforted her after her fiancé's devastating betrayal, before the crash that took away her memory of their time together. But despite his monthly task list, his daily coffee deliveries, he'd allowed the days of silence to stretch into weeks, the weeks into months, the months into years.

Two damned years.

Too many years to have any excuse. It was unforgivable.

"Look at me, Jay!"

Weary and defeated, he opened his eyes.

"Although there are times I wish you were a little less...blunt," Georgia said as she crumpled his coffee-stained handkerchief in the palm of her hand. She reached for her tote and dropped it inside. "I'll get this laundered for you."

"Don't worry about it." He shrugged. "I've got plenty more."

"It'll come clean."

She'd set her jaw in that stubborn way he'd grown to know far too well.

"And if it doesn't, then I'll buy you another." She swung back to face him, suddenly animated. "Hey, you know what? We don't do handkerchiefs. We do scarves. But no handkerchiefs—not in any of our collections. But we should. And not small dainty female handkerchiefs, but larger man-size ones." Her eyes had taken on fire in the way that they did when she was totally consumed by work.

Always Kingdom.

My Kingdom. Anytime. Anywhere.

Jay suppressed a sigh of frustration as the marketing refrain echoed in his head. It all came back to Kingdom. Every time. Yet, yesterday everything had changed. The foundations of her world had been reconstructed, but Georgia didn't appear to have noticed.

Maybe she never would…

"They'd be white—or maybe not quite white. Ivory. And made from the finest cotton." She paused. "Or perhaps linen, a fine light-as-a-feather linen that both women and men would appreciate. I like that! What do you think, Jay?" Then without giving him a chance to retort that he didn't give a rat's ass about handkerchiefs, Georgia added in a rush, "Perhaps with the Kingdom crown motif printed in white. I like it! I'll speak to Charis. Let's see what she thinks."

Then the light went out in her eyes.

"If she ever comes back to Kingdom."

"Georgia—"

She rose in a hurry. "I hate hospitals. This waiting…this sterilized place…is killing me. I'm going to go check if there's any news."

Jay's heart ached for her. What was really killing her was her corrosive fear that the manipulative son of a bitch who was her father might actually die.

Four

Georgia hurried along the hospital corridor and stopped abruptly in a doorway.

Kingston was already back in his private ward. The luxurious suite belonged in a five-star hotel, not a hospital, with its super-sized television, dining table and chairs, not to mention a seating area complete with a pair of leather couches and a coffee table buckling under the weight of floral bouquets. Propped up on a mountain of snowy white pillows, her father was arguing with a nurse, as was to be expected.

"Give me that!" He struggled to sit up.

The nurse ignored the rude demand and calmly pointed the remote she held at the window. "Mr. Kinnear, you won't be comfortable staring into the glare all day," she said in a bright cheerful tone, even as the state-of-the-art blinds whirred shut.

"I want that blind open!"

Georgia rapidly discovered the reason for her father's disgust: he'd been refused discharge. It only took her a moment to get the cardiologist's number from the nurse and update herself, while her father bickered in the background. Although the tests had indicated nothing of concern, the cardiologist was firm about keeping him for a further twenty-four-hour observation period.

Once she'd terminated a second call to the concierge doctor her father paid a fortune to retain, Georgia cast the nurse an apologetic smile, then waded into the fray.

"Dad, give the poor woman a break!"

The nurse shot her father a long look, muttered something and wisely bustled out.

"Must've recruited her from the marines." Kingston's frustration was about to cause him to rupture a blood vessel. "She won't let me smoke, even tried to tell me it's against the rules. Rules? I've never followed any rules. Now open that damned blind."

Jay was right: anyone who had the misfortune of having to deal with her father while he was incapacitated deserved danger pay. "All the other blinds are open. She's only trying to make sure you're comfortable." Georgia told him. Yet, still she found herself pressing the button on the remote so that the blind lifted. The habit of obeying her father was ingrained bone deep.

He blinked against the bright influx of light. "That's better," he persisted. "The day I lie down and listen to some bad-tempered witch is the day I leave here feet first."

"Kingston!"

But he was already looking past her to the door.

"Where is Jay? Call him. Tell him to get his ass up here, will you?"

"He's downstairs. I'm sure he'll be here in a few minutes." Moving to her father's side, she reached out and covered his hand with hers, relishing the warmth of living flesh beneath her touch. He might be impatient, bad-tempered and cantankerous, but he was alive. She stroked his hand. "I'm here."

He shook her hand away impatiently. "I need to speak to Jay."

The rejection pierced her, but Georgia pushed her feelings aside. "You've just had a health scare. Why don't you ease up on meetings for a couple of weeks and take—"

"Ah, good, here's Jay now." He cut her off mid-sentence and sat up.

A wave of energy swept into the ward along with Jay. After she'd been dealing with her father, Jay looked like a glimpse of heaven.

For the first time, she wondered what role he would play in her father's new vision of the company. As her father's confidant—especially if he managed to bring Charis back into the fold as his bride—he'd have untold power.

Would that satisfy him? Or would he want more? He was too clever, too knowledgeable not to know his own worth. She narrowed her gaze as she contemplated him. Tall. Dynamic. Confident. Ambitious. A force to be reckoned with.

"Did you bring the resolutions?" her father barked.

"What resolutions?" she asked Jay.

"Good afternoon, Kingston, glad to hear you're feeling better. Hello again, Georgia."

"What resolutions?" she repeated.

Jay's smile revealed a set of slashing dimples that she couldn't remember ever noticing before. But his smile didn't reach the hazel eyes that saw far too much.

He tapped the leather folio he carried. "Got them right here."

Georgia felt herself stiffen. "Those empower me to run the company while Kingston recuperates, right?"

Jay shook his head, and her blood ran cold.

"Then what are they for?" she demanded.

"They authorize a fresh annual general meeting."

For the board appointments. Nothing ominous in that.

She switched her attention back to her father. She'd had enough of the rumor roller coaster. "Norman and Jimmy are standing down from the board, aren't they?"

"You keep doing your damned job—let me worry about Kingdom," her father snapped.

What was that supposed to mean?

Something dark flashed across Jay's face.

Georgia bit back the torrent of curses that threatened to tumble out of her mouth. "I'm on the Managing Committee—and so is Roberta," she said calmly. "You've taught us everything we know." While they might never have served on the Board of Directors, they were heavily involved in the day-to-day executive management of the company—she pretty much did Norman's entire job already. "Allow us a chance to do what you've trained us to do."

"And where is Roberta now?" Kingston raised his

eyebrows. "Shopping? Or preparing to jet off to flaunt herself in the fashion capitals of Europe again? She's certainly not here!"

"That's not fair!" Georgia balled her fists. "She was here most of the night. Then she took Marcia home."

Jay interjected calmly, "I've spoken to Roberta—she's on her way back."

Georgia smiled across at him in gratitude, and a little of her head-crushing tension eased. "I don't suppose anyone has heard from Charis?"

Kingston snorted. "Charis had better not set foot in the Kingdom offices or in any of my stores. She walked out. Call security the instant she's seen."

A chill spread through Georgia. But business was the only language her father understood. Rubbing her arms, she said, "We need Charis to finalize the spring collection designs."

"*I* do not need her. Kingdom certainly doesn't need her." Kingston's eyes blazed. "She's no daughter of mine. Never speak of her again!"

Shock and something close to horror filled Georgia.

He'd meant it.

She crossed her arms over her chest. She'd been so sure he'd get over yesterday's fit of rage. Although his blatant favoritism for Charis had eaten away at her for years, she was stunned at how easily he'd written her sister off without a backward look.

Fear seeped into her. She tightened her arms over her chest, guarding her heart. A quick glance revealed that Jay was watching her. She hoped like hell he couldn't read her terror.

She might be next…

The click of heels in the corridor outside caused her heart to skip.

What if it was Charis? How would her father react?

"About time you arrived," Kingston grumbled as Roberta breezed into the room in a cloud of French fragrance.

Georgia let out the breath that had caught in her throat and her arms fell to her sides.

"Good to see you're as easy-going as ever, Kingston." Bending over the hospital bed, Roberta blew an air-kiss at their father's forehead.

Roberta's makeup was flawless, her lush figure encased in a wrap dress that accentuated every natural asset she had. From the way Kingston was scowling, he'd noticed, too.

"That dress belongs under a streetlamp."

Roberta did a little pirouette. "You think? I think it's perfect."

Kingston's eyes had narrowed to slits. But instead of getting into an argument, he sat up and growled, "Did you bring that pack of cigarettes?"

Georgia opened her mouth to scold him, but Roberta only laughed.

"You need to take better care of yourself," Georgia warned him.

"The cardiologist said I'm as good as new—"

"Not quite! On the phone, he told me that you need some stress-relief strategies." In his fit of rage yesterday, her father had apparently begun hyperventilating. Both the cardiologist and her father's concierge doctor warned it could happen again. "Why not take it easy for a couple of weeks? It will be a good opportunity to test out the succession plan we've discussed—"

"Bah!" Kingston snorted, his tone full of disgust. "You're not running the company."

Georgia stared at him. "I'm more than capable—"

"I will be back in the corner suite on Monday."

The familiar knot started to wind tight in Georgia's stomach. She drew a deep breath, held it for a second and breathed out. One count at a time.

"Can't you at least activate the backup plan we agreed to, Kingston? For the company's sake? What if something really is wrong? What if you become ill over the weekend?" All the possible catastrophes that had been playing through her mind came tumbling out. "And what if they don't discharge you this weekend—and you can't be at the office on Monday?"

"Then I'll authorize Jay to act as interim CEO."

Jay?

Georgia's breath hissed out and she switched her attention back to where Jay stood silhouetted against the window, the Hudson River glittering in the distance beyond.

Her father *was* lining up Jay to take her place as his successor. She wasn't just being paranoid.

Her throat closed up. Had Jay been angling for this ever since his first day at Kingdom? She hadn't been there when he'd arrived. She'd been in the hospital. Being immobilized following the surgery to her ankle had been bad enough, but it had been the concussion and memory loss that had worried the doctors more.

Despite Jay's easy smile, she'd prickled with hostility from the first day she'd arrived back at work. Jay's competence had radiated from him; he made Ridley look like an intern. Slowly, stealthily, he'd become a greater threat than she'd ever imagined. But she wasn't about to let him oust her from the position that would one day be hers.

Jay finally spoke. "I'm afraid I'm not available to serve as interim CEO, Kingston."

Shock caused Georgia to freeze. Jay was refusing her father? He'd had her dream handed to him on a plate and he was turning the chance to run Kingdom down?

Wasn't this what Jay wanted?

Her father and Roberta both turned to look at Jay where he lounged with apparent unconcern against the window.

"What do you mean you're not available?" Kingston raged.

Jay's tone remained level. "I won't be here."

Georgia finally remembered. "He's going on leave."

"Cancel it!" Kingston was struggling to get out of the bed.

Georgia leaped forward. "Father, settle down."

He ignored her, all his attention on the man behind her. "I need you in New York, Jay."

"Kingdom will run just fine without me." The slight upward kink of his lips didn't change Jay's resolute expression. "I'll check my emails and take some calls while I'm away. But I'll be back before any of you notice I've been gone."

I would notice.

The thought caught Georgia by surprise.

Kingston sighed loudly. "Then I'll have to make sure I'm back at work on Monday. Georgia—"

Shutting down her thoughts, she replied automatically, "Yes?"

"Get Marcia to arrange for Bruno to collect me at the usual time, will you?"

Georgia started to object, but then shrugged. What was the point? "Yes, Kingston."

"Oh, and, Roberta, I'm still waiting for that pack of cigarettes."

"Anything else you need?" Roberta asked, her voice saccharine-sweet.

From under heavy eyebrows, he glared first at her, then at Georgia. "A little cooperation from both of you would be helpful."

Roberta didn't flinch. "Ah, loyalty I think you called it yesterday?"

Georgia tensed, waiting for her father to explode.

But the strident ring of Roberta's phone interrupted the storm. Her sister glanced down at the device and pursed her lush lips. Not for the first time, Georgia noticed the fine lines around her immaculately made-up eyes. Roberta was feeling the strain, too. She'd been… different. Distracted. Distant.

"Give me a moment. I've got to deal with this." Roberta was already on her way to the door. "It won't take long."

Abandoned by her sister, Georgia turned to face her father. But she wasn't alone—Jay still lounged against the window, and Georgia was tinglingly conscious of his narrow-eyed appraisal.

"Forget about your half-cocked succession plan. I need you, Georgia." Her father gave her a weak smile. "Fordyce is a damn fine businessman. He's prepared to do a deal—he needs a wife. And he's exactly what our business needs in the long term."

Our business.

Georgia felt her heart melt. Her father needed her. He'd never admitted that before. The urge to do what he wanted—to gain his approval—pulled at her. But she was uncomfortably aware of Jay witnessing their intimate family drama in silence from the window.

So she brought it back to business. "Kingston, you know my views on bringing outsiders onto the board. It's far better to build succession from within the company."

"That's crap!"

"It's absolutely not!" she argued.

"Georgia is right. Internal promotion means far fewer surprises."

Georgia shouldn't have been astonished by Jay's support. After all, her argument for promotion from within worked in his favor, as well as her own. But he'd just turned down a shot at interim CEO…

What did Jay want?

Was he an ally or a foe?

"We've tried developing internal candidates before." Her father's gaze bored into her. "Haven't we, Georgia?"

Shame stained her cheeks and discomfort crawled in her belly. She didn't want to talk about Ridley. Not now. Not ever. "That was different."

"How?" her father challenged.

She certainly wasn't discussing Ridley in front of Jay. "You're missing the point. I can easily—"

Kingston flapped a dismissive hand. "You're not up to running Kingdom."

"At this stage, it would only be for a few days—"

"A few days too long!" He gave a dismissive snort. "I'm not taking that risk."

Then he collapsed back against the pillows and flung a forearm across his eyes. For the first time, he looked old…and beaten.

"I'm only asking you to do one thing for me—put my mind at rest and marry Fordyce." His lips barely moved. He was asking for her help.

How could she say no?

A piercing pain stabbed behind her eyes. The one thing that she'd learned from the Ridley catastrophe was that she was terrible at romance. She'd sworn off marriage—she didn't even date.

Now, Kingston wanted her to marry Adam Fordyce.

No dating—and no romance—required.

Jay was still watching her from his position beside the window, his expression shuttered.

Her gaze slid away from his scrutiny.

Would marrying Adam Fordyce bring her closer to what she'd wanted since she was a little girl, who visited the Kingdom offices and sat and twirled around in her father's high-backed leather desk chair? Her head threatened to explode. Was her father right? Would Adam mentor her and ensure she got what she'd always wanted? Or would he snatch away her dreams forever?

She'd always obeyed her father. But this…? She needed to list the pros and cons the way she always did when she made a decision. But more than that, she needed space…and a shot of black gold.

Grabbing her tote from where it sat on the chair

against the wall, she said, "I'm going to get a cup of coffee. Can I get you one, Jay?"

He pushed himself away from the window.

She didn't want him accompanying her. She wanted to think. Alone. "I won't be long."

For once, she didn't want Jay's perspective. This was too personal.

But he didn't take the hint. His smile was easy as he came toward her. "It will give me a chance to stretch my legs—and I need to make some calls."

As she reached the doorway, Kingston called out, "And don't forget to bring me back a goddamned pack of cigarettes!"

Georgia stalked out and resisted the urge to slam the door.

It didn't take long for Jay to catch up with Georgia. As he came up alongside her, she quickened her pace.

Ducking her head down, she said, "So tell me...honestly...were Norman and Jimmy really going to retire and stand down had yesterday's annual general meeting gone ahead? Was there ever any chance of Roberta and I being appointed to the Board of Directors?"

Jay wished he could give her the answer she so badly wanted to hear. "Who knows what's going on in your father's head—I suspect he'll persuade his golf cronies to stay another term."

They reached the elevator and the doors slid open, revealing an empty car.

Georgia stepped in. "For one glorious instant, I actually believed my father had recognized all the work I've put into the company. I should've known better."

She laughed, but the sound held little amusement. "He never had any intention of letting me in—not even temporarily. He wants a man in control." She stabbed a button on the control panel. "Someone like you."

Jay moved in front of the elevator doors and spun around to face her, giving her no choice but to look up at him. He was overwhelmingly conscious of her closeness…the fine grain of her pale skin, the bright blue of her eyes, the familiar scent of her…all the intimate details he had no right to appreciate.

He found his voice. "Not me. I'm not available."

A frown pleated her forehead. "You can tell him that all you like. It's not going to stop him. He'll talk you into it once you get back from vacation—he always gets what he wants. And you'll be married off to Charis before you can say—"

"That's not happening, either!"

"Don't be so sure." Her gaze lifted to focus somewhere above his head—the floor indicators, perhaps. "He's already convinced Adam Fordyce to marry me."

"But you're not going along with that."

Georgia gave no sign of hearing a word of what he was saying, whereas he couldn't think of anything but her…

"He'll have his way—just wait and see. He never gives up until he gets what he wants. God knows who he's lined up for Roberta. That's going to cause fireworks, for sure." Georgia's eyes returned to lock with his. "Three successors for his beloved company. Three daughters—who come with stock certificates pinned to their wedding dresses—to dangle as carrots."

Georgia was angrier than he'd ever seen her.

"Roberta and I will never have feet big enough to fill his shoes—" She broke off as the elevator car came to a halt. "And besides that, we have lady parts."

How the hell was he supposed to respond to that?

She didn't give him a chance. Brushing past him, she said over her shoulder, "And who can argue with him? He'll only fire anyone who dissents! He's the boss."

Jay strode after her. "Georgia—"

With increasing frustration, he listened to the rapid click-clacking of her boot heels along the hospital corridor. For all his talk, the old man wouldn't be stupid enough to fire her. Kingston's insane scheme had already cost him one of the most talented young designers in the business. Losing Charis was going to create havoc in the coming months. And it was the same with Georgia. She knew too much about the inner workings of Kingdom for her father ever to risk getting rid of her.

The coffee shop loomed up ahead with its racks of magazines, floral bouquets tied with ribbons and the aroma of strong coffee.

It was now or never…

Kingston was going to be fine. Jay hesitated midstep.

No, not now. She was far too worked up.

Coward.

But he forced himself to commit to some kind of action, saying, "That talk you and I need to have—how about I buy you a drink tomorrow night?"

"What?" She swung around, eyes blank with confusion.

"Careful!"

Jay pulled her to one side as an orderly pushed a patient past in a wheelchair.

"The Bachelors for a Better Future Benefit," he reminded her once the pair had passed by, his heart knocking loudly in his chest. He'd been talked into being auctioned off as a dinner date for the charity. "We can meet for a quiet drink afterward." That way, he'd keep the vow he'd made to himself: to tell her everything before he left for Colorado.

"Oh, my God." Her hands covered her eyes. "I'd forgotten all about that. I swear I'm losing my mind all over again. It's like after the crash." She took a couple of sideways steps and sagged limply against the wall. When she dropped her hands from her face, her mascara had smudged, accentuating the hollows beneath her eyes. "Tell me, Jay, do you think I'm crazy?"

It was the first time she'd ever brought up that period missing from her memory. The night they'd met—the meeting she knew nothing about and had changed the course of his life—and the blanked-out days that followed her subsequent car accident on the way to the airport.

"You're not crazy. You're the most sane person I've ever met." It was more than he could handle to see her wilting like this. But he knew better than to touch her, to offer any comfort. He forced a smile. "At least, most days…after you've had a cup of coffee."

Placing his forearm against the wall beside her head, Jay leaned in toward her.

"I need your help…" He kept his voice deliberately light. "I need you to bid on me tomorrow night."

Her eyes snapped wide. "Me? Bid on you?"

He made himself grin—a shark-like toothy grin, and her eyes narrowed suspiciously. *Good.* "Think of it as act of altruism."

"Altruism?"

"You'll be saving me from hordes of—"

She interrupted him with an unladylike snort. "I can't think of anyone in less need of saving."

His grin widened in appreciation. "Afterward, to celebrate your good taste in winning me, we'll share a bottle of French champagne." He lowered his voice suggestively. "Then I'll sweep you off for that incredible dinner you've paid for..."

He was rewarded with a glint of fire in the depths of her blue eyes, and Jay felt a corresponding flame light up deep in his chest. He held his breath. *Down, boy.* He had to tell her the truth tomorrow night.

"You don't need me to bid on you, buddy. You'll do fine and raise plenty all on your own."

"I dare you to outbid everyone," he murmured.

But instead of rising to the bait, Georgia pinned him with a glittery look full of suspicion. "I don't do dares."

"Too risky?" he taunted.

She shook her head, a couple of strands of hair almost whipping against his arm where it rested close to her head. "Too impulsive."

Jay knew he was pushing hard, but he couldn't stop. "Too scared to live a little?"

She froze. "I'm not scared!"

Gotcha. He raised his eyebrows. "You sure about that?"

"Of course!" Georgia gave a dismissive laugh that he might have thought was real if he hadn't made an art of studying her for the past two years. "Why should I be scared to bid on you?"

He let her question hang, watching her, letting it expand to fill the space between them. "Because you're too scared to be swept away on an incredible dinner date with me?"

Her eyes darkened to sapphire. "I definitely don't do dates."

A second later, she gave another careless laugh. She'd recovered so quickly that if Jay hadn't been watching her, he might have missed the flare of panic.

"Your ego is showing, Jay Black. What a hard life, being *such* an eligible bachelor in New York—and having the privilege to turn down an interim CEO position that I would give my right arm for. Why would you worry about a dinner date?"

Jay stared into her eyes which, despite being shadowed by confusion and antagonism, were still the most beautiful thing he'd ever seen. He wanted to tell her those eyes were worth infinitely more than the CEO position she coveted so highly.

"Oh, God. I'd better not forget to arrange where I'm going to meet Adam."

Suddenly, Jay was no longer in the mood to jest. "You're not seriously planning to attend the benefit with Fordyce, are you?"

Georgia stared at him as though he'd grown two heads. "Of course, I am. Kingston's already arranged it."

A primal, possessive response rocked Jay back on his heels. The hand he had propped against the wall curled into a fist.

"I'm sure Fordyce will have no problem finding another date," he said through gritted teeth.

"It's hardly a date. But I can't just dump the man—he's far too important of a player. And I can't let my father down."

"Can't let your father down?" Jay stared at her. "That's a habit you need to break."

"I don't dare, Jay. If he fires me…" Her voice trailed away. "I'm nothing without Kingdom."

Carefully, Jay pushed away from the wall and uncoiled himself, taking a step backward before he said—did—something that he might regret.

Keeping his voice even with great effort, he said, "Why don't we go get that coffee you wanted?"

Five

They took their steaming cups to a sheltered bench Jay had discovered yesterday tucked away in the landscaped gardens surrounding the hospital. Three nurses stood a distance away, clutching their coffees, while half a dozen sparrows tussled like young thugs on the footpath.

A gust of wind shook a drift of withered leaves from a nearby tree.

"Would you like my jacket?" Jay instantly started to slide it off his shoulders.

"No, no. I'm fine."

Dropping her Kingdom tote on the wooden bench, Georgia drew her jacket more tightly around her, and then took a sip of the coffee he'd bought.

"I could get used to this coffee," she said, as she sat down in the washed-out sunlight.

He hadn't brought her out here to talk about coffee. With his free hand, Jay raked his hair off his forehead and sat down beside her.

"The sooner you tell Fordyce that you're not going along with your father's crazy notions of empire-building, the better."

"Maybe it's not crazy. Maybe it actually makes sense."

"Sense? It's completely mad!" Disbelief took his breath away.

"It'll be business—more like a merger than a marriage."

"But you haven't even met the man," Jay protested, seriously rattled now.

She took another sip. Jay noticed how the morning sun glinted in her hair. "That will change tomorrow night."

Desperation pounded through his veins. He wanted to grab her by her shoulders and warn her that she was making the biggest mistake of her life. Leashing his inner turbulence, he sat still as stone. *Reason, not reaction.* "You'd never do business with a company you hadn't done substantial due diligence on."

She didn't even crack a smile. "I'm not stupid, Jay. I'll certainly weigh up every advantage and disadvantage." Her tone had cooled. She glanced down at her watch. "We can't stay long. Roberta will be wondering where I've gotten to—"

"Roberta will call if she needs you." Jay had no intention of allowing Georgia to run out on this discussion. "Forget the business advantages then, and consider the personal aspects. You can't possibly marry Fordyce."

She flicked him a quick sideways glance, then looked away. "I may not have a choice."

His shoulders grew more rigid from the effort it took to stop himself from leaping to his feet. "Of course, you have a choice. No one can force you into marriage."

"It's not that simple."

"It's exactly that simple. Just say no."

"There are plenty of merits to it—even on the personal level." She began ticking them off on her free hand. "One, I'm hardly likely to fall in love with anyone."

"Why not? You shouldn't allow one bad—"

"Two, I work too hard—you say so yourself." Her middle finger unfurled, as she continued to count out reasons he didn't want to hear. "Which leads me to the next point. Three, I don't have time to date…to meet men."

Jay started to panic. "But you don't want to meet men, do you?"

"Doesn't every woman want to find The One?" She raised an eyebrow. "Someone to love."

The One?

Jay lowered both his eyebrows in response.

"What?" She stared back at him. A fine wisp of silver hair blew across her eyes. She pushed it away, hooking it behind her ear. "Isn't that supposed to be every woman's dream?"

"I never thought it was yours."

"Jay!" She actually looked offended.

Holy crap! How had he misread her so badly? He'd listened so carefully to her no-romance protests that he'd missed the yearning hidden deep below.

"You haven't looked at a man in the two years I've worked with you."

She didn't look pleased with his observation.

"So maybe it's just as well Kingston's come up with this plan. I get the chance to marry someone I'll have business in common with—and I don't need to go through the drama of dating."

"You don't need to marry Fordyce to avoid that fate. You could marry me instead of settling for second best." He grinned, partly to irritate her, but mostly to give himself an out lest she realize how deadly serious he was. "We've got plenty in common."

She gave a snort. "Like what?"

For starters, they both spent most of their waking hours at Kingdom, but Jay decided she might not appreciate that reminder right now. He needed to proceed with care—and humor. He stuck out his thumb, mimicking her actions from moments before. "You like arguing with me—"

"*You* argue with *me*!"

"Two." He flicked out his index finger. "You think my opinions are fantastic—"

"I do not!" Then she relented. "Okay, maybe as far as Kingdom goes—I'll concede that."

"Three," he said, counting the point with his middle finger. "You adore my sense of humor."

She rolled her eyes skyward. "Can't you ever be serious, Jay? This is exactly why I would never marry you."

Ouch!

Before he could react, she blurted out, "Anyway, I'd hate for you to sacrifice yourself."

"But it's okay for you to sacrifice yourself?" he retorted.

She set her jaw in a way that he recognized only too well. "That's different. I'll be marrying Adam Fordyce to get what I want."

Even the wind stopped gusting in the taut silence that followed.

"All you ever think about is Kingdom," he said quietly.

She didn't say a word. Instead, she drained her coffee and carefully set the empty cup down on the sunlit bench between them.

"Georgia, I know you were hurt by Rid—"

She didn't allow him to finish. "Kingdom will never betray me."

This time, her smile turned his guts inside out.

Never betray her? What the hell did she think was happening? What did she think her father was doing?

"And marriage to Fordyce wouldn't be a betrayal?"

"Betrayal of what?" She sounded genuinely confounded.

Of yourself.

Jay suppressed the urge to yell it at her—he didn't dare show the terror that now churned inside him.

"You don't want to do this," he said, the calmness of his voice surprising him. "It would be a massive mistake."

Her careless shrug rattled him further. "Plenty of marriages have worked with less—"

"And plenty have ended in bitterness and acrimony," Jay interrupted her. "Don't you want more out of life than a billion-dollar divorce settlement?"

Georgia glared at him. "You don't understand what it's like to be a Kinnear."

It was his turn to shrug. "Not very different from being a Black, I'd imagine."

"Don't be silly!" Her lips curved up into a smile that held no trace of any real amusement. "You couldn't possibly understand."

"Try me." Jay bared his teeth in a feral grin.

"My life was mapped out long before my birth. From my father's perspective, it went wrong from the moment I was born." She paused. "I was supposed to be a boy."

"George." Jay supplied the name.

"You know?" The bruised look he'd hoped never to see again was back in her eyes. "He told you?"

Jay hesitated, debating with himself how to respond. He let his gaze drift around the landscaped garden. The nurses had vanished. Aside from the squabbling sparrows, he and Georgia were the only ones left.

Slowly, he shook his head. "It's not hard to figure out."

"Father was so sure I'd be a boy. He wasn't interested in hearing some medical technicians' determination of what my sex would be. Because he knew. He even had the christening invitations printed, inviting everyone to 'celebrate the birth of my son, George.'" Her face wore a strange expression. "Funny, huh?"

Even on the second telling, Jay found little amusement in Kingston's arrogant certainty that he could preorder his firstborn's sex. Even less did he like the notion that her father had made his disappointment so evident to Georgia from the day she was born.

"You want to please your father." He knew he had

to proceed with caution. "You want his approval—but you don't need to go along with this…this—" *Insanity.*

"You don't understand. You asked what I want. Well, here's what I want. I want to be the President and CEO of Kingdom. I want it for me—not for my father. I want it because I've worked for it all my life. I want it because it's mine by right, my birthright. I want it because I deserve it."

The words were a death knell.

Hell, he'd known it…but he'd never understood how deep her desire went—nor how far she'd go to secure it.

But he couldn't walk away. He was fighting for her life—and his own.

"So you think by marrying Fordyce you can convince him to let you take charge?" The glitter in her eyes warned him he was on treacherous ground. "Fordyce is an ambitious bastard. What makes you think he'll step aside and let his wife be boss?"

Her chin went up. "I'll persuade him."

God!

Imagining what form her persuasion might take made him go hot…then very, very cold. Jay tugged at the knot of his suddenly too-tight tie. An icy knifepoint of fear cut deep into his heart.

"You deserve more!"

His anger burned a white-hot streak through him. Anger at Kingston for his callous indifference to his daughters. Anger at Georgia for her blind certainty that her father would honor her efforts. Anger at himself for his foolish hopes.

To give himself time to cool off before he blurted

out anything he'd later regret, Jay raised his cup and downed the coffee in two gulps.

The heat scalded the back of his throat.

He set the empty cup down on the bench beside hers.

"I love Kingdom… It's everything," she said quietly.

The vulnerability in her eyes took away his breath, evaporating the sermon he'd been about to deliver. At last, he said flatly, "It's only a corporation, Georgia."

She was shaking her head. "Oh, no. It's much more than that. It's all I have. It's my heritage. My family. My life. My legacy. If I have to marry Adam Fordyce to keep that, I will."

"You shouldn't allow your father to dictate who you should marry." He drew a deep breath. "It wasn't successful last time—why the hell would it work this time?"

She went white. "You know nothing about what happened before!"

Jay winced.

He hated, *hated* to see her hurting. Guilt ate like hot acid at his gut.

But he couldn't keep silent…not anymore.

"Georgia, that night that you…that Ridley—"

"I don't want to talk about it," she cut him off. "And certainly not to you. It's none of your business, Jay."

The words were a punch in his chest.

But it was his business…

He wanted to look away, before she saw into his soul and read the truth that blazed there in ten-foot-tall letters of gold fire.

That she'd changed his life.

That after they'd met, he'd flown home and set the

wheels in motion. That ten days later, he'd called Kingdom International looking for her. Only to learn that she'd been through surgery and was recovering from a head injury. He'd been on the next plane to New York. His first stop had been the Kingdom headquarters. Georgia had still been away on sick leave. There'd been little chance of convincing her staff to give him her contact details. But he'd caught a break. The busy receptionist had assumed he was there for an interview. And in that instant, Jay had taken brazen advantage of the woman's mistake and he'd made his next life-changing decision. It hadn't been difficult to smooth talk his way into Ridley's job.

If he told her the truth now, he'd drive her straight into Fordyce's arms—she was halfway there already. Then he'd lose all chance to win her back. Forever.

"I'd hate to see someone so smart and brave trapped in a miserable marriage," he finally managed. "I'm concerned about you, that's all."

Desperate, seeking to lighten the moment—hell, looking for any distraction—he bent forward, intending to kiss the tip of her nose in an amusing comic fashion.

But it didn't turn out that way.

Instead of brushing her nose, his lips planted themselves on hers. The jolt of the brief impact rocked through him. It wasn't a particularly sexy kiss, as far as kisses went. But his lips lingered longer than he'd intended, refusing to obey his command to back off. Now. Before he blew it all to kingdom come…

Yet, surprisingly, she didn't shove him away.

Her lips were soft beneath his. Then—more surprisingly—her mouth moved slightly, her lips parting a little—probably because she was in shock.

She tasted of strong hot espresso and a sweetness that was all Georgia.

Jay didn't dare press the advantage, nor did he deepen the kiss. Too much lay unspoken between them.

He shouldn't be touching her!

So he retreated, and gave an unsteady laugh, while silently cursing himself.

"Speaking of mistakes, that was a mistake," she said, much too quickly.

Who was she trying to convince?

Him?

Or herself?

But he didn't risk challenging her. His heart was thundering so loudly he was sure she would hear it reverberating around the empty garden.

Her hands came out, warding him off. "Don't move—stay there—I have to work with you tomorrow."

Picking up the empty cups, Jay rose and swung away almost treading on a trio of sparrows bickering amidst a swirl of fallen leaves. He retreated to the trash can nearby and tossed the cups in with barely restrained force. Then, fighting to keep his face from revealing anything of his feelings, he stalked back.

He refused to think of that sweet, gentle kiss as a mistake.

He came to a halt in front of her.

"You don't love Fordyce. It will ruin your life," he said softly, and shoved his hands into his pockets.

She said nothing.

"You'd marry a man you've never met, a man your father picked out for his ability to run Kingdom? *Why?*"

She raised her chin in that maddeningly familiar gesture. "I'll make it work."

Or die trying.

That was his Georgia. The blind tenacity. The pig-headed drive. Everything that made her the most maddening, most fascinating woman he'd ever met.

His eyes locked with hers.

"They call him Mr. Ice," he warned.

Cool, rational logic always worked better. Or provocation. Except, right now, in his desperation, he couldn't summon either…

"Don't give in." He was begging, dammit!

She must have sensed something of his black emotional maelstrom because she tipped her head to one side and considered him with eyes that had cooled to a clear light blue, so disturbingly similar to her father's that Jay was filled with a flood of dread.

"Jay, I'm not giving in. I'm compromising."

"You're damn right, you're compromising. You're compromising who you are."

This was her life—his life—she was talking about. He wanted to shake sense into her. But he kept his hands thrust deep in his pockets and watched the color leach out of her eyes and the wall go up.

Damn Kingston!

So he gentled his tone. "It's your father's loss that he doesn't appreciate you for who you are."

The smile she gave him was brilliant…and utterly fake.

"You're lucky," she said. "You were born the right

sex. I'm sure your father is incredibly proud of you, his eldest son—and of your achievements. You've had freedom to carve your own life."

"I suppose you could see it like that," agreed Jay with little humor.

"I've always been expected to work for the family company. I can't leave."

"Do you want to leave?" Tension vibrated through him.

"No, of course not! Haven't you heard a word I've said? Kingdom is my life."

Kingdom.

That was all that mattered to her. All she wanted. What could he offer to match that? Except the freedom to carve out her own life.

The desperate determination in her eyes warned him that it was pointless to even try to negotiate.

Pivoting away, Jay drew a deep steadying breath.

It was perfectly clear. Pressure would only make Georgia dig her toes in further and push her faster toward the altar. The hell-bent desire to fill Kingston Kinnear's shoes consumed her. She would do anything to be President and CEO of the company she'd been raised to revere.

Even prostitute herself to a man of her father's choosing.

Six

Georgia had intended for her first meeting with the man who she was contemplating marrying to be in private—even if it was in the back seat of a limousine.

Instead, it was taking place in a marble-tiled lobby on New York's museum row in the midst of a high society affair.

Her father's driver, Bruno, had arrived on time to take Georgia to the benefit. But there'd been no sign of Adam Fordyce, apart from the exquisitely packaged corsage on the back seat with a handwritten note from Adam that he looked forward to meeting her at the party.

Now Adam Fordyce's narrow mouth barely moved as he said to Georgia, "I see you received my flowers."

"They're beautiful—thank you." She carefully

touched the corsage on her wrist and silently reminded herself not to rub her eyes any time soon.

"Would you—"

"Should we—"

They both spoke at once, and Georgia laughed awkwardly and felt herself color. This had to be worse than being a teenager on a first date. Tonight had to go well. She couldn't afford to screw this up…

Then she sneezed. And worse, her eyes started to burn.

Of all the bad luck!

Georgia set her cocktail glass down on a nearby pedestal and sent a prayer to the beauty goddesses that her expensive waterproof mascara would hold up.

"I'm so sorry," she sputtered, her vision blurring. She fumbled with the clip of her sequined clutch and dug frantically around inside for a tissue. Her eyes pricked and two more sneezes followed in rapid succession.

"Good evening, Georgia."

Jay.

He thrust a soft linen handkerchief into her hand.

She blew her nose and dabbed at her streaming eyes while Jay and Adam greeted one another. Then she opened her eyes and, to her relief, the world slowly realigned as the noisy chatter echoed around them.

Jay stood before her, immaculate in a black tuxedo and a startlingly white shirt. A black bowtie completed the ensemble. He looked fantastic. The bidding on him tonight was going to be insane.

For some reason, that did not delight her.

"Thank you." She grimaced. "This is becoming a habit." Fluttering his handkerchief between her fingers, she made a mental note to get both handkerchiefs she now possessed laundered and returned ASAP.

"It's the baby's breath," said Jay.

"What?" She squinted up at him.

He raised an eyebrow. "Those little white flowers in the corsage that make you sneeze."

"You're allergic?" Adam was all concern.

"Yes." Once again, Georgia felt awkward, her stomach knotting up. She could kill Jay for drawing attention to her weakness—even if he was right about the allergy. "It's the single-flowered version that's the problem. I'm fine with the double-flowered hybrid." The orchid in the arrangement would be fine—but it would be too difficult to separate it from the baby's breath.

"Here, let me remove it," said Adam.

"I'll do it." Jay moved in between her and Adam, blocking her date from view. His fingers were cool against her skin as he gently removed the corsage from her wrist. This close, his clean-shaven jaw was level with her eyes and she could smell his aftershave—that subtle fresh blend of greenery and wood—as he concentrated on her wrist.

"How did you know I'm allergic to baby's breath?" she murmured to Jay alone.

His head tipped up and his darkening gaze tangled with hers. Instantly, the memory of the last time he'd been this close flashed into her mind.

He'd kissed her.

It had been dizzying, disorienting. She worked with the man… She didn't want to be thinking of how safe, how comforted she'd felt when he'd brushed his lips across hers. Yet, there'd also been a prickle of high-voltage tension…something that had nothing to do with comfort…or safety. And she certainly didn't want to think about—

"I'm observant," Jay said flatly.

Georgia searched her plundered memory bank for an occasion when she'd had an allergic reaction that he might have witnessed and came up blank. But that meant little. There were so many holes where certainty had once existed. The knots in her stomach grew tighter, and she looked away deliberately, and tried to refocus on her date.

She caught Adam studying them.

"Let me fetch you a glass of water," he offered.

"I'll be fine."

The last thing Georgia wanted was for Adam to think she was some kind of freak. But he was unreadable. His dark remote face contrasted so sharply with the pale eyes that revealed no emotion at all. It was easy to see how he'd been nicknamed Mr. Ice.

"Is there anything else I can get you to drink?" Adam's voice interrupted her thoughts. "Another cosmopolitan, perhaps?"

Coffee…

Jay would have offered her coffee. Even on this rarefied occasion, he would've conjured up a paper cup of steaming black gold, and she wouldn't have needed to ask.

She almost smiled—and only just stopped herself from sneaking Jay a sideways conspiratorial glance.

Adam was still waiting for her response. Feeling guilty at the headspace Jay was occupying, she overcompensated with a thousand-watt smile. "Maybe a lime and soda?"

"Done."

She watched Adam disappear into the throng.

"So you're going ahead with this crazy plan to marry Fordyce?"

Georgia's heart sank. Since their confrontation in the hospital gardens, his accusation that she was giving in—and the implication that she was taking the easy way out—had gnawed at her. There was nothing easy about what she was doing. But she couldn't expect Jay to understand. How could he? He'd never been in her position…

She tipped her chin up. "The more I consider it, the less crazy it sounds."

"I've instructed Charis to bid on me if I fail to make the reserve."

"She's here?" The information came as a relief.

"Yes, I ran into her in the lobby—she'll be joining you at the table Kingdom sponsored."

All Georgia's bubbling questions dried up as she gave Jay a slow once-over. He'd make the reserve for sure. The formal evening clothes made him look breathtakingly gorgeous—and his slightly wayward hair only added to the appeal. Working with Jay every day, she'd never even thought of him as handsome.

Where the hell had her eyes been?

"We have a decent budget for this event." Georgia certainly wasn't going to feed his ego. "Charis will make sure you go for a respectable figure. Don't forget to talk up the raffle of the Kingdom trolley bag we're doing tonight. Make sure to slip in mention of the Kingdom brand as many times as you can so that we get some decent media attention. And get some photos with whoever makes the highest bid."

"Thank you!"

Was that a hint of irony she detected?

Before she could call him on it, she spotted the event organizer making frantic hand signals in her peripheral vision. She nudged Jay. "I think that's your cue—and I need to find the cloakroom to fix my makeup."

"The moment of truth—let's see what I'm worth." Jay's smile didn't reach his eyes as he took her in, from her hair styled in an updo to the dark sapphire dress and the diamond drop earrings she wore. "You look beautiful."

The mirror in the ladies' room lounge revealed that Jay had been delusional in his assessment.

After salvaging her eye makeup and repairing the damage caused by her sneezing bout, Georgia went back out and found Adam in the lobby, holding their drinks. Once she joined him, he made short shrift of the rich and famous glitterati crowd that surrounded him.

There was no sign of Jay.

To Georgia's irritation, there was little opportunity for thc social let's-get-to-know-each-other-better chatter she craved with Adam amid waiters circling with platters piled high with canapés, the constant greetings from acquaintances and a never-ending stream of interruptions by Adam's business connections.

Finally, much to her relief, a bell sounded, summoning the crowd to a large triple-height gallery that had been set up for the benefit auction. Adam revealed flawless manners as he seated her at the table sponsored by Kingdom close to the stage, before taking his seat beside her.

Good. Finally they would get a chance to get to know each other.

Georgia smiled a greeting at the others at the table. Roberta was already there, accompanied by a heart-stoppingly handsome man. Then Georgia recognized him.

“Blake. Blake John Williams.” She laughed as he rose to his feet. “How long it’s been!”

He came from one of New York’s wealthiest families. Was he the reason for her sister’s recent surge in texting activity?

Marcia Hall was sandwiched between Roberta and Charis, who had—surprisingly—come alone. Charis looked amazing in a traffic-stopping dress covered with a riot of beaded flowers. It was nothing like the elegant garments Charis usually wore. Georgia had never seen anything like it. It definitely wasn’t her sister’s work. But Charis had discovered some exciting new talent. Once photos got out, the unsuspecting designer was going to be mobbed with orders.

Two other couples filled out their numbers at the table.

As the meal progressed, the conversation predictably turned to fashion. Adam was exchanging small talk with Roberta’s date. Georgia’s gaze strayed to the table where the bachelors were sitting. Jay was seated at the farthest end, head tipped to the side in a pose Georgia knew so well. Another of the bachelors leaned across and said something that made Jay smile, and he laughed as a third chipped in.

Georgia felt her own mood lighten.

When Jay laughed, he was utterly, irresistibly wicked.

If he laughed like that when his turn came to be auctioned, he would have no problem winning a more than desirable figure.

Her glance flicked across to Charis. How far would Charis need to go? But her sister was staring fixedly at the floral arrangement in front of her. Whatever Charis was thinking about wasn't making her happy. Georgia's own heart ached in response. Their father's rejection must be killing her sister.

For the first time in years, Georgia wished she and Charis were closer.

"A glass of champagne?" Adam offered.

It reminded her of Jay's joke about sharing a bottle if she bid on him—and won—him tonight.

Georgia came back to earth.

"Yes, please." She smiled, and the wine waiter at her elbow filled her glass.

"Excuse me for a moment." Adam pushed his chair back. "There's someone I must talk to—I'll be back shortly."

As he left, Georgia glanced back to where Jay sat to one side of the stage. He was chuckling at the antics of the first bachelor getting ready to be auctioned off.

As though he felt the pressure of her stare, Jay turned his head and met her gaze. His laughter froze.

A sharp pang pierced her chest, causing Georgia to draw a quick breath. What was this? She couldn't be jealous of the woman who'd win him…

How ridiculous.

Jay was her rival. A perpetual thorn in her side.

Their relationship was…complicated. Confusing.

But he made her laugh.

And in those unguarded moments, she forgot about her fears. She even forgot about the terror of not being enough.

But Jay wasn't laughing now. His gaze was boring into hers. He alone knew the stakes that faced her tonight, and the magnitude of the decision she'd made. Tomorrow, her world would be different. She'd have Adam.

She'd no longer be alone.

And after tonight's benefit auction, some other woman would be sharing a dinner date and laughing with Jay.

Georgia acknowledged the truth: she envied the mystery woman that carefree, frivolous experience.

One of the other bachelors tapped his shoulder, and Jay's fierce focus shifted, breaking the bond between them. He got up and headed for the stage.

When Jay leaped up the stairs two at a time, and sauntered into the spotlight, Georgia found herself tracking his long strides. He finally stopped and turned to face the crowded gallery, dimples slashing his cheeks as he grinned and adopted a pose so typical of Jay: legs spread apart, hands on his hips, head tilted back. Confident. Arrogant.

Of course, it only served to show off the superb cut of his tuxedo—and the lean body beneath. A charge pulsed through the crowd as the female half of the audience swooned.

The opening bid came quickly from Georgia's left.

Xia. A top fashion blogger. She and Jay had dated a while back. The relationship had fizzled out, but it had led to some fantastic product exposure for Kingdom on Xia's blog. Roberta still raved about the Xia Factor.

"Come, ladies, get out those checkbooks." The auctioneer was extolling Jay's virtues. Cameras flashed.

This was Charis's cue.

Georgia glanced across the table—but the chair Charis had occupied only minutes before was empty. Roberta was no help, either—she was conversing with her date, their heads close together. Quickly, Georgia scanned the gallery. There was no sign of Charis's stunning dress anywhere. Where had her sister gone?

From the lofty height of the stage, Jay's gaze met hers. His eyes were narrowed in challenge.

Of its own volition, her hand lifted.

"Is that a bid?" the auctioneer asked.

Georgia nodded.

Somewhere at a table behind Georgia, a woman whooped with excitement. Her girlfriends giggled, urging her on. Georgia turned in her chair and watched as a gorgeous platinum blonde, poured into a glittering red dress and sporting heavily mascaraed lashes that were too long to possibly be real, raised her hand to place a bid.

An unfamiliar tension curled through Georgia.

She narrowed her eyes. The woman didn't look like Jay's type—too glamorous. Too blond. Then it struck her: as much as she and Jay snarked and argued, she didn't really know what Jay's type was. Xia was beautiful in an exotic kind of way. Then there'd been a willowy fashion model: Dominique, if she remembered correctly. And there'd been a couple of others who had lasted little more than a couple of months. Nic and Carrie. Georgia couldn't believe she remembered their names.

Jay's girlfriends never seemed to last long.

There were no photos of any women in his office. Come to think of it, there were no photos of any description.

She told herself that Jay deserved better. She told herself that Kingdom contributed to the Bachelors for a Better Future Benefit Auction every year. She told herself a lot of things. And she even told herself that it was irrelevant how much fun it might be to call a truce on their rivalry and to spend a carefree evening enjoying laughter and a little champagne.

All the while, Jay's grin taunted her, daring her to do it.

She'd make it quick. Georgia drew a deep breath. "Ten thousand dollars."

Satisfaction filled her at the sudden silence that followed.

Xia was undeterred. "Eleven thousand."

"Twelve thousand." The glamorous blonde in the too-tight dress.

"Twelve and a half." Xia again.

"Thirteen." Glam sounded smug.

Xia shrugged, graciously giving in. Glam grinned, certain of her win.

"Bids?" The auctioneer called. "Ladies! Spoil yourself. You owe it to yourself to have a great evening for a good cause with this fine specimen of manhood here."

Sounds blurred around her. Lights flashed. Adam rejoined the table, sinking back into the chair beside her, and she only spared him one glance—glimpsing his dark frowning face—before swinging her attention back to the stage. Jay was worth blowing the whole budget on. After all, it was for a good cause.

"Fifteen thousand." Her voice rang out, loud to her own ears.

"Sixteen," Glam came back instantly.

Fifteen thousand was the agreed budget. Georgia barely hesitated. She didn't want that woman winning Jay for the night.

"Twenty thousand."

On the stage, Jay stopped grinning, and his eyes locked with hers.

"Twenty-two."

Glam wasn't giving up.

"Twenty-five thousand dollars," Georgia said with grim finality.

"That's more than we allocated from the marketing budget for tonight's event," Roberta chided from across the table as the auctioneer crowed, "Gone."

Georgia didn't spare her sister a glance; she was too busy trying to read the unfathomable expression on Jay's face. Was that a hint of satisfaction? Or a fresh challenge? But she replied, without needing to think too much, "It will be worth it—and it should make a splash in the fashion magazines and the wider media. There are enough cameras here tonight—plus it's tax deductible."

"It will need a fair amount of press coverage," Adam broke in, "to recoup that kind of expenditure."

"Leave it to me." Roberta was grinning. "I'll make

sure I organize photos of Jay and Georgia wearing plenty of Kingdom loot in an A-list dining location that will get us the best kind of exposure."

Before Georgia could respond, Adam said, "Georgia, I'd like a word with you. Alone."

Seven

Georgia was conscious of Jay's eyes boring into the back of her head as she picked up her clutch, slung its delicate silver chain over her shoulder and rose from the table. Adam's hand rested on the base of her spine, and a commanding pressure guided her forward.

A set of doors led to a glass-enclosed balcony that ran along the length of the gallery. Georgia knew that once she stepped over that threshold, her relationship with Adam would change forever.

But she told herself this was what she wanted. She could salvage what she'd worked so hard to attain by marrying Adam. She would be President and CEO of Kingdom one day.

Why should she allow Jay's cautions to spoil her vision of the future?

Drawing a deep breath, Georgia stepped forward.

Beyond the glass walls, the cityscape glittered.

Adam's hand slid down her bare arm and came to rest against her hand. His fingers were cool, his touch curiously impersonal, despite the skin-to-skin contact.

Mr. Ice.

Unbidden, Jay's description of Adam leaped into her mind. Georgia fought to block it out. *Not now.* Not when she needed to focus on Adam, focus on building a rapport with the man.

They were going to be partners. Intimate partners. In business. In marriage. In everything…

"What a beautiful night," she said.

Adam got straight to the point. "Your father has spoken to you—you know why we're here."

She nodded mutely.

This was it, the moment when her life changed. Georgia half expected the earth to move.

"What exactly is your relationship with Jay Black?"

What? She goggled at him. "Jay and I work together."

Adam arched his eyebrow in response.

"We're colleagues. We… We're responsible for a lot of Kingdom's strategic planning," she found herself stuttering. The antagonism and secret rivalry between her and Jay was something she didn't care to share, but Adam needed to understand that Jay was central to Kingdom's success. "And he's my father's right-hand man."

"Women don't bid twenty-five thousand dollars on a colleague."

"You heard Roberta. It was nothing more than a PR stunt."

Except it had felt way more personal than that…

Before she could marshal her scattered thoughts, Adam was already reaching into the pocket of his dinner jacket.

"I've got something for you."

"Oh?"

He drew a small square box from the pocket of his suit jacket. "I think you'll like it." He flipped the box open. "It has all three *c*'s—cut, clarity and color. Four, if you add carat. It's as good an investment as a diamond can be."

Investment. The ring sparkled up at her.

"Try it on."

Georgia slowly took the ring from the box.

"It's impressive." Then, in case that sounded too clinical, she added, "It's magnificent."

The ring was magnificent…in an icy classic kind of way. Was this how Adam perceived her? Flawless and glittering? The perfect trophy wife?

As good of an investment as a woman could be?

And why not? Her father measured her worth in the same terms.

"We will be married next June."

A summer wedding…

But instead of a warm wave of pleasure, Georgia felt flustered at his haste. He was talking of wedding arrangements already. What had happened to courtship? To getting to know each other? He'd taken her assent for granted. Was that her father's doing? Had he assured Adam she would not object?

Anger started to smolder deep within her heart. *Fine!*

She'd let Adam find out who she was through negotiations—nothing new to her about that.

"We'll need to hammer out a prenup first." She spoke carefully, giving herself time to think and get her emotions under control.

"Sure." He shrugged. "But we already have an agreement in principle."

He stepped forward and his hands slid around her shoulders. He was tall—well over six feet. And solid. His chest rose like a fortress in front of her.

Reaching out a hand, she placed it on the wall of hard muscle that blocked out the light around her. Adam tensed. Panic crushed her. For an awful moment, Georgia felt…trapped.

She fought the suffocating claustrophobia that had come out of nowhere.

Deep breaths, she cautioned herself. It was okay. She was okay. Or she would be, as soon as she pulled herself together.

Adam was going to kiss her…

She couldn't afford to screw this up. It had to work. And it was up to her to make sure it did.

She turned her face up and closed her eyes, dreading what was coming.

When his lips landed, they were firm…and cool. Adam Fordyce kissed with technique. That, at least, was a relief.

Yet, instead of being swept away by lust, as she should have been, Georgia found herself waiting…

And waiting.

For what, she wasn't sure. Whatever it was didn't happen.

He slid his hands along her back and pressed her closer. Out of nowhere came a stab of stark terror. She went as stiff as a board.

He raised his head.

"Nice," she choked out.

Made of ice, she found herself thinking.

Damn Jay! And why was she thinking of Jay, anyway? Or the coffee-flavored kiss full of care and tenderness he'd bestowed on her yesterday…?

The memory of their too-short moments of warmth and comfort in the garden's pale sunshine contrasted with the darkness that surrounded Adam. She pulled away a little more.

"Yes."

It took Georgia a scattered moment to realize that Adam was agreeing with her assessment of that cold kiss as *nice*.

In the dim light, she couldn't read his expression. It might've helped ease the tension in her stomach, the thunder in her head. She drew a slow steadying breath.

Nice.

She'd lied.

And the earth hadn't moved.

Beyond the glass walls, the buildings dominating the skyline stood glittering and silent. Nothing had changed.

Only the hammering of her heart.

She immediately grew impatient with her own reaction. Why should the earth have moved? She wasn't some teen princess with grandiose expectations anymore. She was a grown-up woman, with a hotshot position on the executive team at an iconic fashion house.

Hey, she knew that the earth didn't move because of a kiss. That fireworks and glass slippers and golden rings forever were nothing more than fantasy. She understood reality. Adam was a real man—not a fairy tale prince.

She and Adam shared a common vision: commercial success.

It was a start—they would build on it.

She couldn't afford to think about the urge to flee; she wouldn't think about Ridley…and she wouldn't think of Jay. She had to think of Kingdom.

"Very nice," she amended, trying harder. *Throw more heart in, Georgia.* They would both have to work on this. She'd do more than her bit. Like she always did.

Georgia tried to forget that moment of panic when he'd taken her into his arms, that sensation of being trapped and crushed, that terrifying spike of adrenaline. It had come out of the blackness at the bottom of her brain… It had happened before, when she thought of Ridley, of that moment she'd walked into the hotel suite and found him with a sales assistant on the bed. While the woman had struggled to get her dress back on, Ridley had lit into Georgia, telling her it was her fault. She didn't have what it took to hold a man.

And after that, a big dark blank…

Not now. Please not now.

So she filled her lungs with air, and tried to smile at Adam.

If she tried a little harder, if she invested some more enthusiasm, it might ignite some magic. But searching for the positive side was hard work.

Especially when she longed for Jay. For the barbs and banter that had become so familiar. At least she knew where she stood with him. Most of the time. She longed to use him as a sounding board to clear this confusion that kissing Adam had evoked. To clear the sudden doubt she was experiencing…

Grow up, Georgia.

This is your life. Nothing to do with Jay...

Another thought struck her. Had Adam's cold kiss been intended to seal the execution of an agreement? Had it been that calculated?

She was a person, dammit. Someone with emotions and dreams, who possessed a heart, as well as a brain.

"There are some…" *terms* was too unromantic a word, Georgia decided "…things we need to discuss before I agree."

"Things?"

She shrugged, feeling unaccountably foolish. *Negotiate.* She gritted her teeth. "How this marriage is going to work."

"It'll work like any other marriage."

From nowhere, Jay's voice flashed into her head. *And plenty have ended in bitterness and acrimony. Don't you want more out of life than a billion-dollar divorce settlement?*

"Really?" She arched her eyebrows. "Most people don't marry for the reasons we will be marrying." *Most couples are in love, actually.* But of course, she didn't say that.

"So what things do you want to discuss?"

Now she felt even more idiotic. But Jay's sweet kiss of comfort in the hospital garden yesterday had let a whole lot of emotions out of the box. What with her father's dramas, and now this…. Boy, over the past few days, she'd discovered emotions she hadn't even known existed.

"Uh…how we will communicate—"

She broke off. Adam was staring at her as though she were crazy.

"How we will communicate?" he repeated. "Like most people do, I should think."

She could feel herself flushing. She tried again, "I'm talking about…"

Sex.

Adam's face darkened.

For a moment, she thought he understood.

But then he swung away from her, presenting her with a broad shoulder. Half his face was in shadow. The ring she still clutched mocked her. She caught a flash of cold fire and glanced quickly away, reluctant to fit it on her finger yet.

Turning back to face her, he spoke again. "You're aware of my relationship with Charis?"

Georgia sighed a small sigh of relief. It was too soon to be discussing intimate details—his change of subject was a good idea. Rapidly, she reviewed which of Charis's current projects Adam might be involved with. She drew a blank. "I didn't know you and Charis had any business dealings."

"My relationship with Charis has nothing to do with business." There was a husky undertone to his voice, a smoky heat in his eyes that belied his nickname.

That caught Georgia's attention. On rewind, her sister's silence this evening played through her mind, and understanding dawned in a flash. "Oh, my God. You're talking about a personal relationship, aren't you?"

Adam stared back at her, unblinking.

There was an instant of disbelief.

Then the outrageous idea coalesced into certainty. “You’re lovers!”

The silence stretched as she waited—in vain—for a denial that never came. Tightness bubbled at the back of her throat as she thought about the kiss he’d given her while her sister sat inside the ballroom.

“Uh…the relationship is over?”

Of course, it must be. She couldn’t believe she was even asking.

Otherwise—

His silence took on the quality of cold forged steel.

Otherwise…how could he possibly propose to her? Or kiss her? Her stomach twisted, a sick sensation filling it as the silence grew colder.

Georgia held up the glittering diamond engagement ring he’d given her like a talisman. “It’s over as of now. Right?”

Adam’s head jerked back. “That ring changes nothing. You need to understand that our marriage will not change my relationship with Charis—that’s non-negotiable.”

“You mean…you’re going to…” she broke off, seeking a sanitized way of uttering the unspeakable “…you’re going to keep…” *sleeping with* “…seeing… my sister while you’re married to me?”

“I’m glad you understand.”

Understand? Georgia stared at him. Had she gone completely crazy? Or was he crazy?

“So,” she drawled, her brain working overtime to catch up, “you’ve discussed this with my sister? She knows you'll be married to me, even while you sleep with her?"

He gazed at her through slitted eyes, his face an iron mask. "Charis will do exactly as I want."

What he wanted was to marry Georgia and sleep with her sister. Have his cake and eat it. Bile rose at the back of her throat. Georgia's heart ached. For Charis… and for herself. The situation was ghastly beyond anything she'd ever contemplated.

Finally, she said, "So I guess our marriage will be in name only."

Adam didn't reply.

A numbing emptiness invaded her. Was this what she wanted? A marriage that was nothing more than a business arrangement? Marriage to a man who was sleeping with her sister?

You deserve more...

Jay was right. This travesty wasn't what she wanted.

"I want children," she said at last. The thought uncurled out of the secret mists of her mind. It was something she'd never contemplated, but which had always been there. Except she hadn't known it existed.

Adam was saying something. She hadn't heard a word of it.

"What?"

He spoke again, slowly, as though she were simple. "A child is no problem."

"No problem?" She tried to grasp what he meant by that. "You mean IVF, right?"

"There are easier solutions." His voice dropped, each word softly clipped.

Her whole being rocked as the words sunk in.

"Easier solutions?" she echoed the heresy he'd uttered and stared at him, shocked. He didn't just mean to marry her and sleep with Charis—he meant to sleep with them both! "But..."

How would her sister feel about that?

Certainty settled in fast. Jay was right. Adam Fordyce truly was made of ice. There was no humanity in the man who stood before her, his eyes so dead. Nothing. Jay might be maddening and infuriating. But at least he still had feelings. Emotions. This man had none.

Amoral asshat!

Poor Charis.

No wonder her sister had looked so miserable.

But Georgia knew how she felt about it. And that made her decision easy.

She handed the ring back to him.

Damn. Jay had been right. Again.

"I can't marry you, Adam. I'm sorry."

Why was she apologizing?

"Your father—"

Georgia shook her head. "No. Not even for my father."

He stared icily down his long straight nose at her. "Sleep on it."

Nausea rose in her throat at his phrasing.

"Keep the ring." His confidence was staggering.

She shook her head and thrust it back at him.

"At least take the weekend to think it over. Once you've had a chance to think about it, you'll realize there's no point throwing away everything we'll have together." He smiled. But the thin smile didn't reach his remote colorless eyes. “Call me on Monday morning—we’ll talk some more. This is going to work.”

Georgia knew she was going to be sick.

“Shall we go back in?”

Unable to speak, Georgia nodded. She hitched the chain of her clutch higher up on her shoulder. His hand rested lightly on her hip as he escorted her toward the gallery filled with chatter and laughter.

A sideways glance revealed that he was smiling, a hard savage smile.

“I need to go to the cloakroom.” And then she needed to find Jay. He was the one person she could rely on to help her.

Without a backward glance, she left Mr. Ice standing alone on the threshold of the crowded room.

Georgia slunk into the ladies’ room. Beyond tall urns overflowing with fragrant lilies and a velvet-covered chaise, she spotted a familiar exquisitely beaded gown.

Charis.

Her sister had seen her enter and was watching her in an ornately framed gilded mirror.

Despite her inner upheaval, Georgia flicked her a quick awkward smile. But Charis didn’t smile back.

“Your lipstick is smudged.” Her sister’s face was pale and tight.

“Oh.” Georgia flushed, and humiliation crawled through her. Damn Adam for putting her in this situation! She extracted Jay’s crumpled handkerchief from the clutch slung over her shoulder and rubbed frantically at her mouth.

“It’s fine now.” Charis’s voice was flat.

Nothing was fine. God, this was awkward. "We need to talk."

Charis's gaze shifted to her own reflection. She pursed her lips into a moue. "Come hell or high water, I'm going to finish the spring collection if it kills me."

"Father doesn't want you in the build—"

"He doesn't need to know!"

Georgia started to argue, then thought better of it.

"Why didn't you say you were dating Adam Fordyce when Kingston made his announcement?"

"I don't want to talk about it."

"Charis—" Georgia broke off, searching for an easy way to say this. "Listen, I'm not going to marry him—"

"Have you told that to our dear father?"

"No." Georgia's stomach seized up at the thought. "But I will."

"Good luck with that." Charis tossed the soiled towel in the disposal slot.

Then, for the first time since Georgia had entered the cloakroom, her sister swung around to face her.

"He won't let you back out."

She wasn't sure whether her sister meant their father or Adam Fordyce.

Tonelessly, Charis added, "You're welcome to Adam."

Georgia said in a rush, "I don't want him. Adam Fordyce makes me sick!"

"Then that makes two of us." There was such savagery in Charis's voice that Georgia recoiled.

Jay's provocative question rang in her head. *You'd marry a man you've never met, a man your father picked out for his ability to run Kingdom? Why?*

It had seemed so clear-cut, so logical.

Until Adam had kissed her…and then, to her appalled shame, her body had taken over…and the reaction had not been good. She'd found herself thinking of Jay…

So she'd turned Adam down. For the first time in her life, she'd gone against her father's wishes.

Once Kingston found out…

Georgia shuddered with dread.

But her father didn't know what she'd done. Not yet.

She felt a flare of hope. There had to be a solution. A way to keep her father happy…and keep her position safe. An overwhelming desire to talk to Jay filled her. Jay always gave her perspective. He had the ability to ask questions that made the solutions to whatever was bothering her so obvious.

She glanced at Charis. Her sister was blotting her lips with a tissue. She looked composed…but ghostly pale.

"Are you okay?"

Charis's eyes were dark and distant. "Why wouldn't I be? I have a collection to finish. I'm going to make it the biggest success Kingdom has ever seen. Then I'm going to live my life—without all the never-ending drama that comes attached to Kingdom."

Georgia wanted to argue—to convince Charis that Kingdom was what kept them together. Kept them family. She ached for what might've been. For all the years that had been lost. But Charis was clearly in no mood for a heart-to-heart.

She touched Charis's arm. "I don't suppose you know where Jay is?"

Charis shook her off. "He went home."

“Home?” Georgia realized she didn’t even know where Jay lived. No matter. Bruno would know.

“He’s flying out on vacation.” Her sister opened the cloakroom door.

“No he’s not!”

Georgia grabbed her clutch. Jay wasn’t going anywhere. Not until he’d helped her sort this mess out.

Eight

It was already after midnight.

Jay had just finished packing the last white professionally pressed T-shirt into his bag and was about to zip it shut in readiness for his early morning flight when the doorbell chimed. Before he had a chance to react, it sounded again.

"Hold your horses!" He strode through the apartment and yanked open the front door.

Georgia stood in front of him.

To catch his breath, Jay leaned against the doorjamb and folded his arms across his chest. Even as he examined her, he prayed she wouldn't detect the sudden drumroll in his chest.

Jay didn't bother to ask how she'd gotten past the doorman; Georgia on a mission could achieve anything she set her mind to.

Under her evening coat, she was still wearing the midnight blue couture slip dress she'd worn to the benefit auction—and she clung to the silver-sequined Kingdom clutch that Jay had recognized from last fall's collection. Her silver-blond hair was still drawn off her face in a stylish knot although several tendrils had escaped, adding to her air of fragility. The stark simplicity of the look was broken only by the stunning pair of art deco diamond drop earrings he knew were her sole legacy from her mother…and a stain of red on her lips.

His gaze narrowed. Her lipstick was slightly smudged around the edges, showing signs of hasty repair. Her lips were full, ripe. Kissed.

Jay suppressed the surge of raw emotion that shook him. He might not know where she'd been, but he had a damned good idea who she'd been with…

"What do you want, Georgia?"

"May I come in?"

Cocking his wrist, he glanced at his watch. "It's late."

"You promised to share a bottle of champagne with me if I bid on you—so here I am."

Too late for champagne now, too late for the intimate tête-à-tête he'd planned to soften her outrage. He thought of all the great intentions he'd had to tell Georgia the truth.

But now it was too late to confess that he'd lied from the outset. That he'd never been recruited to fill the position Ridley—her errant fiancé—had left vacant at Kingdom. While she'd been recovering from a car crash that had sheared away a portion of her memory, he'd taken advantage of being in the right place at the right time so that he could have second chance to get to know her better.

He risked another glance at her tempting strawberry-red lips as the dreams that had sustained him for two years turned to dust.

He should've told her the truth, instead of being such a damned coward.

But he hadn't—and now it was too goddamned late.

There was no point in discussing the night they'd first met—a night she'd long since forgotten. Why open an old wound that held so much trauma for her? There was no point in convincing her to give him a chance to start over. Georgia was lost to him.

She'd followed her father's orders.

Yet, still, Jay found himself unable to resist the inexorable force that caused him to step back, allowing her space to pass and enter his apartment, even though the tightness in his lower gut warned him this was a dumb idea. Despite an urge to slam it, he shut the door with a dull click.

She shrugged off her coat, and he hung it up on one of the coat hooks that lined the hall alcove.

He flat-handed a control panel on the wall as he passed by, and the apartment exploded into bright light. Now was not the time for dim mood lighting. He waved her into the living space ahead of him. At the island of Carrara marble that functioned as a dining table and divided the streamlined butler-style kitchen from the lounge, he stopped, keeping the slab between them.

He didn't want her anywhere near him—not now, looking so well-kissed by another man.

A man she intended marry…for Kingdom's sake.

"You want a drink?" He sure needed one. "Tequila?"

Her shoulders hunched. "Not tequila!"

Stop being an ass, Black!

"What about a glass of that champagne you offered earlier?" Her brightness sounded forced.

He was in no mood to celebrate. Instead, he said, "How about coffee?"

"Much as I'd love a cup, the caffeine will keep me awake."

Jay clawed a bottle of whiskey out of the liquor cabinet and poured two stiff fingers of amber liquid into a tumbler. The time had come for him to cut his losses. To leave Kingdom, the cold corporation that had chained Georgia's soul. To find some distant place to lick his wounds in peace—preferably across a wide stretch of ocean.

London. Paris. Sydney.

Whatever. He certainly had no intention of dancing at Georgia's high society New York wedding.

For the first time, he was grateful that he'd be out of town for the next couple of weeks.

The tumbler thudded against the marble. He reached for a second glass, poured in a shot and pushed it across the slab to her. "Why did you come here?"

She set her glitzy clutch down and faced him across the sleek black-veined slab, her eyes unexpectedly shadowed. "I need…advice."

"Has something happened?" Giving a silent snort of derision, he picked up his glass and swirled the whiskey around the glass when she didn't answer.

Dammit, he could see what had happened. It didn't take a genius to work it out.

Genius? He was an ass!

He contemplated her over the lip of his glass. "It's Fordyce, isn't it?"

She nodded. "He asked—or, should I say, expected—me to marry him."

No surprise there.

"Congratulations." Jay took a slug of whiskey, set the half-empty glass down and wiped the back of his hand across his mouth to stop himself from swearing violently.

His pain would go away. Someday. On his deathbed.

Georgia leaned toward him and spread her hands out on the marble countertop. "Do you see a ring?"

He stared at her fourth finger.

It was bare.

The breath left his lungs, and his gaze skittered across the marble before rising to her face. "You turned him down?"

"Stone cold."

Stepping around the cold sleek slab, all he could see was the fullness of her bottom lip. "But you kissed him."

"*He* kissed *me*."

Under the stain of strawberry-red lipstick, her mouth was trembling. The tip of her tongue slid along the inside of her lip, and he wrenched his eyes away.

"I couldn't go through with it."

She was pale, her eyes stricken. What the hell had caused her to look so wounded? Instead of a surge of triumph, Jay quelled an overpowering desire to go and hunt Adam Fordyce down. To pummel the tycoon to a pulp with his bare fists. Leashing his rage, he asked levelly, "What happened?"

Georgia wrapped her arms around herself and rubbed her palms over her bare shoulders. "You say he's made of ice. You're wrong—he's colder than ice."

Jay clenched his hands into fists at his sides. There wasn't a trace of ice within him. Only a raging molten heat.

"What did he do?"

"Nothing. He didn't hurt me—at least not physically." She shivered and goose bumps rose on her arms. "Sticks and stones—it's not true."

What the hell?

"Tell me!" Jay insisted.

She shook her head and winced. Uncrossing her arms, she smoothed her hands over her face, over her hair, coming to a stop as she encountered the topknot. "My head hurts too much."

Restraining his impatience to know what Fordyce had said to rattle her so deeply, Jay murmured, "Your hair is tied too tight. Take out those pins."

He moved so close that he could see the flecks of silver in her bewildered eyes. His fingers were already unclenching to help her. Her hair came down in a swath of soft silk. Jay's fingers tangled in the silver mass, threading through it, combing it until it fell around her face.

"Better?" he asked as gently as he could.

She nodded. "Jay, I'm so glad you were home."

Unexpectedly, she leaned forward to rest her forehead against his chest.

Jay went rigid with shock. He forced his hands down to his sides. She nestled against him, tucked against the white fabric of his dress shirt, while his heart rattled an erratic tattoo beneath. It was hard to remember that

Georgia never liked being touched, that she held herself separate, distant. But not now. Not tonight.

If he bent his head, his lips would touch the fine silver hair—

Fool!

One. Breathe in.

Two. Out.

All Georgia wanted was a confidant. A little comfort. She'd had one hell of a week. He needed to keep reminding himself of that simple fact, until his moronic body got the message.

She lifted her face. "Can I ask you something?"

His hands wrapped into fists to stop himself from touching her.

"You can ask," he said warily.

"Is…is—" she stammered. "This is harder than I thought it would be."

Uh-huh. "What?"

"Um—"

"Spit it out!"

She bit her lip, and a pink flush warmed her cheeks. "Do you have a dream woman?"

He felt himself flush in turn. Saw her eyes register his discomfort.

"Oh," she said.

He felt awkward and exposed. "What nonsense is this?"

"Charis is your dream woman?" she asked.

"Charis?" It was the last thing he'd expected her to say.

"My sister."

"I know who Charis is," he growled.

Jay held back a curse. The woman he wanted was far from a dream. She was real. Flesh and blood. And she was cuddled up against him. Yet he didn't trust himself to touch her.

"Jay?"

There was a strange expression in Georgia's eyes. Was that yearning he read there? Or was he indulging in another futile fantasy?

"No," he finally said, "Charis is not my dream woman."

"I'm so glad to hear that."

His heart thumped in his chest, and he silently cursed the leap of hope. "What's this about?"

"So there's no chance that you might want to marry Charis?"

"I've answered that before." He knew he sounded terse. "Why all these questions?"

"Adam and Charis are lovers." She dropped her head down, and her voice was muffled by his shirtfront again. "I didn't want you to get hurt…if you felt something for Charis."

Jay almost laughed. Jesus…what a royal screwup Kingston had made.

"Did Fordyce tell you that?"

"It was obvious—and he didn't deny it when I blurted it out. It gets worse." She sucked in a deep shuddering breath. "I thought he was telling me their affair was over. He'd just proposed to me—if one could call it that. Whatever it was, he'd given me a ring. Stupid me." Her whole frame shook against him. "God, I was wrong. So wrong." Another shiver went through her, and she buried her face deeper against him. "Adam told me he would continue to sleep with my sister…that it wouldn't interfere with our marriage."

Damn Fordyce!

"I didn't even know Charis was seeing him."

Georgia's hurt and bewilderment hung between them, and Jay couldn't think of a single platitude that might ease her pain. Finally, he allowed his fists to uncurl and let his arms steal up around her. Bowing his head over hers, Jay couldn't escape the soft feminine scent of her. To his horror, blood rushed to his groin.

"How did you respond?" His voice was husky.

Georgia's head came up so quickly that his lips brushed across her forehead. She pulled back a little, putting space between them, and his arms fell away.

Had she felt his arousal? God, he hoped not.

"What do you think I did? I told him I couldn't marry him." Her chin came up. "I told him I needed the bathroom—I felt sick."

Jay forgot his own dilemma. He snorted. "You actually told him that? That he made you sick?"

"Not quite." For the first time, a spark of her familiar feistiness showed through her anguish. "Trust me, there was nothing funny about it."

"I'm not laughing." But he felt a rush of very male satisfaction. In all their barbed exchanges, he might have annoyed her, frustrated her, but he'd never made Georgia sick…

"I ran into Charis in the ladies' room." Her words tripped over each other. "I don't understand her. I don't think I ever have."

The pain that underpinned her confession made Jay swallow. God help Fordyce when he found the man…

"She told me she intends to be part of the launch of the spring collection—and to hell with whether Kingston lets her or not."

"Well, I suppose that's one bit of good news."

His response didn't help.

"It's not! I don't think she intends to stay at Kingdom. She didn't even want to talk to me. She's always been as stubborn as a mule. She even told me I was welcome to Adam—and then she picked up her purse and walked out." Georgia gulped in a deep breath. "I couldn't bring myself to go back into the ballroom, but Adam was waiting for me in the lobby. That's when I got really scared because he looked so terrifying. He said I had to marry him, it was all arranged—" She broke off.

The wild despair in her eyes tore his heart out.

Under his intense scrutiny, Georgia colored. "So I ran."

"To me."

"It was run to you…or throw up that five-hundred-dollar-a-plate dinner onto his highly polished handmade shoes."

That was his Georgia!

Something like euphoria made him feel as high as a kite. He stepped forward and took her into his arms. It felt…right.

"You don't have to do anything you don't want."

She sighed. "Just hold me, Jay. Please?"

God.

Torn between the need to give her the comfort she craved and his fear of what might happen next, Jay shuddered. There was no way he could disguise the effect her closeness was having on his body. But there was no chance that he'd resist her request.

Even if it cost him his peace of mind.

When his phone buzzed in his pocket, Jay cursed silently at the sudden tensing of Georgia's body.

"Is it Kingston?" she whispered, her fear tangible. "Charis?"

The spell was broken.

Jay moved away and pulled his phone out.

"It's my mother."

"Answer it—something may be wrong."

He bit down on a tide of four-letter words. Against his better judgment, Jay accepted the call.

His mom was loud and enthusiastic. He made himself wink at Georgia as he waited for his mother to run out of steam, and as soon as she slowed down, he said, "Mom, I'll call you back later. I'm in the middle of something."

"You work too hard, Jay. You should consider coming home. Permanently."

He didn't intend to have that discussion right now—not with Georgia watching, and a hard-on to end all hard-ons filling his pants. "Mom—"

"It would make your father so happy. And Suzie is looking forward to seeing you again. We all are. You've been gone too long."

He was relieved to hear that Suzie actually wanted to see him again. Georgia shifted from one high-heel clad foot to the other in obvious discomfort. Before he could smile at her, she drifted farther into his apartment, clearly intent on giving him some privacy.

"Mom, I have to go. I have someone with me." He cut off her rush of questions. "I'll see you tomorrow."

Jay killed the call and went in pursuit of Georgia.

Through an open door, Georgia spotted what had to be Jay's bedroom.

The enormous windows on the opposite wall framed the brightly lit city skyline.

Wow!

Fascination drove her into the room. It was decorated in shades of navy and dull gold brightened with an ivory knit throw draped across the bed. Over the headboard hung an abstract canvas full of stormy movement, dominated by midnight blues and inky grays, a narrow shaft of light piercing the dark turmoil.

Then she spotted the open steamer bag beside the bed. The sight drove all other thoughts out of her head.

She heard footsteps behind her.

Without taking her eyes off the bag, she asked, "When exactly do you leave?"

"First thing in the morning."

Georgia wished she could escape like Jay. Fly away. Go home to a family where everything was simple and uncomplicated. Before she could stop herself, she found herself saying, "Can I come with you?"

"What?"

Trying not to feel foolish, she considered pretending she'd been joking—as Jay had been when he'd invited her to marry him. But the impulsive idea wouldn't go away…

In a rush, she said, "I could check online and see if there are still seats available…" Her voice trailed away when she got no response. Maybe it was a stupid idea. “We don’t even need to sit together.”

“Why?”

At last, she turned to him.

He stood a couple of feet behind her. The dark intensity in his eyes unsettled her.

“Why don’t we need to sit together?” By deliberately misunderstanding his question, she tried to inject some humor into an exchange that had grown astonishingly awkward.

For the first time, she became aware that it was well past midnight…that she was standing in his bedroom… that several buttons of his rumpled shirt were undone, revealing the chest she’d buried her head against. And his feet were bare. It was intimate. They were asking for trouble.

Yet, she wasn’t the least bit afraid.

This was Jay…

Although she had to admit, after the auction earlier tonight, she was seeing him in a different light. He was a very attractive man. It would be all too easy to fall for him.

But Jay had never had any interest in her. She simply wasn’t his type.

Jay still hadn’t smiled. “Why would you want to come with me?”

“I need a break.”

God, she hoped she didn’t sound like she was begging, but she was at the end of her tether.

“You want to avoid your father,” he said slowly.

“No,” she denied too fiercely. She looked down, away from that penetrating gaze. “I just need to leave.”

Escape. Her father was going to kill her when he found out she'd turned Adam down.

The air vibrated with her desperation.

Jay blew out a breath in an explosive gust that sounded loud to her ears. "Georgia, you have to tell your father that you're not going to marry Adam."

"I know. I know. I will." *Someday.* "Just not yet."

Jay went silent again. From under her eyelashes, Georgia watched him, trying to read his thoughts. He must be thinking she was the biggest coward on earth.

As the seconds passed, the mounting tension started to get to her. Even taunts and rivalry were better than his silence.

Well, she'd better get used to it. Jay was going to be gone for two weeks.

It would mean two weeks without his heckling. Without his laughter and lame jokes. Without that crooked smile at her office door each morning…and two takeout coffees in his hands. Without someone to argue with and bounce her ideas off—and share the triumph of success with. The place was going to be dead without him.

She swallowed, stunned at how forlorn she felt.

Somehow, Jay Black had become so much more than a threatening rival. More than a colleague to collaborate with.

An astonishing realization struck her.

Jay had become a friend.

A friend she could turn to for support…and comfort. She remembered the electric brush of his lips against hers. That had been something more than friendship…

No!

She couldn't afford any disturbing thoughts about Jay.

He was her friend. Better to have him as a friend than a lover who would betray her at the first opportunity.

She gazed at him, silently imploring.

Jay thrust his hands through his hair, causing the espresso-brown strands to stand up untidily. "Georgia, it's my parents' wedding anniversary—"

"You're right. I'd be party-crashing." Embarrassment seared her.

"It's nothing like that." He gave her a long look. "But you'd be better off facing up to your father."

Watching Jay cross the room and hunker down to zip the steamer bag shut, she tried to imagine his parents' home in some pretty, small town. It would be modest. With a white picket fence. No doubt, his mother and father loved Jay to death. She seemed to remember that his family had visited him over the past couple of years. Jay had taken them to shows on Broadway, done family stuff. Not that she'd given it much thought; she'd been focused on work. Now she wished she'd paid more attention...even asked to meet his family. She thought of how fondly he'd smiled a few minutes ago while he'd spoken to his mom. A wave of something close to envy swept her.

It had been a long time since she'd had a mom.

Only a dad. Her mom had driven away one day and she'd never come back. It had been left up to Kingston to tell them weeks later about the helicopter crash that had claimed the life of their cheating mom and the boyfriend she'd loved more than her daughters.

What would it be like to have grown up in a safe, secure environment like Jay's family? To be loved for oneself? To have no expectations placed on you from the moment of birth? To have a mom—and a dad—who loved you?

To her surprise, Georgia discovered she wanted to find out. She wanted to feel what it was like to live in the warm surroundings of a normal family.

If only for a week…

Except she had to be back at work by Monday. Kingston would be there—supposedly taking it easy.

But if she could escape for the weekend…

"Jay?"

He looked up, his eyes unfathomable.

Hauling in a deep breath, she said with raw honesty, "I haven't taken a vacation in years. I'm not coping well with the decisions I've had to make this week. Going away for a couple days will give me a chance to get some perspective. Please, may I come?" Laying herself open like this was hard. She tried to smile but her bottom lip trembled. "I won't stay long—only until, say, Sunday night."

"What about your father?"

She fought the claustrophobic fear of her father's displeasure when he learned she'd left without a word. Even worse would be his rage when he learned she'd turned Adam down. She couldn't face him. Not yet. He'd steamroll her to change her mind, to go prostrate herself to Adam.

"I'll make sure Marcia and Roberta take care of him until Monday."

"You know that's not what I mean." Jay's eyes didn't leave hers.

Beneath her apprehension about telling her father that she'd turned Adam down lay the haunting terror that her father was going to disown her. Abandon her. Just like he'd done to Charis…

Without Kingdom, she had no family.

No future…

"Putting it off never makes it any easier. Trust me on that." Jay's smile was crooked. "I speak from experience."

"I know. I know. I'll do it. I won't put it off indefinitely. I'll do it on Monday."

"You don't want Fordyce telling him first—"

"Adam's so sure I'm going to change my mind that he told me to take the weekend to reconsider. He won't say anything to my father. Please, Jay. I need this time away to think about how I'm going to handle Kingston's reaction when I tell him that I've turned Adam Fordyce down." Just thinking about confronting her father caused her stomach to churn anxiously.

Jay's face softened, and her frantic fear eased a little.

Finally, he rose to his feet and placed his hands on his hips. He studied her in a way that was a little too calculating.

"What?" she demanded.

"Okay, if there's a seat, you can come."

She gave a squeal of relief and delight and rushed toward him to throw her arms around him.

"Wait!" He warded her off with one hand, and gave her a ghastly grin. "There's one condition."

"Anything!"

"You should know better than to agree before hearing the terms." His grin grew feral. "Haven't you learned that much this week?"

"Better the devil I know," she teased, back on familiar territory. "What do you want?"

There was an abrupt shift in his expression, and he stopped grinning. "You'll come along as my fiancée."

"What?" She hesitated, uncertain now. "What do you mean, your fiancée?"

"Don't worry. It won't be the real deal."

Were his parents really so conservative? "Uh, surely you can tell your parents we work together…that we're colleagues? We don't need to be engaged to spend a weekend together."

Jay's expression lightened as he gave a chuckle. "My parents haven't spent the past couple of decades buried in the woods. But they're hoping to persuade me to return for good. A fiancée with a career and a family in New York would convince them that's not going to happen."

Georgia was so relieved she would've promised anything. Besides, she couldn't wait to meet Jay's small-town family.

"Oh, I can do that. And I can tell them how indispensable you are to Kingdom, how much Kingston relies on you and what a great future you have ahead of you. They'll be even more proud of you when they find out what a hotshot you are in the Big Apple."

She gave him a smile full of eternal gratitude.

"Thank you, Jay. You're the best—the very best friend I could ever have!"

Nine

Aspen, Colorado.

Jay had collected a sporty black SUV rental at the airport, and now, as they drove through the town bustling with Saturday morning activity, Georgia looked about with interest. Last night, when Georgia had begged Jay to take her home with him, she certainly hadn't expected their destination to be one of the premier ski resorts in the country.

She'd never been to Aspen—clearly, a big mistake. There certainly weren't many towns that boasted Louis Vuitton and Prada stores—Kingdom ought to have had store presence here, too. Georgia made a mental note to follow that up as they left the heart of the town behind, and Jay swung through a roundabout onto the picturesquely named Castle Creek Road. She wondered how far away from Aspen his parents lived. She'd love to come back for a look around the town.

"I thought you might like to see some famous Aspen Gold," said Jay, tossing her a quick grin.

They passed under a bridge, and the road opened out ahead. Georgia bit back a torrent of questions and sat back to enjoy the ride.

The road snaked upward as the dark blue-green mountains rose steeply around them. In the distance ahead, snow-capped peaks jutted out against the Colorado blue sky. The beauty was breathtaking. Her heart soared as they sped into a tunnel of ghostly silver-white trees topped with clouds of golden foliage. Too soon, they emerged on the other side. Seconds later, they swept through a bend, and the next flurry of slim silver-and-gold aspens flashed by. Georgia smiled in delight.

About ten minutes later, Jay slowed and pulled over.

"Why are we stopping?" she asked, turning away from the awe-inspiring landscape.

Jay killed the engine and swiveled to face her. "You'll need an engagement ring."

That brought her swiftly back to reality.

"It's not necessary—it's not a real engagement."

"It is for this weekend. My parents will never believe our engagement is real without a ring." Jay's eyes glimmered. "They'll be annoyed enough that I didn't let them know before."

"But they know I'm coming?"

He shook his head. "It'll be their anniversary surprise."

"You didn't call ahead to let them know you were bringing a guest?"

"You worry too much."

He leaned toward her and she caught a whiff of the delicious woody notes of his aftershave as he reached for his shearling jacket in the back seat. From one of the pockets, Jay extracted a small velvet-covered box and flipped it open.

The ring inside made her gasp.

A gorgeous round art deco diamond—the biggest blue-white she'd ever seen—blinked up at her. Set in white gold, with four diamond-studded petals folded back down the sides, it looked like a flower smiling up at her.

Georgia's heart sank. "My God. What if I lose it?"

"In one weekend?" Jay lifted a brow. "Unlikely. Anyhow, it's insured. Do you like it?"

I love it.

She controlled her impulsive response, but honesty compelled her to say, "It's the most beautiful ring I've ever seen."

Part of her was horrified. Jay earned a very good salary, but he wasn't wealthy…at least, not compared to her family. What he must've spent on that ring wasn't worth a one-weekend charade—unless he had it on loan. But even then, the insurance premiums would be horrific. A ring like this hadn't come from a last-minute foray into one of the airport shops. By some magic, Jay must've pulled strings to have it couriered to him this morning.

His attention to detail left her gasping.

Georgia's lips parted, but when Jay took her hand, all her questions scattered.

"Here, let me put it on." Cradling her hand between

both of his, he stroked the length of her fingers. Her skin started to tingle. Then he slipped the ring onto her finger.

A perfect fit.

Adam had never even gotten his as-good-an-investment-as-any-diamond-can-be ring onto her finger. The memory of another engagement ring—Ridley's—crowded in. Shuddering, she blacked out those disastrous associations.

Thank God, this time it was only a pretense.

Because she truly wasn't any good at this engagement stuff…

Jay's ring winked up at her. She thought of her mother's art deco earrings, which were all she had of the woman who had walked away from her three young daughters. She stared at the exquisite ring for a long moment, wishing, wishing… For what? She gave up trying to figure out what she yearned for, and lifted her gaze from the most beautiful ring she'd ever seen to the man beside her.

"Jay, it feels like it's never going to come off."

He was smiling at her, his hazel eyes warm and amused.

Georgia took in his features. The firm chin and angled jaw, dark with rough stubble. The good-natured curve of his mouth. Her gaze lingered. Why had she never noticed until recently the deep slashes beside his mouth that gave his face such rugged masculine appeal? Or the spark of bright green in his eyes? Like moss in the depths of a dark pine forest.

She worked with the man every day and all she'd ever allowed herself to focus on was their rivalry. For good reason. Every secret, silent SWOT analysis she'd ever done had convinced her that Jay was her biggest threat.

Yet, when offered the chance to usurp her place in her father's life, he'd turned it down.

He did her head in.

"Good," he said easily. "I'm glad it fits. Now you don't need to worry about losing it."

Unexpectedly, he lifted her hand and brushed his lips across the backs of her fingers.

Her heart bumped in her chest as the moment stretched between them, oddly intimate…and so very sweet.

It was friendship, Georgia told herself firmly. That's what the warm glimmer in his eyes signified. No point making more out of it.

So, instead of leaning across the space between the seats and seeking the shelter of his arms as she had last night, she simply smiled at him. "Thank you, Jay."

She was thanking him for the surprising comfort she'd discovered in their friendship—and the opportunity he'd offered for her to be part of a loving family for a brief time, giving her time to heal, to become whole again. It was friendship. She needed to keep reminding herself of that. Because there were other unfamiliar yearnings beneath the warmth of gratitude, yearnings that felt nothing like friendship.

As she studied him, his expression grew serious. "There's something we need to talk about."

The sudden intensity in his eyes caused her to still. "What is it?"

Georgia might not be aware of it, but she wanted him to kiss her.

The dewiness in her eyes, the lush, ripe fullness of her pink mouth told Jay all he needed to know.

Even as hope fired up within him, he suppressed it. He understood her hunger. That desperate desire to seal lip against lip. But he could no longer be satisfied by kisses. He wanted more. Much more. Just for starters, he wanted to slip his hands under the soft sweater she wore, strip it away and touch her skin. He wanted to shuck off his clothes. He wanted her naked against him.

But he had no right to any of those things.

The moment he'd put the ring he'd inherited from his grandmother on her finger, he knew that he couldn't leave any unspoken deceit between them. He had to face his fear…and tell her the truth.

Even though it meant he risked losing her.

Forever.

So don't screw it up this time, Black.

Jay hauled in a deep breath to steel himself against the terror.

Cupping his hand under her jaw, he tipped her face up to his. Looking into dark-lashed eyes, he said in a rush, "What if I told you that we'd met before?"

As always, the beauty of her eyes, clearer than Colorado summer skies, enthralled him. Right now, they glistened softly.

"This is going to sound…weird. Sometimes I feel I've known you all my life, Jay." Her throat bobbed. "You understand me—almost better than I understand myself."

"That's not exactly what I mean."

She blinked rapidly. "Then I don't understand."

Jay decided to sidestep the thorny issue of that powerful sense of connection he, too, knew so well. It had hit him the very first time he'd seen her in the hotel bar. Bam! Between the eyes. He hadn't understood it, either. So, for now, he was sticking to what could actually be explained.

"I'm talking about two years ago," he said softly, his heart pounding against his ribs.

"Two years ago?" she repeated slowly, her eyes never leaving his.

Jay nodded, watching her, his chest tight. Georgia—of all people—wouldn't have missed the significance of the timing. "Before I came to Kingdom."

"No!" She pulled back and laced her fingers together. His hand fell away. "I don't believe you. I would've remembered meeting you."

The interior of the SUV closed in on him.

To escape the sudden claustrophobia, Jay thrust the car door open.

"Let's walk," he commanded gruffly. Without waiting for an answer, he climbed out, dragging his jacket with him.

He led her down a short track between the quivering aspens to the edge of the bubbling creek. The wind blew off the distant peaks with a snow-chilled edge so typical of the Rockies, and Jay slung his jacket around her shoulders to block out the worst of it. The jacket was long enough for Georgia to sit down without getting her jeans damp. She did so, and then he settled himself on a tussock beside her.

A splash in the water caused her to jump.

"Trout. Brown trout," he told her.

Her profile was etched against the silver tree trunks that surrounded them.

"Where?"

Jay didn't pretend to misunderstand. She wasn't asking about the trout, and he knew he'd run out of time… and distractions.

"Las Vegas. I was attending a conference—you were there, too. With your fiancé." *Good-riddance Ridley.*

Georgia went very, very still.

The creek babbled busily in front of them as he waited for her response.

An aspen leaf drifted past on the surface. The current swept it between two rocks and it spun into the eddies below and down toward the deep rocky overhang where he knew lazy fish loved to lurk. All the courage he'd summoned threatened to drown along with the golden leaf.

She pushed her hair—paler than the silver bark of the aspen trees—off her face, and finally she looked across at him.

"When, exactly, did we meet?"

"On the Friday night." He waited.

There was an explosive silence as she absorbed that.

"I don't remember."

Jay had to ask. "How much do you remember about that night?"

"I don't want to talk about Ridley." Her tone was flat. There was no emotion in the words. He'd heard far more enthusiasm in her voice about the rising costs of Italian leather for next season's totes.

Tipping his head back, Jay stared at the blue sky visible between the gold leaves above. Hell, she never ever talked about the damned man. Why had he thought she would now?

Her eyes were bright with accusation when he glanced back at her. “You should’ve told me we’d met.”

“I…tried.”

He told himself he had. When she’d returned to work on crutches, her broken ankle encased in a moon boot, she hadn’t shown any hint of recognition. That had been when he’d learned what hell was. It had been blisteringly clear that Georgia didn’t remember him. The concussion she’d suffered in the car crash had wiped out several days afterward…and parts of the time just before. Jay hadn’t realized how much he’d been banking on her favorable reaction to finding him in the office next door. She’d refused to discuss the car accident, her injuries, any loss of memory and her ex-fiancé. And Jay hadn’t wanted to rub her nose in whatever she remembered of her humiliation.

“Not hard enough!”

At her stony expression, the ache in his chest swelled.

He hesitated, loath to confess that he’d been afraid. Afraid of exposing himself to her ridicule as their relationship settled into habitual snark and rivalry. He was still afraid. But now, at least the past was out in the open—she knew they’d met before.

“I thought it would be better if you remembered by yourself.”

“What do you know that I don’t?” She shook her head and her hair swirled around her shoulders. “Dammit, Jay. You kept this from me, every day. For two years.”

Anger and distrust cooled her eyes; he’d expected that. Hell, he deserved every bit of it.

“I’m sorry,” he said.

"You're sorry?" She glared at him. "You think that's enough?"

"I know it can never be enough, but I'm very sorry—I shouldn't have kept it from you."

What he badly wanted was her forgiveness. Day after day, he'd held stubbornly on to the hope that she would remember. One day. How could she not? The bond that had linked them from the moment they'd met had blown him away. She had to remember it.

So each morning, he'd resolved that he would tell her the truth, while secretly hoping she would remember him. Each morning, he'd brought her a cup of coffee.

Each day, she'd greeted him with a wide smile, a clever quip and suspicious eyes filled with fear that he was trying to edge her out of Kingdom.

And each day, it had nearly killed him. And he'd put it off for another day.

Two years of his life—and hers—had ticked by. He'd hidden his desires by playing the fool. He'd made her laugh. He'd driven her crazy. But he'd also worked to help her chase the dream she wanted—a dream of a future that every day took her further away from him.

But Jay wanted more than a dream woman. He wanted Georgia. He loved her mind. He loved her spirit. And he wanted his ring to stay on her finger.

More than anything, he wanted her love.

A wave of self-disgust at his own impatience swept him. He was pressing her too hard. He'd harbored a selfish hope that telling her that they'd met before might jog her memory. It hadn't happened. And it was probably for the best. While she might get to remember him—the first time he'd held her, comforted her—on the flip side, she'd also get to remember everything else about good-riddance Ridley that she'd so carefully blocked out.

He sucked in a deep breath. "Do you want to call this off? Do you want to go back?"

"Back?" Her eyes were dazed.

"Back to New York."

Georgia stared at Jay. His normally smiling lips were pressed into a grim line and there was no laughter visible in his eyes.

"No, I want to stay!" Despite the shock he'd delivered, she wasn't ready to face her father. At least not until she'd decided how she was going to appease him without giving in to his wretched demand.

Jay gave her a long considering look and got to his feet. He stretched out a hand to help her up, but she ignored it, brushed past him and marched back up the trail. All too soon, they were back in the SUV. He restarted the vehicle and spun it around to head back the way they'd come—back to Aspen.

Thoughts tumbled through her head as she tried to make sense of what Jay had told her, what it meant for her. For them. For their working relationship.

Jay had lied to her.

Turning her head away, she looked out the window. Around them, imposing mountains dominated the vast landscape. But this time, instead of driving through the town, Jay headed into the surrounding hills. She caught a couple of the road names as they climbed higher and higher through the switchbacks and the homes became increasingly more exclusive.

Hunter Creek Road.

Red Mountain Road.

When a pair of stone gateposts set with heavy black wrought-iron gates came into sight, Jay slowed. He pressed a code into a keypad beside the gate, and the heavy gates swung swiftly and silently open.

As the SUV purred along a driveway lined with aspens that shimmered in the sunlight, she realized her assumptions about Jay's family might have been a little off. The driveway ended in a spectacular sweep in front of a house.

No, not a house. Forget that. A luxurious Colorado lodge rose out of Red Mountain to a haphazard height of at least four stories. Not even the warm rays of the morning sun could soften the craggy lines of the stone structure that had been built to withstand storms and snowfall in the harshest of winters.

Georgia stared. "*This* is where your family live?"

So much for a white picket fence…

And what about the party tomorrow?

Any chance that it would be a low-key family affair went out the window. She thought frantically about the casual selection of garments she'd tossed into her Kingdom carry-on for a small-town family visit. She'd deliberately dialed it back, not wanting to arrive with a mountain of luggage looking like some super-spoiled big-city fashionista.

Aside from the French blue jeans and turtleneck sweater that she was wearing with a pair of flats, and her Kingdom coat with its distinctive crown-pattern lining on the back seat, there wasn't much in her carry-on.

Mentally, she listed the contents. Fawn riding-style pants that never creased. A white shirt—not silk, because she'd foolishly decided silk would be too over-the-top. A plain wool cardigan—not cashmere. A white long-sleeved T-shirt. Apart from her Kingdom coat, her favorite pair of well-worn Chelsea JJB boots was the only recognizable brand she'd packed. One pair of modest heels—nothing like the sublime skyscraper works of art she wore most days to work. One dress. God. The dress! It was an ode to understated mediocrity.

Her confusion and shock crystallized into anger.

She could kill Jay for not warning her!

Before she could give voice to it—or the million questions bubbling in her head—a small crowd spilled out of the lodge's enormous wooden front door and tumbled down the stone stairway.

Later, she promised herself. She would kill Jay later. He'd die a slow death. A very slow death…

She was out of the vehicle before he could come around and open the door. More shaken than she would ever have admitted by the discovery that Jay didn't come from some average small-town home, Georgia hovered beside the SUV as a woman wearing Western-style jeans, a pale pink cashmere sweater and a pair of black suede Jimmy Choo boots rushed down the stairs to fling her arms around Jay and kiss him soundly.

A moment later, the woman turned to Georgia and examined her. She had Jay's hazel eyes. It was his mother. There was no doubt about those eyes.

Georgia smiled hesitantly at Jay's family.

The people who loved him. The people to whom she and Jay were about to pretend they loved each other and intended to marry…and live happily ever after.

For the first time, the stark reality of the deception

they were about to enact struck Georgia. If there was one thing she was worse at than engagements, it was telling lies.

Unlike Jay…

How would she convince anyone that she was a besotted bride-to-be? Aside from that fiasco with Ridley, she'd never had much practice.

Her palms grew clammy.

There were two more women and a man behind Jay's mother. The younger woman was more casually dressed than Jay's mother in a pair of JJB boots—newer than those Georgia had packed—along with black jeans and an oversized white linen shirt. Once again, Georgia thought of the sorry contents of her overnight bag.

Jay moved closer. When he took her clammy hand in his, it eased her fluttering nerves. The sense of relief she felt further confounded her.

He gave her hand a gentle squeeze. "Mom, Dad, Jennifer, Betty…meet Georgia Kinnear. My fiancée."

Everyone appeared to freeze.

"Did you say fiancée?"

As Jay might have expected, his mother was the first to speak, even as his father's face grew tight-lipped with disapproval.

"Kinnear? Isn't that the name of that man you work for?" His father's dark brown eyes bored into him.

Here we go, Jay thought. His father knew the industry inside out. J.J. knew exactly whom Jay worked for. This was simply the next salvo in a long running battle. Their relationship had gotten no easier with absence.

Georgia was smiling at his father, a careful, charming little smile. Jay noticed she hadn't offered her hand. Clearly, she feared his curmudgeonly parent might choose to ignore it. He rather suspected she'd read the situation correctly. Sometimes, she could be the most astute woman he'd ever known—yet, at other times, she remained as blind as a newborn mouse.

"I'm Kingston Kinnear's eldest daughter, Georgia." She was still smiling. "Nice to meet you."

Her hand had gone cold in his. Jay gave it another gentle squeeze.

"Georgia, this is my family. My parents, J.J. and Nancy, my sister, Jennifer…and Betty, who has looked after our family for decades. You'll meet more of the extended family and plenty of friends at the anniversary celebration tomorrow." Turning his attention to his family, he said, "I'm fortunate that Georgia has agreed to marry me." Jay raised the hand he held and kissed it.

He heard her breath catch. He froze, too. The slanting sun caught the ring on her finger, causing it to glitter with fierce blue fire. He felt Georgia jerk, and looked up.

Their eyes caught…tangled…held.

He forgot everything. His family receded. His whole awareness centered on the pair of clear sky blue eyes.

The moment shattered as a furry body barreled into his legs.

A golden Labrador grinned up at him, and he heard Georgia laugh.

"I see I forgot to introduce Zeus," he said ruefully.

She rubbed the dog's head.

Jay looked up. Everyone appeared to be transfixed at the sight of the ring on Georgia's hand as she caressed Zeus's ears. No one could have missed what he'd known the moment he met Georgia: the ring was perfect. The blue of the diamond reflected the brightness of her eyes, while the silver setting glittering with pavé diamonds matched her hair. With his grandmother's ring on her finger, Jay had sent a message: he expected his family—every one of them—to honor his choice.

"Don't let Zeus jump up—his feet are all muddy."

His mother was the first to step forward, gently kneeing Zeus out of the way. She kissed Georgia, first on one cheek, then on the other.

"This is such happy news," she said, her voice thick with emotion.

Thank you, Mom. A wave of love for his mother filled Jay.

His sister hadn't moved. She stood beside his father, a question in her eyes. Jay read it as easily as though his sister had yelled it at him.

What about Suzie?

Dammit!

The old guilt stirred deep in his gut. He pushed it away. He'd deal with Suzie later. Tomorrow. She'd be at the anniversary celebration. Unlike the old man, Jennifer would reserve judgment—even though her loyalties would be torn.

Jay headed back to the SUV. It only took a moment to heft their bags out of the trunk. Georgia, thank God, had traveled light. He retrieved their coats from the back seat. His mother had finally released his brand-new fiancée, who looked a little dazed as he dropped her coat over her shoulders.

"Let's go inside," Jay said brusquely. For now, she had endured enough. There was more to come—her weekend escape was the beginning of his purgatory. There was little hope of forgiveness: he'd left it too late for that.

"Give me one minute. I need a word with Betty to sort out a few last-minute details." Nancy Black touched her husband's arm and fixed him with a look that Georgia guessed held a warning. "Darling, prepare Jay and Georgia something refreshing to drink—I'm sure they're parched after the trip."

"I'll get Zeus cleaned up." Jay's sister grabbed the Labrador by the collar.

Georgia's desire to murder Jay escalated another level.

He hadn't been joking. He'd given his unsuspecting family no warning that he was bringing a guest—much less a fiancée. His mother's need for time to consult with the housekeeper revealed that much. Not that Nancy had made her feel like an interloper; to the contrary, Nancy's welcome had been the warmest of all.

Nor had Jay been joking when he'd said his parents would expect her to be wearing an engagement ring, although she hadn't anticipated that they would be quite so riveted by the sight of the ring on her finger.

This was far from the modest, ordinary family she'd expected.

Jay's mother exhibited the easy style of a woman comfortable with wealth, while his father wore jeans, a Western jacket and, once again, the ubiquitous JJB boots—although his were the scuffed cowboy kind.

And then there was the house…

Once inside the heavy front door, Georgia found

herself standing in a double-height—or was it triple-height?—foyer. Never-ending living spaces unfolded before her, with fabulous mountain vistas visible through the surrounding windows. In the distance, a curved staircase in black wrought iron with a carved wooden bannister rose to the upper floors. From the marble-tiled lobby, two steps led down to a spacious living area arranged around a stone fireplace. Wooden floors—walnut, she suspected—were scattered with large hand-woven rugs. On the far side of the fireplace, Georgia glimpsed a dining space surrounded with vast floor-to-ceiling windows that framed more spectacular views.

She wanted nothing more than to get Jay alone. To demand some answers. Why had he never said a word about his family's wealth? In all the time she'd known him, all the time she'd worked head-to-head with him, he'd never discussed it. He'd mentioned parents and a sister in passing. But nothing had prepared her for this—this—

Words failed her.

Murder might not be enough…

As she and Jay trooped down the two stairs behind J.J., Georgia tried to fathom the family dynamics that were swirling around them. There was clearly a bond of deep affection—love—between Jay's parents. But the relationship between Jay and his father was not as easy to decipher. Jay gestured to a leather sofa. Once she sat down, Georgia glanced around with interest, taking in the pewter chandelier overhead and the pair of bronze elk statues beside the hearth. But when Jay settled beside her, his thigh close to her own, any curiosity instantly evaporated.

All she could focus on was the pressure of Jay's thigh against hers.

"So, you want to marry my son?" J.J. had taken the leather armchair directly across from where she and Jay sat.

Before she could respond, Jay spoke from beside her. "I proposed—I want to marry Georgia."

But J.J. appeared deaf to the warning note in Jay's voice as his bitter brown eyes drilled into Georgia.

J.J.

The name nagged at her. Jay's father looked vaguely familiar. But she'd swear they'd never met. Georgia took her time studying him. The broad shoulders and head of gray hair. The heavy brows over measuring eyes. He was the picture of a successful, wealthy man comfortable in his skin right down to the scuffed Western boots he wore. JJB boots. Like hers.

J.J. Black?

As in JJB Boots? Iconic Western boots. She and Roberta both loved them. She'd had a vague idea that the company was based out west. In Colorado?

Oh, my God!

Jay was one of *those* Blacks.

And he'd never told her?

JJB Boots!

Deep inside, something twisted painfully at that thought. Despite all their skirmishes, despite her fears that Jay was after her dream job, she'd always known he shared many of her own visions and values. She'd spoken the truth down beside the creek: Jay understood her better than anyone she'd ever met, and that only intensified the hurt she was feeling. He'd confessed to lying to her about the past. Now she'd discovered he'd chosen to tell her nothing about his family business—yet he knew everything there was to know about Kingdom.

How had he come to work for Kingdom? How had he learned about the post Ridley had vacated?

Jay had risen to his feet. A dark wood unit opened to reveal a liquor cabinet and a fridge. "What would you like to drink, Georgia?"

A destructive impulse to demand a triple tequila before noon overtook her. Georgia stifled it. Jay might be amused, but she doubted J.J. would appreciate it. Getting off on the wrong foot with the man would only make what was starting to look like a challenging weekend more difficult.

"May I have some water, no ice, please?"

"Sure." Jay took a bottle of mineral water out of the concealed bar fridge, then twisted the top off and poured it into a tall glass.

Georgia felt ridiculously obtuse. Part of it was Jay's fault—he'd never given her any hint. How could she have guessed? It wasn't as if Kingdom ever had any business dealings with JJB Boots.

Although that wasn't such a bad idea…

"—and I'll cut down on my working hours once you're back. Your mother will be pleased."

What? Ripped out of her thoughts, Georgia's sudden movement caused the ring on her finger to flash blue fire. All at once it no longer mattered how or why he'd come to work for Kingdom.

Her gaze meshed with Jay's.

"You're planning to leave Kingdom?" she whispered.

"Of course, he's going to leave!"

She blocked out J.J.'s loud voice and kept her eyes on the man who had become her rock. Jay's expression was unfathomable. It had been bad enough to think about him leaving her for a vacation, but for Jay to leave Kingdom forever…?

"My son was never going to stay at a New York luxury label when he has the solid family tradition of JJB Boots waiting for him back home."

There. If she'd needed confirmation, she had it in J.J.'s contempt. Anger, hurt, a raw pain contracted her chest.

But Jay's eyes remained steady on hers. "My fiancée would be the first to know if I were considering such a drastic step."

Fiancée. His warning was clear: she'd better not give the game away.

Even as he handed her the soda and sat down beside her, a frantic desire to slip into the bracing chill outside overcame her. Anything to get away from the suddenly oppressive mood in the room and to clear her thoughts.

Jay was part of JJB Boots. He had a career—a life—waiting for him here. A life he'd said he didn't want to be pressured into going back to. But someday, he would realize the value his family and the JJB Boots brand held.

Someday, he would leave Kingdom.

All Georgia's anger at Jay evaporated as a greater dread set in.

They made a great team. How often, during the worst moments of her day, when she was bogged down with stress and deadlines, would Jay arrive brandishing a cup of coffee just as she liked it and flash that lazy grin, his eyes glinting with devilry. Tension would seep out of her. Life would instantly become simpler, more fun for a few moments. Solutions to all the problems plaguing her would fall into place.

What would she do when Jay decided to leave?

A shocking realization struck her: she didn't want him to leave. Ever.

Really rattled now, Georgia couldn't hide her relief when light footsteps sounded, and Nancy reappeared.

"Ah, good. J.J., I see you got Georgia a drink." No one disabused her of the notion. "Everything is sorted out, Jay. The guest suite is ready for both of you."

The guest suite is ready...for both of you?

Georgia blinked. Twice. Her lips parted. "Um—"

"Thanks, Mom." Jay was already on his feet. "I'll take our bags up."

Georgia was left with no choice. Flashing a polite, vacant smile in the direction of her hosts, she abandoned her untouched drink and dashed after him. He took the wooden stairs two at time, his black boots thudding against the wooden stairs.

Black leather boots…

JJB Boots.

How could she have been so blind? She could've screamed. Had Jay been laughing at her all the time that he'd had her fooled?

"Wait," she called out as he reached the top.

"We're just through here." Without slowing, Jay vanished through a stone arch.

Ten

"You have some explaining—"

Georgia came to an abrupt stop under the arch. Through the rustic doorway, she could see Jay setting their bags down on an antique blanket chest at the foot of the bed.

She did a double take as she took in the size of the sleigh bed that dominated the guest suite. It was ginormous.

"—to do." Her voice fizzled out.

And just like that, Jay's relationship to JJB Boots became the least of her worries.

One bed… Two people.

And not another bed in sight. Tension gripped her belly. Refusing to acknowledge it, she reminded herself that she and Jay were colleagues.

No, they were friends.

Only friends. Nothing more…

She thought of the skimpy lace and satin pajamas in her trolley bag and drew her brows together.

"I am not sleeping here, Jay." She fought to keep her voice from rising. "Not in one bed."

"And if there were two beds? Would that make a difference?"

Georgia narrowed her gaze. She was starting to suspect that the lazy mocking smile, the good-humored teasing masked a more intense, far more complex man. This Jay was all too familiar. Maddening. Provocative. Engaging. Amusing. But not even an invitation to debate the matter was going to distract her. Not this time.

"That hardly solves the problem," she said firmly.

The corners of his mouth kicked up into a crooked smile.

Oh, she knew that smile…

Except this time, her reaction was different. More complicated. For once, she didn't rise to the bait. Instead, her eyes flickered to the undone top button at the neckline of his white shirt and the sliver of bare skin revealed at his throat, then quickly away…back to his face.

From the light in his eyes, she knew he'd recognized the heat she'd felt.

"We don't even have to sleep, you know." He followed that smile up with a wicked growl. "Not if you're so dead set against it. That should solve the problem, right?"

She swallowed hard.

Suddenly, she was finding it hard to breathe.

While that magnificent maple bed behind her was simply waiting…

Georgia's heart started a slow thud in her chest.

He was coming closer. The wickedness in his widening smile caused her throat to tighten further and her skin began to tingle.

How had she never noticed the sensual ease with which he moved…or the sexy slant of his cheekbones? The catalog of her oversights was growing longer by the hour.

"Hey." She struggled to laugh.

Too late. Way too late. It came out breathy and expectant, and the awful sound hung between them.

Nice work, Georgia!

Warmth flooded her face. Striving for firmness, she channeled her most businesslike boardroom voice. "Don't tease, Jay."

His smile was all teeth, and his eyes gleamed.

"Whatever makes you think I'm teasing?"

At the low husky note, a pang of yearning—just short of pain—stabbed at her heart. A memory of that instant she'd uttered the reckless bid that had won her Jay at the Bachelors for a Better Future Benefit Auction swept over her. His stunned expression and the surge of triumph that had seized her in that moment came sharply back into focus.

When his gaze dropped to her mouth, the tingle flared into heat, shocking her with its intensity. Georgia resisted the urge to run the tip of her tongue over lips gone suddenly dry.

But she couldn't stop her heart from slamming against her ribs.

"Stop it!" she croaked.

"Okay." He looked up from her mouth and met her gaze full-on. "So what do you want?"

That huskiness in his voice—her heart recognized it. Even though she could've sworn she'd never heard it from Jay before. She backed up a couple of steps. The drumbeat against her ribs grew heavier.

"Your parents will be wondering where we are." Desperation called for desperate measures.

"My mother knows we'll be taking time to freshen up a little."

She took another step back. The big bed banged into the back of her legs, and she stilled in surprise.

"So, you never did answer my question."

She was aware of his intent gaze, of his lean strength, of the heat of his body in front of her. *Oh, dear heaven.*

"What question?" She shuddered inwardly at the squeakiness of her voice.

"What do you want?"

Her heart jolted. His closeness—

The rustle of denim, the smell of suede and the fresh mossy, woodsy scent of his aftershave filled her senses.

"Georgia…"

At last, she lifted her gaze. The final traces of a smile still lingered. But as their eyes connected, it vanished. The diamond hard-edged intensity in his expression caused her heart to splinter painfully.

Jay wanted her.

In the absence of his teasing smile, the hard slash of his cheekbones and the tight line of his mouth were a revelation. Again, that Alice-down-a-rabbit-hole sense of not knowing, not seeing the real Jay filled her.

Her breath caught in the back of her throat. She placed her hands on his forearms, the suede jarringly rough beneath her touch. “I don’t think we should—”

“Don’t think,” he ordered.

His head came down.

“Feel,” he whispered against her mouth.

Her heartbeat went through the roof.

Excitement tore through her. This kiss was nothing like the sweet, chaste kiss of friendship they’d shared in the hospital courtyard. This time, there were no preliminaries. His mouth was hard and hungry. His tongue lashed into her mouth, tasting her…scorching her.

Digging her fingertips into the thickness of his jacket, Georgia made a little sound in the back of her throat.

It was part surprise. Part something…darker, far more frightening.

Then she released her grip on him to edge her hands down around his hips. As he groaned and pushed closer, she clutched at his jeans, the ridge of the pocket edges rough against her fingers. Beneath the denim, she felt the tight butt she’d so covertly admired on the stairs only minutes before, and arched up against him.

He felt hard and unmistakably male against her.

Panting, she tore her mouth from his. Instantly, he eased back so that her hands slid from his buttocks to his hips.

Her hands tightened on the waistband of Jay’s jeans.

Did he know what he was doing to her? Did he know about the desire that pulsed through her veins? She flipped him a quick upward glance from under her lashes. He was watching her, disconcertingly composed, his gaze steady. No glint of mockery in sight.

"Are you okay?" he asked, utterly serious for once.

"Of course!" She tried to smile.

But was this a good idea? They worked together. She was terrible at romance. And worse at reading men's intentions. Now was the time to tell him that the only thing they had in common was business. The fashion industry. Work. Kingdom.

Only…

That wasn't true. Not anymore. Something had changed.

She had changed.

And Jay had changed, too.

He desired her.

Despite his level gaze and apparent calm, the evidence she'd felt pressed against her had been unmistakable.

Maybe she had it all wrong…

Maybe she *was* his type. Maybe he really did want her, Georgia, the woman she was under the Kinnear veneer.

Beneath the churning uncertainty and confusion, it was as if a dam wall had broken and a torrent of emotion had been released. For the first time in years, she no longer felt shamed by what she felt. By what she wanted.

Or by doing something about getting it.

So what did *she* want?

Right now, she wanted to be kissed by Jay…

A real kiss, not some sweet innocent kiss between friends. A real rip-my-heart out kiss, wherever that led.

"Oh." The sound burst from her in frustration.

Releasing his hips, she brought her hands up, sliding them over the rough suede past the buttoned edges until they closed on the lapels of his jacket. His eyes blazed as she gave a little tug. Then he laughed and twisted around, leaving her holding the abandoned jacket. She flung it onto the bed behind her.

His hands came down on her arms as she plunged forward, grasping a fistful of his shirtfront.

He steadied her. “Slowly, sweetheart.”

“Don’t you dare laugh!”

He didn’t want her. The heat of all-too-familiar doubt rose through her. The fear of humiliation, of making a fool of herself all over again seized her gut. She swallowed.

Jay’s hazel eyes were unexpectedly serious as they searched hers.

“Do I look like I’m laughing?”

His mouth was at eye-level. It was a beautiful mouth. It spoke to her in ways her heart understood. And it wasn’t laughing.

Georgia wanted to sob with frustration, even as her grip on his shirt tightened, her emotions seesawing wildly between desire and betrayal. She twisted her hand. A button threatened to pop.

She didn’t want it to be like this.

Forcing herself to look away from that mouth that was driving her crazy, Georgia released her grip on his shirt, and smoothed down the creased fabric.

The hurt that had been festering since she’d put two and two together about JJB Boots spilled over.

“Why didn’t you tell me, Jay? About JJB Boots? Why the secrecy?”

Lifting his hands away, he speared them through his hair. She felt bereft at the loss of his touch.

"It was always on my résumé."

Which she'd never seen because she'd been convalescing when Jay had been hired. And why bother when every frenetic day, Jay's actions spoke louder than any testimony ever could? He'd proven himself an excellent hire. "You never talk about your family."

"You never ask," he countered.

Silently, Georgia acknowledged her blinkered absorption in all things Kingdom.

"I told you a couple of times that my mom and sister were visiting New York. You didn't show interest in hearing more."

"Your dad didn't come?"

His mouth tightened. "No." He ran his hands through his hair again and hunched his shoulders. "Who my family is doesn't change who I am. JJB Boots—and J.J. Black for that matter—do not define who I am." He looked up, his gaze direct. "I'm sorry. I screwed up. I hurt you."

His hair stood up in spikes where his fingers had mauled it. Without laughter, he looked older, resolute, disturbingly serious.

The maddening rival was nothing like the man who faced her now. He'd withheld so much of himself. She couldn't dismiss that. But the man hidden behind the mocking mask was so much more. Her apprehension lifted, causing her to blurt out, "You're my rock, Jay. I never want to lose that."

"You won't. I promise."

It was enough.

"What do I want?" She tipped her head. "More than anything, I want you to kiss me again."

The fingers that brushed against her chin, cupping her cheek, shook a little. His free hand came up to her shoulder. With a jerk, he drew her closer.

Caught in his embrace, held against him, despite everything she'd discovered about him today, despite everything he'd withheld, Georgia felt safe. She leaned into him and his arms tightened fiercely around her. He nuzzled her, and his breath warmed her neck. She needed that warmth. *His* warmth.

Then his lips were on hers, her lips parted and he sank in.

His leg shifted forward, sliding between her thighs. One hand closed on her breast, and his fingers stroked. Slowly, deliberately, he caressed the tightening peak under her sweater, causing bursts of arousal. Georgia's knees almost gave way again.

She closed her eyes, lost in the fresh flare of desire.

A little gasp escaped against his mouth.

A loud knock shattered the hot daze, and the bedroom door flew open.

"Georgia, we don't dress up fo—" Nancy stood in the doorway, her mouth a perfect *O* of surprise. "I'm sorry. I thought you might need some towels."

Flushing wildly, conscious of his hand on her breast and the solidness of the big bed behind her knees, Georgia tried to extricate herself from Jay's hold. But he held her close, refusing to let her go, his body shielding her from his mother's view.

Over Jay's shoulder, Georgia could see Nancy clutching a pile of towels.

Jay's mother cleared her throat. "Uh. Dinner will

be ready in less than half an hour—we don't dress up. Please join us for a drink."

"Thanks. And, Mom..." Jay said as his mother paused "...wait a little longer after you knock next time, okay?"

Nancy's eyes were wide with shock. She dropped the towels on the tallboy just inside the door, nodded and fled.

Eleven

Jay's frustration knew no bounds.

After retreating to take a shower so cold that his skin still stung, there was no relief to be found back in the bedroom where Georgia stood in front of the dresser, brushing her hair. He pretended not to watch—all the while itching to run his hands through the soft silver strands as he had last night.

Hell, he'd need another cold shower if this carried on.

She'd swapped the sweater she'd been wearing earlier for a snowy white shirt tucked into her jeans and a wide woven belt. She didn't spare him a glance as she secured her hair in a loose knot at the nape of her neck. He wanted to rip the pins out.

"Are you ready?" His voice was husky.

She nodded and moved to the door.

Jay slung an arm across her shoulders once they exited the guest suite. Downstairs in the dining room, his mother and Betty had their heads bent over a piece of paper on the dining table, while Jennifer watched them approach from across the table.

"That's the final list?" he asked the women.

"The final-final list." His mother peered at him over her reading glasses, revealing no sign of the awkward moment in the guest room as she smiled at Georgia. He loved his mom!

"More like the final-final-final list." Jennifer grimaced. "Between Mom and Betty, tomorrow is going to run like clockwork."

"They're a pair of dynamos—they wear the rest of us out." Jay tipped his head toward Georgia, allowing himself the surreptitious pleasure of inhaling her perfume. He pulled out the chair at the table for her.

"We kept it small," his mom was saying to Georgia. "Only a hundred and eighty guests. That way, we can enjoy ourselves."

"Is there anything I can do to help?" asked Georgia.

"Yes, you can help with all the last-minute details after dinner. Jennifer, I'll need you, too, please."

"With pleasure." Georgia sounded a little more relaxed.

He could tell that his mother already liked Georgia. How could she not? Jay felt a swelling of warmth in his chest as he sat down beside Georgia.

"So long as I'm excused from the flower arranging." His father's gruff voice interrupted his thoughts. The last to arrive, J.J. took his customary place at the head of the table.

Jay didn't register his mom's response because Georgia chose that moment to turn her head and give him a small smile, slashing his guts to ribbons. He slowly smiled back, and instantly the sizzle of awareness reignited between them. Then color rose in her cheeks and her gaze fell away, breaking the connection.

The meal passed in a blur.

"That was delicious." Georgia's knife and fork clinked together as she set them down on the plate.

"Betty is a marvel," his mother responded with pride in her voice. "What do you say, Jay?"

"The fish was good," he managed, scrambling to remember what he'd eaten. He'd been too conscious of Georgia's denim-clad thigh beside his own, his shoulder brushing against hers as he reached for the salt, her scent drifting across, intoxicating him.

"Of course, it is. Freshly caught by your father." His mother caught his eye and smiled.

Jay felt himself reddening—something he couldn't remember happening since he was a teenager. Was his enthrallment with Georgia so obvious?

"You used to come with me, Jay. Remember the bighorns in the high country pastures? The water holes where we'd find fish under ledges no one else knew about?" His father grimaced. "But these days, you have more important fish to fry."

"Jay and Georgia could visit over the winter. We could all go skiing." His mom looked hopeful. "And Georgia might even want to tag along next time you and Jay go out fly fishing."

"What would a New York fashion plate know about tying a fly?"

Jay winced at his father's rudeness, even as Georgia flinched beside him.

Georgia spoke before he got a chance, her chin rising a notch. "I can get by on a pair of skis—and I can certainly learn to fly fish."

His father snorted. "You'd get wet."

All Jay's muscles went rigid. His father was spoiling for a fight. With barely concealed anger, he said, "Dad, there's no need for—"

A chair scraped as his mom rose hurriedly to her feet. "Betty is sorting the cutlery and linen for tomorrow's party. I need to check on the apple pie and make sure it's not burning. J.J., you can come and help me."

His father clambered to his feet, pointedly ignoring Georgia.

Jay opened his mouth to blast his father, but was stalled by the touch of Georgia's hand on his thigh.

"Let it go," she murmured so only he heard.

"Suzie makes some of the best flies in Colorado." J.J.'s truculence sliced through the distance between them. "You should be marrying her."

"J.J.!" His mother's voice was sharp. "Now!"

"Uh, I think I might go help, too." Jennifer shot to her feet.

The moment his family disappeared, Georgia swiveled her head and Jay received a hard stare.

"Suzie?"

She began to remove her hand from his leg. He brought his hand down, enfolding hers, forestalling her withdrawal. He rubbed the back of her hand, luxuriating in her soft skin under his palm. "I apologize for my father's rudeness."

She didn't acknowledge his apology. "Is there something else you've forgotten to tell me?"

Jay didn't want to talk about Suzie. Not with his parents and sister about to return at any moment. "Let's discuss this later."

"I think you need to fill me in now."

The tilt of Georgia's jaw warned him that she was not about to be deterred.

"Who is Suzie? Your girlfriend?" she persisted, picking up the paper napkin laid across her lap and tearing it in half.

"Ex," he muttered.

Georgia narrowed her eyes until the flash of blue through the cracks of her black lashes glittered brighter than the diamond on her finger. "How ex?"

"I haven't seen her in years."

Georgia's look of relief caused the oppressive weight in his chest to lift a little.

Crumpling the shredded napkin into a ball, she dropped it onto the table. "Well, I suppose I should be thankful you haven't put me in the unsavory position of being the other woman."

Jay winced.

The sound of his mother's raised voice chastising his father wafted from the direction of the kitchen.

Georgia drew a breath. "My presence here is causing friction."

Damn the old man! "This friction between my father and me is nothing new."

"I feel so guilty for misleading your family. Your mother is so lovely. She believes I'll be back to visit with you. She's already including me in future skiing trips. I can even understand your father's hostility—he resents me because he believes I'm keeping you away. I shouldn't be here."

It was all his fault that Georgia felt like an outsider. By convincing her to agree to a sham engagement, he'd created this situation—not his father.

But the alternative was to lay his heart on the line… and have her stomp all over it. Because of his own male pride, he'd made it harder for her, not easier.

Tightening his hand around hers, he said, "The truth is, my father finds it hard to accept I'm a man, not a boy any longer. I'm not coming back. He knows that—but he refuses to accept it."

"He wants you to take over the legacy he's built," she said softly. "It's his dream."

The irony of that wasn't lost on Jay. Georgia craved most what she thought Jay had walked away from. Families could be hell.

He drew a deep breath and said, "But it's not my dream."

"He loves you, Jay." The sparkle in Georgia's eyes had gentled. She turned her hand over, threading her fingers through his, and Jay's heart contracted. "He wants what's best for you."

Jay shook his head. "No, it's not what's best for me that he wants. It's what's best for him. And that's not love."

"You need to talk to him." There was concern in her eyes.

Her compassion loosened a tightness deep within him. But he concealed his vulnerability by arching his eyebrows and saying with pointed irony, "*I* need to talk to *my* father?"

Georgia shifted in her seat, her cheeks reddening. "I'll talk to Kingston on Monday. Honestly, I will."

Instantly, Jay felt bad. Georgia's relationship with her father was far more complex than his with J.J.

He squeezed her hand, then released it and rose to his feet. "Okay, I'll go talk to J.J."

"Be gentle," she murmured so softly he had to strain to hear the words. "For both your sakes."

From the doorway of the den, Jay shook his head and smiled at the sight of Zeus sprawled across the leather chesterfield, snoring.

Wooden bookshelves packed with books on fishing, business management and the craft of boot-making lined the walls. A box-frame filled with the first flies that Jay had tied under his father's tutelage still held pride of place, and the almost-buried memory of that long ago time tugged at Jay.

"So the prodigal son has returned."

His father rolled the leather executive chair away from the window and set his whiskey glass down on the antique walnut desk next to a box of carefully crafted flies. The eyes that inspected Jay were filled with a critical glint that was all too familiar.

"About time, my boy."

Jay shoved Zeus to one side to make space on the couch. Settling himself beside the snoring dog, he crossed an ankle over his knee and strove for calm.

"Dad, we need to talk."

"This nonsense about an engagement must end."

Already, his father was hijacking a conversation that hadn't yet begun. "I want you back home."

Slowly, Jay shook his head. He allowed a slight smile to tilt his mouth as he rocked his boot-clad foot back and forth.

"I'm not coming back."

His avoidance of the word home was deliberate.

Home was where the heart was, and his heart had taken up residence elsewhere.

"Of course, you are!" His father gave an impatient snort. "You've had enough time away. It's time for you to come back and marry Suzie."

Once again, his father was treating him like a boy, rather than the man he'd become. Keeping his voice steady, Jay said, "I'm not going to marry Suzie."

There was only one woman he planned to marry.

"You're engaged—"

"That's over. You know that, and Suzie knows that."

"Suzie still wants to marry you—she'll jump at the chance."

Jay doubted it.

Some of the residual guilt about his old friend stirred. He forced it down. Guilt was the last thing Suzie—or he—deserved. "What Suzie really wants is to be a permanent part of JJB Boots—marrying me would've secured that."

"That's not the point. Suzie needs you—she needs a husband," his father insisted. When Jay refused to respond, J.J.'s hands balled into fists. "The business needs you, too, Jay."

They'd finally gotten to the crux of what his father really wanted.

The old tightness was back in Jay's gut, winched tighter by the steel chain binding him to dreams that had never been his.

This time, when he shook his head, it was with finality. "You're looking at the wrong Black."

"What the hell is that supposed to mean?"

His father's bull-headedness was as frustrating as always. Colorado would never be big enough to hold them both. Jay felt his hard-won calm slip. "You know what it means, Dad. Open your eyes to what's in front of you. Jennifer—"

"Jennifer has done her best to help hold things together while you've been gallivanting around New York. You've gotten the qualifications we decided you needed, and I've given you enough time to gain the necessary industry experience to run our business."

Jay steeled himself not to react. Zeus pressed up against Jay's thigh. Absently, he scratched the dog behind his ears.

"I need you here running JJB Boots! Jennifer will get married someday—"

Jay's hand stilled as he cut his father off. "I'll be married first."

"It's not the same, Jay."

If Georgia had been here, she would've have accused him of being deliberately provocative. She would have probably been right. But his father's stance would have infuriated her, too. J.J. was almost as bad as Kingston.

Dinosaurs, both of them.

Zeus's nose nudged at his hand. Jay recommenced rubbing the soft feathery ears and the dog settled his muzzle onto his paws.

"The world has changed, Dad. There is life after marriage. Jennifer and Suzie will make fine business partners in JJB Boots—even if both of them decide to get married someday."

"Don't be flippant, boy! You're my son. My successor. Your place is at the head of JJB Boots."

Jay didn't allow his rising annoyance to show. "I'm not coming back. It's not what I want."

They lapsed into uncomfortable silence.

He'd promised Georgia that he would be gentle, so he searched for words to soften the blow. "Dad, I'm a man, not a boy anymore. I will visit you and Mom. And I hope you take time out to come to New York next time Mom visits." But Jay wasn't holding his breath. It hadn't happened in two years.

With a violent kick of his foot, his father swung his chair away to stare out the window into the darkness that had settled over the jagged peaks. "I will cut off your allowance."

At his father's raised voice, Zeus whimpered. Stroking the dog's head in reassurance, Jay almost smiled. J.J. was using the same tactics Kingston had used so successfully on Georgia. But it was an impotent threat—and J.J. was enough of a realist to know it.

"You will find I haven't touched that for years." It had been longer than five years since Jay had spent a cent of the quarterly allowance he received from the trust fund set up by his grandfather. Nor had he touched the parcel of stocks his grandfather had left to him—as the sole grandson. "I'm quite capable of fending for myself."

"And what of your fiancée?" The chair spun back. His father's mouth was clenched as tight as a trap.

His fiancée…

A vision leaped into his mind. Of Georgia grabbing his shirtfront, pressing up against him, careless of his clothes or hers. Of the wild kiss that had followed. Of her hot little gasps against his mouth…

Whoa! He had to crawl into bed beside Georgia tonight…and sleep. He'd be awake all night if he started to think about the wild little sounds she'd made in the back of her throat.

"I wouldn't be so sure that little lady agrees with your high moral stance, my boy. She's accustomed to the best in life. Luxury labels. High heels and charity balls. Not hiking boots and wading in mountain streams. That high society lifestyle, it doesn't come cheap. Will you be able to fend for her and keep her happy?"

His father had no idea what would make Georgia happy. But Jay rather suspected he might. If only she gave him the chance.

"I think I'll be able to keep my fiancée happy."

"Don't be so sure. Her father will expect—"

"Now that brings me to what I came in here to talk to you about." Jay's voice lowered as he lifted his foot from where it rested across his other ankle and set it firmly down on the rug. He sat forward on the chesterfield. "Why don't you tell me about the mission you've been on to buy up stocks in Kingdom?"

Twelve

With the heady scent of gardenia soap clinging to her, Georgia stepped out from beneath the shower and quickly wrapped herself in one of the soft luxurious bath towels that Jay's mom had left. The last thing she wanted was for Jay to walk in and catch her naked.

It was absurd to feel so nerve-rackingly aware of him.

They'd worked together in adjacent offices for years. But that was before that sizzling kiss. And now, the treacherous tingle that prickled along her skin refused to be doused by the rough rub of the towel.

Clothes, she needed clothes.

Back in the bedroom, she shimmied into her pajamas, covering up her shower-dampened body. Catching sight of her reflection in the armoire mirror, Georgia quivered. Pale aqua satin clung revealingly to her hips and bottom. The V-neckline of the flagrantly feminine cami top gaped wide, while lace side panels revealed still more skin. It looked like she was doing her best to stage a deliberate seduction.

What she needed was body armor, Georgia decided grimly. The corporate kind. A smart no-nonsense big-name jet-black designer pantsuit would work just fine. But she was stuck with what she'd packed.

She rolled her eyes. Of course, there was an alternative!

Ever conscious that Jay might stroll in at any instant, she sped to the armoire and emerged—triumphant—with a long-sleeved white T-shirt. She whipped it over the cami, and then scrutinized her image critically.

Not quite boardroom armor, but an enormous improvement.

Deciding that the chairs grouped by the glass door presented a better option than waiting in the bed, she made her way across the room. The damned satin pajama bottoms whispered against her sensitized skin with every step. Perching on one of the straight-backed slipper chairs, Georgia picked a fashion magazine off the coffee table. Her fingers trembled as she flicked through the glossy pages. Not even an interview by one of her favorite fashion feature writers could hold her attention as her stomach twisted into convoluted knots.

So much had happened today. The ring. Jay's confession that they'd met before he'd come to Kingdom—and she didn't remember. Meeting Jay's parents—and finding out that they owned the iconic JJB Boots brand.

Then there'd been the discovery that his family expected Jay to marry another woman.

And the cherry on top: the shock that Jay actually desired her.

Restlessly, Georgia shut the magazine with a snap and shoved it aside. Once on her feet, she started to pace.

Jay wasn't engaged to Suzie; he was free to kiss whomever he pleased.

Georgia chewed her lip. Did it matter that he hadn't told her about his family's business? The JJB Boots brand held no threat to Kingdom. Did it even matter that Jay had never mentioned the first time they'd met? He'd done her a favor. It was a day she never talked about—she didn't even remember most of it. The little she did remember, she'd worked hard to forget.

If there was one thing her experience with Ridley had proved conclusively, it was that she was useless at relationships. She certainly wasn't expecting love and commitment from Jay. But she wouldn't mind another one of those knee-weakening kisses.

Shock caused her to stop in her tracks. She wanted—

Even more than kisses, she wanted to sleep with Jay.

She closed her eyes.

What was she thinking?

God, it was hard to admit. She wanted pleasure. The kind of mind-blowing pleasure that kiss earlier had promised. Opening her eyes, she stared blindly at the carpet. They were two consenting adults with no reason not to indulge in a no-strings fantasy for a night.

Maybe even two nights…

She could change her flight—and fly back early

Monday morning. Excitement and nerves churned in her stomach.

Even as she considered the possibility, footfalls sounded on the wooden stairs and the door handle rattled. Her heart jolted, and the tension inside ratcheted up another notch. Georgia hesitated for only for a fraction of a second before diving into the big bed, sinking into the indulgently soft linen as the door swung open.

Jay had arrived.

The wooden door shut behind him with a heavy clang, causing the drapes that framed the glass doors leading to the terrace to flutter. Georgia's pulse rocketed from zero to a hundred when Jay strode in. Determined not to let the sudden intimacy rattle her nerves, she drew a deep breath to ask him how the talk with J.J. had gone.

But as he strolled forward and began to unbutton the tiny buttons at the cuffs of his shirt, the unspoken words dried up.

After shaking the cuffs loose, Jay started on the buttons down the front. Georgia could only stare as the shirt's edges parted to reveal an impressively muscled chest and a washboard stomach, both of which confirmed he was no stranger to a sweaty workout.

Georgia's fingers played frantically with the corner of the sheet as she watched him shrug off his shirt. With his hair mussed and his shirt billowing, he looked deliciously disheveled.

She tingled as acres of male skin were laid bare.

How had she missed that he was simply gorgeous for so long? Was she completely blind?

"You were right that I needed to talk to J.J." Jay

fished into his pocket and dropped his wallet on the nightstand.

Then, to her relief, he walked across the room, giving her plenty of opportunity to admire the surprisingly well-developed laterals sloping to a narrow waist. With a flick of his wrist, he tossed the shirt over one of the chairs beside the glass doors.

He headed for the armoire. “Plenty of positives came out of it.”

Jay lifted an arm, and Georgia couldn’t help noticing the rounded peak of the bicep and, below, the bulge of his triceps as he rubbed his hand back and forth over the back of his neck. Somehow, he’d found time in his awful work schedule to do a fair amount of serious curls. A flush of warmth came with the discovery that the man who walked in and out of her office every day had a body worth lusting after—had she been given to lusting.

The sound of a zipper severed the sudden silence. Then he kicked off his boots and shucked off his jeans, and her brain stopped working.

Georgia tried—unsuccessfully—not to gawk at the muscled ridges on his chest. The taut, tight abs. Was she the only one who had never noticed? He’d certainly aroused enough feminine interest at the benefit auction. She discovered she didn’t care for the memory. She didn’t like the idea of Jay being pursued by every Dom, Nic and Carrie. She didn’t like the idea of his being engaged to another woman—any woman!

Except her.

She was jealous.

Even as the realization dawned, her stomach clenched. After a final wide-eyed gawk, she forced her gaze away from his lean, taut body and bare muscled thighs, his snug-fitting black briefs—all that kept him decent—and fought to concentrate.

But she had to ask. "Your family clearly regard Suzie as much more than an ex-girlfriend."

He shot her a quizzical look. "Suzie and I had an understanding."

"Understanding?"

The word was jarring. It reminded her of her father, and that terrible, distasteful confrontation with Adam which, in truth, she hadn't understood at all. Dread weighed down her stomach.

"Exactly what kind of understanding?" she prodded.

"Suzie wanted children—and so did I. One day." He shrugged one beautiful bared shoulder. "Neither of us had found anyone better. We'd been friends—and work colleagues for years—she was Jen's best friend. There was no good reason why marriage between us shouldn't work," he said, his voice growing muffled as he bent down to pull off his socks. "It was convenient."

Jay disappeared into the bathroom, closing the door with a click.

As she stared at the closed door, Georgia wrestled with the uncomfortable emotions coursing through her. Jay wasn't in love with Suzie. He wasn't in love with anyone. He'd told her himself he had no dream woman. She slowly let out her breath and felt her tension ease. Her jealousy was unfounded...and simply silly.

By the time Jay reappeared a few minutes later, his hair damp and his jaw smooth, with a thick white towel slung low across his hips, Georgia had recovered her composure.

Raking a hand through his hair, he came toward the bed.

He sat down on her side of the bed, and the towel slipped a little lower.

Georgia sneakily side-eyed Jay's mouth to see if he was grinning. Only to discover that his lips were firmly pressed together, the bottom one full and surprisingly sensual.

"What Suzie and I shared…wasn't enough. Something was missing." He planted one hand one either side of her shoulders and leaned toward her, the fresh tang of soap mixed with the woodsy smell of him surrounding her. "There wasn't any chemistry," he murmured.

Excitement started to spiral in the pit of her stomach. She ached to touch the rough dark stubble on his jawline, to run a finger over that unexpected bump on his otherwise straight nose.

"I wanted more," he whispered, his eyes smoldering like molten embers. "I wanted this."

He cupped her cheek, his fingers gentle, and her heart contracted. And then he kissed her.

The hunger of it seared her.

This was hot and burning. This was a flame igniting potassium. She saw flashes of lilac. White. Silver. Burning.

A frightening emotion shifted deep in her chest. A new shivery, painfully raw pleasure. If this was chemistry, well, she couldn't get enough of it.

Drawn by the unnamed need, she confessed, "I've never felt anything like this before."

Summoning all her courage, she wound her arms around his neck and tugged him close, closing the gap between them. Maybe Jay was right. Maybe chemistry was worth everything.

"Do you want to do this?" he asked against her lips.

"Oh, yes!"

He moved his hips. "Are you sure?"

Georgia moaned and arched against him. "Very."

She wanted to see if she could lose all sense of time and place like that again or whether she'd imagined it. She wanted to experience the excitement, the rightness of his mouth against hers. For a moment, she thought about where they were, in his parents' home, then discovered she didn't give a damn.

Her breath caught, freezing in her throat.

She'd always worried about doing the right thing, about what people thought, about the consequences. But she wanted this more. Much more. She wanted Jay.

All of him.

Body. Heart. And soul.

She reached up and stroked her index finger along the blade of his nose, curiously exploring the jagged ridge where he must've have broken it at some stage. He'd gone very still, watching her.

His pupils flared. In retaliation, he trailed a fingertip along the sensitive skin of her neck, along her jawline. Her head fell back, her lips parting.

Then he touched her mouth.

"You have a beautiful mouth. Made for kisses." His voice held a dark deep edge, as one finger outlined her lips.

They felt full and swollen. His face was at an angle, throwing his cheekbones into sharp relief. No vestige of humor remained in his intent eyes. Only heat.

“So kiss me,” she invited.

With a hoarse groan, Jay hauled her closer and licked her open mouth. His mouth sealed hers shut and their legs tangled, the satin of her pants slippery between them.

“How have I managed to resist you?” he murmured.

She didn’t think she’d ever get enough of touching him. Her arms crept up around his broad shoulders. She reveled in his skin, sleek and supple, beneath her fingertips.

His hand smoothed over her shoulder and traveled down until it rested, strong and steady, on the curve of her breast. His fingers stroked, and she gasped.

He kissed with fierce intensity, and Georgia responded kiss for kiss. When his hand edged under the T-shirt, she aided him, lifting, twisting, breaking the kiss, impatient to get the garment off, craving the caress of his hands on her bare skin.

When he touched her, she transformed into someone else.

Someone more than Georgia Kinnear, daughter of Kingston Kinnear, gifted student and hotshot executive. Jay made her feel like the most amazing, tempting woman in the world. Sexy. Desirable. Special.

He was nothing like any other man she’d ever known. Her father. Ridley. Adam.

He made them all look like greedy, controlling jerks.

No wonder she loved him.

She *loved* Jay?

Georgia’s breath caught, freezing in her throat.

But he allowed her no time to ponder the discovery. He ran two fingertips along the lacy neckline of her camisole, his lips following the invisible tracks he'd traced. Then the camisole, too, was stripped away.

He tasted her. The soft hollow at the base of her neck. The valley that lay between her breasts. And finally, when she thought she might go mad, he tasted her taut nipples.

Then he returned to her lips and kissed her with a passionate intensity born of desperation.

They only had tonight. Or maybe, if she got very lucky, two nights…

When he shifted again, and his hands sought the waistband of her pajama bottoms, she was quick to help him, dying to feel her bare body against his.

His fingers stroked. Heat scorched her. Her breath hooked in the back of her throat, then hissed slowly out as his fingers retreated. A heartbeat later, they slid forward again, teasing her nub with sure purpose. Her hips twisted. She bit her lip to stop the squeak that threatened to erupt.

She'd never considered herself vocal. Jay had discovered a side of her she hadn't even known existed.

Two—God, she thought it was two—fingers slid into her. Deep. She arched off the bed and her breath caught on a sob.

"Jay!" It wasn't a protest.

"What do you want?"

She cast around for words. Polite words. Words that wouldn't make her blush. "I want you. There. In me."

Jay seemed to know exactly what her jumbled words meant. He shifted to rummage on the nightstand. Then he was back. He moved over her, above her, resting his weight on his elbows as he nuzzled her neck. Then his hardness found her.

Georgia gasped at the tightness.

There was a moment when she thought it would be impossible. Then he slid a little deeper. The tightness expanded into a painful tautness. She tensed.

"Relax," he whispered.

The sensual tickle of his tongue against the sweet groove beneath her ear caused her to shiver, then convulse into giggles. And the tension drained out of her.

When Jay moved again, her arms closed around him, pulling him deeper. She walked her fingers down his back, adoring the way his body stiffened, and dug her fingers into the mound of muscle on either side of his spine. He groaned. Her fingers crept lower…lower…

"Don't touch," he managed to say. "Or I will come."

The threat—if that was what it was—caused her to raise her hips a couple of inches off the bed, arching against him, then sinking down onto the mattress again. It was Jay's turn to gasp as the friction notched a turn tighter.

"Do. Not. Move."

"Yes, Jay."

She whispered the obedient words against the curl of his ear. Then her own tongue snuck out and she experimentally licked the edge. He hissed.

The friction of his body quickened against hers. Georgia felt the edge of tension rising. Hot and tight. Her feet came off the bedding, her knees hugging his hips, deepening the pleasure. Her eyes shut tight and she focused blindly on the driving desire. Then, unexpectedly, she came apart.

Georgia gasped.

Sheer delight rippled through her.

His body jerked. Once. Twice.

Then he fell forward, and buried his face in the crevice where her neck met her jaw. With a groan, he murmured, “Georgia, you are the most unforgettable joy of my life.”

Thirteen

Jay stared down at the woman asleep in the bed.

She lay on her side, knees bent, her cheek resting on her palmed hands. The diamond he'd placed on her fourth finger winked at him. Jay wanted nothing more than their engagement to be real. For the ring that Georgia said fit so perfectly to stay on her finger. Permanently. With another simpler gold band beside it.

And he was determined to make her happier than she'd ever been.

Dark eyelashes lay peacefully against cheeks flushed with sleep. Unable to resist, he bent down and brushed his lips across hers.

She opened her eyes, stretched languorously. Then her eyes widened.

"Jay?"

"Good morning." He set two cups down on the nightstand. "I brought you some coffee."

"You must've read my mind."

He gave her a slow smile.

Leaning forward, he kissed her again. This time, she was fully awake and her lips parted beneath his. Placing his hands on either side of her, Jay braced himself against the onslaught of desire that rushed through him.

Lifting his head, he groaned. "We can't afford to get distracted. It's almost time for the party."

Georgia wound her arms around his neck. "Thank you for my coffee."

"Any time."

The mood in the room was imbued with an intimacy and sense of promise, filling Jay with a surge of renewed hope. Yesterday, he'd come clean with Georgia. And last night had been incredible. Now he simply had to convince her they belonged together.

Forever.

Then her phone rang.

Where had she put her purse last night?

Catching a glimpse of it buried under Jay's shirt on one of the chairs by the window, Georgia slung her legs out of bed, remembering too late that she was naked.

Flushing, not daring to look at Jay, she grabbed a throw off the bed and pulled it around herself. When she reached the chair by the window, she clutched at the throw and clumsily dug the now-silent phone out of her purse, glancing at the screen.

Roberta...

Panic instantly had her wide awake.

She frantically hit the redial button and stared blindly out over the private terrace to the mountains beyond, counting the rings and silently urging Roberta to answer.

When, at last, she heard her sister's voice, she said, "Please tell me Kingston is okay."

"He's fine." Roberta sounded loud and comfortingly familiar. "Breathe, sister. Be very grateful that you're not here. He's making everyone's life miserable."

"Oh." Georgia shut her eyes as the waves of panic subsided. "I'm so glad."

"Glad that we're suffering?"

Georgia stifled a sob of laughter. "Glad that he's back to his normal self. Glad he hasn't had a relapse."

"I'm still not sure there was much wrong with him to start with," Roberta said tartly. "But the stock price at markets' close on Friday? Now that's a different story."

Hunched over her cell phone, Georgia felt the familiar anxiety rise. "What do you mean?"

"Someone is buying up Kingdom stock." Roberta's voice took on a hard edge. "And that is enough to give our beloved father a real heart attack."

Georgia's grip on her phone tightened. "I'll fly home immediately."

"Don't bother to reschedule." Roberta's sigh came loud and clear over the miles that separated them. "There's nothing you can do—certainly not until Monday. But I called to tell you…" Roberta's voice trailed away.

"What?"

There was a pause, then Roberta said, "I just wanted to remind you that I'm not in the office for the next few days. You're flying back tonight, right?"

Georgia hadn't gotten around to changing her flight to the morning. "At this stage, yes."

"The sooner, the better. With the weather closing in, the airports may close."

So it was done. There would be no second night with Jay. The disappointment was crushing.

Georgia ended the call and turned to find Jay watching her from the bed, his arms linked behind his head.

How would she react when he breezed into her office bearing cups of coffee after he finally returned from vacation? She froze. Would she ever forget how he'd kissed her, licked her, loved her last night?

Would they be adult and pretend it had never happened? Or would they revert to the snarky, energetic rivalry they'd shared before? Would they still be able to work together? Or would awkwardness take over?

Georgia faced the reality of loving Jay. She wasn't dumb enough to pretend to herself that Jay felt the same about her. He wanted her. Sure. He liked her—she was pretty sure about that, too. They had their shared work ethic in common. She simply had to keep her emotions under control. It shouldn't be difficult; she'd had enough practice.

"Is everything okay?" he asked.

She slipped her phone back into her purse. "Kingston is giving everyone hell, the weather's terrible in New York and Roberta reminded me that she won't be in the office tomorrow."

"Sounds like business as usual."

About to tell him about Roberta's concerns about the stock price, she hesitated. There was nothing Jay could do about it until tomorrow. For now, she was going to enjoy the rest of her escape with Jay. Tomorrow, she'd be back in New York—and back to reality.

She flashed a smile at him. "Time for us to party."

The celebration was in full swing.

Tall stands of exquisite flowers and masses of colorful balloons filled the airy space. A quartet played, and there was a roaring fire in the fireplace.

Everyone had been so welcoming, so pleased to meet Jay's fiancée. In addition to family friends, plenty of Aspen's well-heeled crowd were present. Georgia had taken the opportunity to add several valuable contacts to her network.

Yet, with Jay's arm hugging her to his side, the feeling of being a total fraud swamped Georgia.

"This is awful," she whispered to him after the dozenth time his mom had excitedly dragged another of her friends over to introduce her only son's fiancée. "Your family doesn't deserve this, Jay."

Jay tilted his head closer. "Let's talk about this later—"

"That was your mom's best friend—your mom told her I'm her new daughter. I can't do this, Jay. We need to tell your parents the truth."

"Okay. But after the party. I'm not going to ruin this occasion for my mother. There's not long left, people will start leaving soon."

"Sorry to interrupt you lovebirds." Betty's arch tone caused Georgia to start. "Jay, can you give me a hand moving some of the anniversary gifts into the den? They're almost spilling out the front door."

"Of course." He shot Georgia a brooding look. "I won't be long."

He wound his way through the crowd with the housekeeper bustling behind him. Georgia watched him pause to respond to a greeting from a multimillionaire who'd made his fortune in retail. Then Jay turned to kiss a renowned actress on the cheek, before shaking hands with another couple. Georgia watched how the faces of men and women alike lit up. Jay was well-respected, and an easy authority radiated from him.

How had she ever missed that authority?

Shifting from one foot to another, casting little glances in the direction where Jay had disappeared, Georgia felt like a teenager in the throes of a crush, hyper-aware of Jay's every move.

She slipped outside.

On the covered terrace that faced the majestic Rockies, the guests had broken up into groups. Some stood clutching tall glasses bubbling with the best champagne, and others congregated on built-in seating around the edges of the terrace, while waiters circulated with trays still piled high with food.

Jennifer was chatting with a group of beautifully dressed women.

As Georgia approached, Jay's sister rose to her feet and came toward her. In a low voice she said, "That's Suzie in the red dress."

Georgia glanced past Jay's sister. A jolt of shock caused her to catch her breath.

"But she's—"

"Yes. And, in case you didn't know, Suzie also worked with Jay and me at JJB Boots." Jennifer bent her head closer and lowered her voice. "Mom had already consulted with a wedding planner. The caterers had been booked. The dress and the bridesmaid's dresses had been ordered when Jay dumped her for you."

"Jay jilted her?" Georgia knew she was gaping. How could Jay have done that to Suzie?

"You didn't know?"

She shook her head. "No."

"Don't feel sorry for Suzie—she'd hate it. I was so pleased they were getting married—my best friend and my big brother. Everyone was thrilled. We all knew it was only a matter of time before Dad retired and Jay stepped into his, uh, boots."

Despite the joke, there was real anxiety in the other woman's face. Jennifer honestly believed that Georgia had been the cause of her brother's breakup with her best friend.

"Jay had never done anything unexpected in his life. Sure, he and Dad fought, but we all knew they'd hammer their differences out eventually. But then he met you and broke off his engagement to Suzie. He walked away from JJB Boots and he hasn't been back since. Dad wants him in the business…but Mom and I would settle for having him come home from time to time. We hope you'll persuade him to visit—even to spend Christmas."

"You think Jay will do what I want?" breathed Georgia. The idea was so preposterous she almost laughed out loud. Only Jennifer's set expression stopped her mirth from spilling over.

"My brother is so in love with you that if you asked

him to mortgage his soul to buy Kingdom International for you, he would."

In love with *her*?

Georgia nearly admitted that Jay didn't love her at all, that this engagement was one big sham. But she came to her senses just in time. Of course, Jennifer believed Jay loved her—after all, they were engaged, and she had a great big glittering rock on her finger to prove it.

Georgia curled up a little more in shame at the charade she and Jay were perpetrating on his family. It needed to end. And she needed to leave. She didn't belong here.

She itched to reassure Jennifer, to tell her that she was no threat, that she would never keep him from his family…that she didn't have the power to break his heart. She wanted to tell her that she and Jay were only friends.

But that, too, had become a lie.

She realized Jennifer was still waiting for a response.

"I'll talk to him," she said lamely.

"You'd better come and meet Suzie—you'll be seeing plenty of her when the two of you visit."

There was no way out.

Suppressing her own discomfort, Georgia approached the pretty blonde in the red dress. An uncomfortable silence fell as they reached the group. After the introductions, Suzie gave her a sweet smile. Georgia could only admire her.

To break the ice, she smiled back. "I understand you work with Jennifer at JJB Boots."

Suzie's eyes lit up. For the next few minutes, Georgia forgot her discomfort and listened with interest to Jennifer and Suzie kidding around. When a break came in the conversation, Suzie glanced around and said easily, "Ladies, why don't you give Georgia and me a chance to get acquainted?"

The women in the tight-knit group looked at each other and then rose to their feet in unison.

"Come, sit." Suzie patted the cushion beside her.

Georgia sat, smoothing the skirt of her simple pink knit dress around her knees.

Suzie touched her hand. "Don't worry. J.J. is not going to get his way. Jay finds working with him stifling—they fight like bears. J.J can be quite something and he's never understood what makes Jay tick. But he's never worried me. I love it here. By taking over JJB Boots and marrying me, Jay would've done what he considered his duty. But then he met you. If we'd gotten married, it would have ended in divorce at some stage. Jay did us both a favor."

Georgia stared.

How could the other woman not have been in love with Jay?

But then relief surged through her. Under different circumstances, she would have liked to have been friends with Suzie. A pang stabbed her heart. Deep down, she knew that when this charade was over, she would never return to Colorado.

How on earth was she ever going to be able to face Jay every day at work?

"J.J. believes that the end always justifies the means. That's why he's blackmailing Jay."

Suzie's words jerked her back to the present. "Blackmailing Jay?"

"Manipulating is probably a better word. Jay hasn't told you?"

Slowly, Georgia shook her head.

Suzie rolled her eyes. "Jay's always been protective. J.J.'s not going to get anywhere, but Jay should have told you. You're a big girl—and he can't play the knight in shining armor forever. Honestly. Men!"

"I'm sure Jay will tell me," Georgia defended Jay, despite an inner twinge of unease.

Suzie's gaze moved to a point behind Georgia. "Speak of the devil."

Jay guided Georgia down a set of steep stone stairs to the pool deck below. Inside the stone pool house, the distant chatter of the guests dimmed and all that could be heard was the tap of her heels.

"The water is heated—my parents swim most days," he said, leading her to a pair of oversized wrought-iron chairs with plump overstuffed cushions set amidst a forest of greenery.

But Georgia didn't take the time to study her surroundings—or to sit down. Instead, she impaled him with suspicious eyes. "Jennifer tells me you jilted Suzie practically at the altar."

Jay winced.

"Is J.J. blackmailing you?"

"Who told you that?" he demanded.

"Suzie."

Jay drew a deep breath and sat down. "My father has been buying up stock in Kingdom—"

"J.J.'s behind the erratic stock prices?" Georgia interrupted him. "How long have you known?"

"I noticed the shifts in the stock a few months ago—"

"A few months?" She frowned down at him. "When did you plan to enlighten me?"

"At first, the movements were irregular…with no obvious pattern. It could have been a variety of factors. Last week, an earlier sequence of patterns was repeated. I confronted my father. He admitted he was responsible. I've dealt with him." His father had miscalculated—and he would not be doing so again.

"You've dealt with him?" Georgia still hadn't sat down. "You should've told me."

"I only spoke to Dad last night, after dinner." Jay knew he was on thin ice. He'd intended to tell her last night…but once he'd gotten to the bedroom and found Georgia in his bed, all good intentions had flown out the window. He'd abandoned his strategy of playful patience…and given in to desire.

"You've been keeping me in the dark. You're supposed to be my—"

"What? Colleague?" He raised an eyebrow, suddenly tired of watchful caution. "Friend?"

"No! Yes. You're both of those. But you're more." Her expression shifted.

Jay held his breath, waiting.

"You're my lover." At last, she answered his silent question.

Somewhere deep in Jay's chest, a warm glow ignited.

"Georgia—" He reached forward and snagged her fingers between his. "I'd never let my father harm you. Believe that."

She resisted. "I need to call Roberta—"

Jay tightened his grip on her fingers, restraining her. “Listen to me. I’ve sorted it out.”

He yanked her hand; she lost her balance, toppled over and landed sprawled across his lap. Her blue eyes blazed up at him. He pulled her close, securing her in his hold. However much he stood to lose, there would be no secrets between them. Never again. “Hear me out. My father has sold the stock he purchased to me.”

“To you?” She stared up at him, emotion shifting in her eyes. “Why would you want to own Kingdom stock?”

Why indeed?

He’d been asking himself the same question.

“I don’t,” he said tersely. “I did it—” He broke off.

For you.

But Georgia was frowning. She was adding up the limited pieces of information she had at her disposal and coming to God only knew what conclusion. In his arms, he could already feel her stiffening. She moved restlessly in his lap and against his will, his body reacted to her abrupt movements.

“Sit still,” he growled.

“The takeover—”

“Listen,” he said roughly, determined not to be distracted by the dictates of his body. It was imperative for them to talk. “My father has no ambitions to stage a hostile takeover.”

“How can you say that?”

“Dad had some mad scheme of using his newly-acquired stake in Kingdom to force me to do what he wanted—return to JJB Boots.”

Her frown had deepened. “He thought that would work?”

He shrugged. "He thought if he had a decent block of Kingdom stock, he could lean on the Kingdom board to fire me."

"Why did you resign from JJB Boots?"

Jay hesitated. "When I went to that fashion trade show I was seeking…something. I thought I was looking for a new challenge…but I couldn't crystallize what I needed. All I knew was that I no longer knew where my life was headed—or what I wanted." There was no harm in admitting any of that. "I was in danger of becoming one of those sad sons who can never make a decision without running it past Dad's master plan first. One of those men who never stand on their own two feet, and live out their lives as sad shadows of the men they might have become."

Georgia shifted. "Sometimes it's easier just to be swept along with the current."

"But it's harder, too." Jay wanted her to understand. "You lose yourself—and finding that inner certainty again takes strength."

"And Kingdom offered a bigger and better challenge?" Her voice was as brittle as glass. "One that would make you strong again?"

He didn't respond as she wriggled in his lap, and he loosened his grip so that she could sit up to face him.

Pulling the hem of her pink dress straight across her knees, she said, "Was that first meeting that Friday night really a fortunate coincidence, Jay? Or did you—and J.J.—plan that, too?"

"My father had nothing to do with it. Our meeting was nothing I'd ever planned for." But it wasn't the whole truth. There was more. "I didn't come to Kingdom to apply for a job. I came looking for you."

"Oh, God." Georgia stiffened in his arms. "Let me go."

Let her go? Anything but that!

But she was so tense in his hold, so rigid, it was clear she didn't want to be anywhere near him. The battle inside him was fierce, and the familiar fear was consuming. If he let her go…he was going to lose her. Forever.

But he was out of alternatives. He had no choice but to release her. So Jay opened his arms, and she scrambled off his lap.

Her chest rising as she drew a breath, Georgia pushed her hair off her face and finally looked at him.

"That Friday night did we…?" Her throat bobbed. "Did I know you were engaged?"

"No."

There was a sudden spark in her eyes. "Did you take advantage of the situation…? Did you take me to bed?"

"What do you take me for?" The ache in his chest deepened. "I was engaged… You were in a state of distress. We didn't sleep together—at least not in the way you're asking."

The tough, determined set to her jaw was one Jay knew all too well.

"What's that's supposed to mean?" she demanded.

"In the interests of full disclosure, you should know that we stayed together that night. You shared my room. And I held you—until you fell asleep."

Her hands came up to cover her eyes. "Oh, my God."

"You didn't want to go back to your room because your fiancé and his—"

Georgia's voice cracked. "You know about that?"

Her hands dropped away from her face, and she stared at him, flushed deep, deep red with a humiliation that made him want to draw her into his arms.

"That you caught your rat-shit fiancé in bed with another woman? Yes, I know about that. You told me."

"*I* told you?"

He nodded.

"So you thought it might be a good idea to take me back to your—"

"There were no other rooms available. The hotel—and the adjacent hotels—were jammed to the rafters with conference goers. You were distressed. You had nowhere to go. You slept in the bed. And once you were asleep, I moved to the couch. A very uncomfortable two-seater couch, I might add, but I'll forgive you for not thanking me for my gallantry."

A little of the tension went out of her. "Well, thank God for that."

"I'm not that much of a bastard. You were very shaken after breaking up with Ridley."

"How I wish my memory about him had been blanked out." She stared at Jay bleakly. "That…incident…has replayed in my mind over and over, thousands of times."

He'd been so sure the traumatic memory had been suppressed that he'd never dared bring it up to her. "Georgia, none of it was your fault."

Her expression didn't change. "My father doesn't agree. He blamed me. Ridley was the perfect son-in-law as far as he was concerned."

Jay gave a snort of disgust. "Then you had a lucky escape."

He was tempted to tell her that Fordyce would've been a far worse mistake, but managed to bite the barb back.

He'd never given up hope that Georgia would remember him. But she never had, not even now when he'd filled in the gaps she deserved to know.

"What is it, Jay? What's wrong?"

"You were gone when I woke up on the Saturday morning," he told her.

Slowly, she shook her head. "I don't remember. Days…that entire weekend…is simply gone."

"I know. I tried to contact you—only to learn that you'd crashed the rental on the way to the airport. You'd been hospitalized. I was worried." Nothing as mundane as worry. When he'd heard that she'd been in an accident and was awaiting surgery…he'd been truly terrified. He'd sweated bullets. "I wanted to see for myself that you were okay."

"I was fine."

The sound he made was not pretty. "I got to see you several weeks later, and you were not fine! You returned to work far too soon, hopping around on crutches—"

She shrugged. "Kingdom needed me. Besides, I'd heard Ridley's position had been filled, and I was eager to meet his replacement."

Jay knew she'd been worried her place in her father's life…in Kingdom…might be usurped. The day she'd met him, she'd been bristling with suspicion.

Even though he doubted Georgia would ever admit it, the period after her accident had been one of crisis. Her faith in herself must've been badly shaken by her memory loss, by Ridley's betrayal and her father's angry disappointment. Hardly surprising that she'd turned, as always, to work.

Kingdom had always come first, and Jay knew it always would. The company pulled at her…even as her father pushed her away. And it saddened him to see how hard she worked to try to gain her father's approval and love.

"You should've been resting, keeping your ankle elevated." He didn't want to nag, but he couldn't help himself. "That's what non-load bearing means."

"Well, you certainly reminded me of that often enough."

He had. He'd tried his best not to hector her, and had taken refuge in the taunting rivalry that had grown between them.

"And you brought me coffee…" her voice softened at the memory "…whenever I needed it."

But bringing her coffee was never going to be enough.

For him.

Or for her.

Despite everything, he couldn't help her attain what he knew she really wanted: to prove herself by getting the top job at Kingdom and winning her father's love. And Jay was in danger of doing what his father had done to him: smothering her with protection and expectations.

If he loved her, he had to give her the freedom she needed.

Even if that meant losing her forever.

Fourteen

Fake.

Their engagement was fake. She was an imposter…a fake. She, who worshipped at the altar of honesty, had lied. To Jay. To herself.

She'd been so scared of becoming lovers with Jay, so fearful of jeopardizing their working relationship, so terrified of risking the tentative friendship between them, that she'd been blind to the fact that she was falling in love with him.

Forget blind. She'd been asleep.

For years!

What if she took a chance and told him how she was starting to feel?

As Georgia stared at Jay, a vision of all the possibilities filled her mind. They were dynamite together.

She wanted to share her slice of Kingdom with him… the plans and projects and shining success she'd plotted for years.

But before she could get up her courage, he spoke. "Do you ever think about what you want? Deep down?"

She was shaking inside when she said, "I want to be someone people respect and—"

"People? Or your father?"

Jay's interruption jolted her.

"Are you sure that's what you want?" He tipped his head to one side, studying her. "What you really want most?"

She wanted more than one night... She wanted a future with Jay.

Georgia drew up her shoulders and let them drop. "There are other things I want."

"Like what?"

The impossibility of Jay falling in love with her made her hesitate…

Her mind veered away and she thought of her weariness. "Well, a vacation would be nice." Not running away or avoiding, but simply a time to relax and reflect.

"What else?"

"I've been meaning to spend more time with Roberta. I missed her when she lived in Europe. Yet, since she's returned to New York, we haven't spent much time together." All they seemed to do was work.

"You two are close." His voice had dropped.

"Very. It's quite strange because when we were children, she was much closer to Charis."

"Did you resent that?"

"No. I don't know. Maybe."

"Perhaps much of the tension between you and Charis comes from your father's dominance and manipulation?"

"What's this? Psychoanalysis 101?" But she had to admit that her father had always made it clear that Charis was his favorite—even when she pretty much killed herself to be everything he'd ever wanted from the son he'd never had.

"No. I have no desire to fix you—you are perfect the way you are."

She blinked in disbelief. Had she heard right? Had Jay actually told her she was perfect? With no gleam of mockery in his eyes…eyes that were already glancing away at the watch on his cocked wrist.

"What time is your flight?"

Her heart contracted. She told him, even as she tried to fathom what he was thinking.

But his face gave away nothing.

"The guests will be leaving soon, and then I'll give you a ride to the airport."

She'd half expected him to ask her to stay.

But he hadn't. Something inside her withered.

"I suppose you've got what you want all figured out?" She flung the words at him, feeling curiously defenseless.

If it hadn't been for his stillness, and the slight narrowing of his eyes, she would've thought he was quite at ease.

"Yes, I know exactly what I want." His lips curved up, but his eyes remained watchful. "Two years certainly gave me plenty of opportunity to work that out."

The fears that had always been so much a part of her

everyday life bubbled up. She hesitated, and then said in a rush, "Is Kingdom part of it?"

"If you have to ask that, you don't know me at all." He took a few steps away, making her feel more alone than ever. "Come, we need to go back to the house."

What did Jay really want? There were so many more questions she wanted to ask, but Jay was waiting, his body tense.

So, she would be leaving…

There was the confrontation with her father that lay ahead. Her heart plummeted. She was dreading it. But she couldn't prevaricate anymore; she had to tell her father the truth that she'd turned Adam's down proposal. But she was not going to allow him to banish her from Kingdom as he had Charis. And before she left Jay's parents' home, she owed them an apology for the sham engagement. She wasn't much looking forward to that, either; but at least then her conscience would be clean. She wanted Jay's parents to remember her as someone with integrity. Even though there was no reason she would meet them ever again.

"Come on." Jay had paused on the stone stairs. He held out a hand to her. "Let's go say goodbye."

All the guests had finally left, and the anniversary party had been a stunning success.

While Georgia packed her bag, Jay had disappeared to check his email and make a couple of calls. Once she was all packed up, conscious that she would be leaving very soon and that she still had to undo some of the damage she'd done this weekend, she made her way downstairs.

In the den, J.J. was at his desk and Nancy sat on a couch with Zeus asleep at her feet. J.J. narrowed his eyes over the top of his spectacles as Georgia entered.

Once again, the shame about lying to Jay's parents washed through her. So much for her high principles. "I've come to say goodbye," Georgia announced.

"No doubt we will be seeing more of you, for those skiing trips at the very least." Nancy rose to her feet. "The snow will be here soon."

J.J. removed his spectacles and set them down on the desk. "You do know that Jay is only marrying you because you're your father's right-hand man, don't you?" He paused. "Jay has always wanted to call the shots."

"Stop it, J.J."

Georgia gave Jay's mom a grateful smile, before turning her attention back to J.J. "Jay could've taken over JJB Boots, if that's all he wanted, and he would've gotten total control far more easily." Suzie was right. J.J. had no idea what motivated his son. "But that's immaterial, and you have no need to worry about me keeping Jay away, because I won't be marrying him. Our engagement was a facade. Fake."

There was a gasp. Then Jay's mother was at her side. "What's this nonsense about a fake engagement? The two of you are perfect for each other. We—I—would welcome you with open arms."

Bemused, Georgia stared at Jay's mother. For the first time in years, the yearning for a mother flared. Then she threw her arms around Nancy and hugged her. A real warm hug. Tears pricked at the back of her throat. "I'm so sorry for deceiving you. Thank you for being so welcoming. Whoever gets to be your daughter-in-law is a very lucky woman."

Nancy hugged her back. "Georgia—"

From behind her, she heard a curse.

Georgia let go of Nancy and spun around. Jay stood in the doorway, her trolley bag at his feet. Now that it was finally time for her to leave, Georgia felt a lump in her throat.

It was time to finish what she'd started.

She hurried to Jay's side.

"This belongs to you." She tried to wrest the beautiful ring from her finger, but it refused to budge.

"Don't," said Jay, his jaw tight.

"I've already told your parents that our engagement is not real—and that I'd never stop you coming back."

"I'm not coming back to JJB Boots. My father knows that."

J.J. muttered something Georgia decided it was better not to hear.

"Your father can come along to New York next time Jennifer and I visit," Nancy said quickly.

This time J.J.'s muttering was louder.

Nancy rounded on her husband, her hands on her hips, her eyes flashing. "It's time we traveled together. Why, I was speaking to Joyce earlier, she and Bill have been wanting to go on a cruise for years, but they've never gotten around to it. She invited us to go along."

"Wait a minute." J.J. looked concerned. "I can't simply leave our business—"

Nancy tossed her head. "If you want, you can stay here and run JJB Boots, but I'm going on a cruise."

"You can't expect me to leave the company for months—"

"One month, that's all." Nancy brandished her index finger at J.J. "I intend to go once a year. While I certainly don't expect you to do anything you don't want, I've been dreaming about this for a long time. Now I'm going to do it."

"Go, Mom!" Jennifer's voice rang out from the doorway. "Make your dreams happen."

"Dad, you could always leave JJB Boots in Jennifer and Suzie's more-than-capable hands." Jay's suggestion broke into the cacophony. "Who knows? You might even find they do an outstanding job."

It was the baffled expression of blank shock on J.J.'s face that caused Georgia to interject, "Don't make the mistake my father made two decades ago. He was married to his business. He put Kingdom ahead of my mother's needs. He drove my mother into another man's arms. And then she died—they both died—and she never came back."

And her father was still putting Kingdom ahead of his daughters…

She thought about Jay's reasons for walking away from JJB Boots. He'd said something about needing to become his own man…not a boy in the shadow of his father. Was she in danger of having her growth stifled by her father?

She'd always held her father up as an ideal—a role model. He worked hard, he'd built a successful brand, he struck fear and awe into the hearts of everyone who knew him. She'd long ago decided that the only way to gain his respect was to rise to the top in the family business.

J.J.'s astonishment had turned to real horror, bringing Georgia back to the present. "Nancy would never leave me. I doubt she'll even go through with this cruise nonsense, either."

"Oh, I'm going through with it. I'm booking that trip first thing tomorrow. I'm going to have fun!"

Jay crossed to hug his mother. "Way to go, Mom!" Then he straightened, and said to his father, "Georgia's right. You should think about having some fun, too. Before it's too late." Then he added, "Now, Georgia has a plane to catch."

"Don't let her get away," his mother called from behind them. "Keep that ring on her finger."

In the doorway, Jay paused, and said over his shoulder, "I have no intention of letting her get away."

The SUV swept down Red Mountain, and Georgia felt like part of her heart would remain behind. This was the place where she had first realized how deep her feelings for Jay went…how much she loved him. This was where they had first made love.

Her thoughts were interrupted by the vibration of her phone.

"Leave it!"

Irritated by Jay's peremptory tone, she ignored him and hauled the phone out of her purse to check the screen.

"Oh, no! My flight's been canceled. I'm going to have to call the airline to rebook." Another thought struck her. "I'll have to book myself into a hotel, too."

"You're welcome to stay with my parents."

"I don't think so—not after dropping that bomb that we're not really engaged."

Jay steered the SUV toward the town center and threw her a mischievous look. "Maybe we can finally share that bottle of champagne I promised you if you bid on me."

"Never mind a bottle of champagne.... You still owe me the fantasy date I won." Then she had second thoughts. "We'd better not do that today. Roberta would go nuts. She'll want to leverage every PR angle. She'll make sure our *date* takes place in some A-list restaurant and that we're appropriately dressed in all things Kingdom with a photographer of her choice on hand to document it."

"God help us both." Jay gave a theatrical shudder that had her laughing, even as he pulled the SUV into the forecourt of one of Aspen's luxurious hotels. Within minutes, they were ensconced on a terrace with the mountains looming all around.

Once the sommelier departed after a lively discussion with Jay, he turned to face her. "There's something I need to discuss with you," he said quietly.

The energy that came off him in waves made Georgia feel decidedly on edge. "What's wrong?"

"I've resigned from Kingdom, Georgia."

"Resigned?" The bottom dropped out of her stomach. This was worse than anything she could have anticipated.

A mix of emotions swamped her. Complex feelings of bewilderment, betrayal and a sense of being utterly abandoned when she'd least expected it. Her worst fears had come to pass. She'd known this would happen. Now it had.

She was losing Jay…

"Does Kingston know yet?"

"I emailed him my resignation before we left my parents' home."

Then on the heels of her inner turmoil, she said, "Does that mean you're going back to JJB Boots?"

He shook his head. "I think you know better than that. JJB Boots does not—"

"Define you? Own you?"

He nodded. "It took a while to break those bonds."

"Was it worth it?"

He nodded, his eyes intent. "I will never regret it."

"Will you stay in New York?" She asked the question, though she dreaded the answer.

"I don't know yet."

Georgia had never considered leaving New York, never considered leaving Kingdom. But if Jay was not there…

Something inside her shriveled up.

Raising her chin a notch so that he wouldn't see how devastated she was, she asked, "So what's next? Another journey? Where to this time?"

He gave her a smile that was all too familiar…and more than a little wicked. "Now, that rather depends on you."

"On me?"

He nodded. "A couple of hours ago, you asked if I knew what I wanted. I do. I want you, Georgia. I would like to ask you to marry me—to spend your life with me. That's what I most want."

Her throat closed. She had to choose between Jay… and Kingdom. She couldn't have both.

"You don't need to give me an answer right now. Take all the time you need."

"I have to go back to New York—"

There was a slight change in his expression, a tension in his body. Did he think she was trying to escape?

"I have to tell my father I can't marry Adam," she said.

Jay hadn't asked her to choose, of course. But she knew she had to be clear in her own mind about what she wanted. She didn't ever want to feel regret. Or to feel she'd been coerced into making a choice she wasn't ready to commit to.

Could she do it?

She didn't even have to weigh up the pros and the cons.

Because she wanted Jay more than she wanted Kingdom. The contentment, the laughter, the feeling of being valued that Jay brought to her life.

It was a shock to acknowledge. And it had happened slowly, so slowly that she'd never even noticed he had become more important to her than her very reason for being.

The sommelier came back, bearing a bottle of champagne and two flutes. He filled their glasses with a flourish before retreating.

Jay lifted his glass to her. "Here's to you, Georgia."

"And you." Her glass chinked against his. "I—"

Her phone rang. She set her glass down to pick it up and glanced at the screen.

"Bingo." She glanced across at Jay as illumination

struck. "It's my father. Do you want to guess why he's calling?"

She didn't wait for an answer but pressed receive.

Her father's voice was loud in her ear. "Jay has resigned."

"I know," she said.

"You know?"

"I'm with him right now. And Kingston, there's something I need to tell—"

"So what are you doing about it?"

The look she shot Jay said it all.

"Kingston—"

"Roberta says you've been in Aspen. What kind of crazy, irresponsible move is that?"

She rolled her eyes at the interruptions. "Think of it as business."

"Business? What do you mean?"

"We should open a store here."

For the first time, there was a pause.

"Do a cost analysis," her father commanded.

Georgia remembered saying something similar that first day they'd driven through the town. It made her feel distinctly uneasy. She was nothing like her father.

"Kingston, I'm not going to marry Adam Fordyce."

"I'll hire someone first-rate to manage—" There was an abrupt pause. "What did you say?"

"I'm not going to marry Adam."

Her father actually snorted. "Of course, you are—we've agreed to it."

"*I* haven't agreed. And as the bride, I'd say I have some choice in who I marry."

"Don't be silly now, Georgia."

He was still treating her like a child. But then she had never fully stepped out of that role. She'd kept him on a pedestal as a way to avoid having to create an intimate relationship. She was no longer a girl, it was time to become her own woman.

"I'm not being silly at all. I'm perfectly sane. Probably for the first time in my life. And I'm going to marry Jay."

At that, Kingston exploded. Georgia held the phone away from her ear.

There was a wild joy in Jay's face. He threw his head back and laughed, then raised his glass to her in acknowledgement.

Finally, when her father paused to draw a breath, she said into the phone, "My mind is made up. And I'm taking a week's vacation—maybe even two weeks."

She shot a look at Jay to assess his reaction.

He just grinned.

She was done arguing with her father. "Disinherit me if you like—I'll only quit. Then you won't have as much time to play golf."

Georgia's heart was pounding in her chest as she killed the call and smiled across at Jay. "That was far easier than I thought it would be. He needs to face reality. He can't run my life anymore—because I'll be spending it with you."

Jay raised his champagne flute, his face alight with admiration. "To you, Georgia. My fiancée."

But he hadn't finished yet.

Leaning forward he brushed his mouth against hers and murmured, "I knew from the moment I met you that there was no one else like you. How I love you."

There was so much pride in his voice that her heart melted like honey in the sun. She wished she could remember that first moment they'd met. But it didn't matter, because she'd grown to love the man who challenged her more than any other, who understood her, who matched her. He was her future.

Epilogue

It had been an hour since the crash of the phone hitting the desk told Marcia Hall the call had come to an end. It had been awfully silent in the massive adjoining corner office since then. Marcia was starting to feel a little concerned about her boss.

From the parts she'd overheard, the call had not gone well.

She rose to her feet and made her way to the watercooler beside the group of sofas across from her workspace. Through the wall of glass windows, the predicted storm clouds were closing in, darkening the sky outside. She was a little worried about Roberta and Georgia flying in these awful conditions. She poured a glass of water—chilled to the exact temperature her boss demanded—and made her way through the adjoining door into his office. It was more than an office. It was the archive of his life. The photos on the walls documented his meetings with stars and fashion icons.

He sat there, staring at the blotter. His gaze lifted as she stopped before the desk.

"That stupid girl turned Adam down!"

When he spoke of any of his daughters like that, it upset her. "Don't work yourself up, Kingston. We don't want another trip to the hospital."

"Bah."

She set the glass down on the leather mat in front of him. "Here, have a sip of water."

He glared at the glass.

"She's taking a vacation." He looked dumbfounded. "She's not coming back to New York tomorrow. She doesn't even know how long she intends to be gone."

Marcia suppressed a smile of glee at the news that Georgia wouldn't be flying in this weather. "Kingdom is not a prison. She's allowed time off."

Kingston let out a growl. "Her refusal to marry Fordyce puts me in a goddamned uncomfortable predicament."

Marcia couldn't have stopped the smile that split her face if her job had depended it.

Had Georgia finally realized what had been there in front of her all this time? She hoped so. No point telling her boss that his predicament was one of his own making. Instead, she said, "Kingston, she's a grown woman. Let her go… Let her make her own decisions."

"I need her here. With me. With Kingdom."

"If you don't let them go, you may have no Kingdom." Nor any family, either.

He laid his head back. “Marcia, this isn’t how my plan plays out.”

“Sometimes life has a way of upsetting those rigid plans.” Then more softly, she said, “You need to learn to let go, Kingston.”

His eyes were closed, and he gave no sign that he’d heard her.

“What the hell am I supposed to tell Fordyce? How will I ever face the man over the negotiating table again?”

So, this was about loss of face rather than about the loss of another daughter. “I’m sure you’ll find a way.”

From the outer office came the sound of a ringing phone. She glanced toward the door, and then back at the man she’d worked with for almost three decades. The man she knew better than anyone else in the world. He was as deaf to reason as he was blind to the truth.

Marcia Hall shook her head and went to answer the phone that wouldn’t stop ringing.

The show must go on.

* * * * *

The fate of Kingdom lies in the balance.
Find out what happens next as Takeover Tycoons continues with Roberta’s story, coming soon from
USA TODAY *bestselling author*
Tessa Radley
and Harlequin Desire.

COMING NEXT MONTH FROM

Available August 6, 2019

#2677 BIG SHOT

by Katy Evans

Dealing with her insufferable hotshot boss has India Crowley at the breaking point. But when he faces a stand-in daddy dilemma, India can't deny him a helping hand. Sharing close quarters, though, may mean facing her true feelings about the man...

#2678 OFF LIMITS LOVERS

Texas Cattleman's Club: Houston • by Reese Ryan

When attorney Roarke Perry encounters the daughter of his father's arch enemy, he's dumbstruck. Annabel Currin is irresistible—and she desperately needs his help. Yet keeping this gorgeous client at arms' length may prove impossible once forbidden feelings take over!

#2679 REDEEMED BY PASSION

Dynasties: Secrets of the A-List • by Joss Wood

Event planner Teresa St. Clair is organizing the wedding of the year so she can help her brother out of a dangerous debt. She doesn't need meddling—or saving—from her ex, gorgeous billionaire Liam Christopher. But she can't seem to stay away...

#2680 MONTANA SEDUCTION

Two Brothers • by Jules Bennett

Dane Michaels will stop at nothing to get the Montana resort that rightfully belongs to him and his brother. Even if it means getting close to his rival's daughter. As long as he doesn't fall for the very woman he's seducing...

#2681 HIS MARRIAGE DEMAND

The Stewart Heirs • by Yahrah St. John

With her family business going under, CEO Fallon Stewart needs a miracle. But Gage Campbell, the newly wealthy man she betrayed as a teen, has a bailout plan...if Fallon will pose as his wife! Can she keep focused as passion takes over their mock marriage?

#2682 FROM RICHES TO REDEMPTION

Switched! • by Andrea Laurence

Ten years ago, River Atkinson and Morgan Steele eloped, but the heiress's father tore them apart. Now, just as Morgan's very identity is called into question, River is back in town. Will secrets sidetrack their second chance, or are they on the road to redemption?

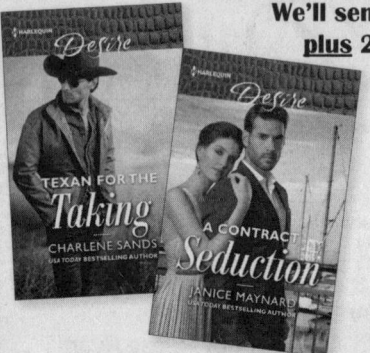

SPECIAL EXCERPT FROM

Gabe Dalton knows he should ignore his attraction to Jamie Dodge…but her tough-talking attitude masks an innocence that tempts him past breaking point…

Read on for a sneak preview of
Cowboy to the Core
by New York Times *and* USA TODAY
bestselling author Maisey Yates.

"You sure like coming up to me guns blazing, Jamie Dodge. Just saying whatever it is that's on your mind. No concern for the fallout of it. Well, all things considered, I'm pretty sick of keeping myself on a leash."

He cupped her face, and in the dim light he could see that she was staring up at him, her eyes wide. And then, without letting another breath go by, he dipped his head and his lips crushed up against Jamie Dodge's.

They were soft.

Good God, she was soft.

He didn't know what he had expected.

Prickles, maybe.

But no, her lips were the softest, sweetest thing he'd felt in a long time. It was like a flash of light had gone off and erased everything in his brain, like all his thoughts had been printed on an old-school film roll.

There was nothing.

Nothing beyond the sensation of her skin beneath his fingertips, the feel of her mouth under his. She was frozen beneath his touch, and he shifted, tilting his head to the side and darting his tongue out, flicking it against the seam of her lips.

PHMYEXP0719

She gasped, and he took advantage of that, getting entry into that pretty mouth so he could taste her, deep and long, and exactly how he'd been fantasizing about.

Oh, those fantasies hadn't been a fully realized scroll of images. No. It had been a feeling.

An invisible band of tension that had stretched between them in small spaces of time. In the leap of panic in his heart when he'd seen her fall from the horse earlier today.

It had been embedded in all of those things and he hadn't realized exactly what it meant he wanted until the right moment. And then suddenly it was like her shock transformed into something else entirely.

She arched toward him, her breasts pressing against his chest, her hands coming up to his face. She thrust her chin upward, making the kiss harder, deeper. He drove his tongue deep, sliding it against hers, and she made a small sound like a whimpering kitten. The smallest sound he'd ever heard Jamie Dodge make.

He pulled away from her, nipped her lower lip and then pressed his mouth to hers one more time before releasing his hold.

She looked dazed. He felt about how she looked.

"I thought about it," he said. "And I realized I couldn't let this one go. I let you criticize my riding, question my authority, but I wasn't about to let you get away with cock-blocking me, telling me you're jealous and then telling me you don't know if you want me. So I figured maybe I'd give you something to think about."

Don't miss
Cowboy to the Core *by Maisey Yates,*
available July 2019 wherever
Harlequin® books and ebooks are sold.

www.Harlequin.com

PHMYEXP0719

SPECIAL EXCERPT FROM

Dealing with her insufferable hotshot boss has India Crowley at the breaking point. But when he faces a stand-in daddy dilemma, India can't deny him a helping hand. Sharing close quarters, though, may mean facing her true feelings about the man...

Read on for a sneak peek at
BIG SHOT
by New York Times *bestselling author Katy Evans!*

I hate my boss

My demanding, stone-hearted, arrogant bastard boss.

You know those people in an elevator who click the close button repeatedly when they see someone coming just to avoid human contact? You know what?

That's my boss. But worse.

As I settle in, I notice that my boss, William, isn't around.

He's the kind of person who turns up early to work for no good reason. It's probably because he has no social life—he's a lone wolf, according to my mother, but to me, that translates as he's a jerk with no friends. Despite the lackeys who follow him around everywhere, I know he doesn't have any real friends. After all, I control his calendar for personal appointments, and in truth, there aren't many.

But where is he today? Not being early is like being late for him. Until he arrives, there's little I can do, so I meander to the coffee machine and make a cup for myself. As the machine is churning up coffee beans, the elevator dings and William appears.

I'll admit, something about his presence always knocks the breath from me. He stalks forward, with three people following in his wake. His hair is perfectly slicked, his stubble trimmed close to his sharp jaw. His eyes are a shocking blue. I can picture him now on the front cover of *Business Insider*, his piercing eyes radiating confidence from the page. But today his eyes are clouded by anger.

He spots me waiting. The whole office is watching as he stalks toward me with a bunch of papers in his arms. His colleagues struggle to keep up, and I discard my coffee, suddenly fearful of his glare. Did I do something wrong?

"Good morning, Mr. Walker—"

"Good morning, India," he growls.

He shoves the papers into my arms and I almost topple over in surprise. "I need you to sort out this paperwork mess and I don't want to hear another word from you until it's done." When he stalks away without so much as a smile, I notice I've been holding my breath.

And this is why, despite his beauty, despite his money, despite his drive, I can't stand the man.

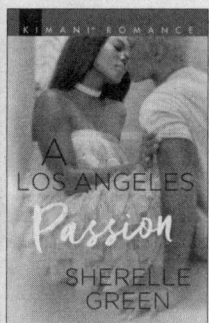

Happily-ever-after.
It's our promise,
whatever kind of love story you're seeking—
passionate, dramatic, suspenseful,
historical, inspirational...

With different lines to choose from
and new books in each one every month,
Harlequin has stories to satisfy even the most
voracious romance readers.

Find them in-store, online or subscribe to
the Reader Service!

ROMANCE WHEN
YOU NEED IT

SeriesIBC2018

She must marry a stranger or lose a fortune.

But she'll be another man's fake fiancée first...

Georgia Kinnear's tyrant of a father has a new demand for his daughters: wed men of his choosing or lose their legacy. But Jay Black, Georgia's sexy corporate confidant slash nemesis, makes Georgia his fake fiancée first! Neither can deny the explosive chemistry that could blow up her father's plans. Unless Jay's secrets catch up with them...

$5.25 U.S./$6.25 CAN.

ISBN-13: 978-1-335-60378-4

CATEGORY
PASSION

harlequin.com

valueBOOKS

First and Ten

FOOTBALL FUN, FACTS, AND TRIVIA

FOOTBALL FUN, FACTS, AND TRIVIA

Compiled by
Daniel Partner

BARBOUR
PUBLISHING, INC.
Uhrichsville, Ohio

ISBN 1-57748-435-5

Published by Barbour Publishing, Inc., P.O. Box 719, Uhrichsville, OH 44683, http://www.barbourbooks.com

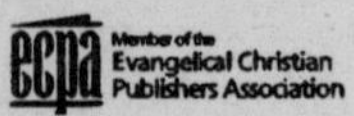

Printed in the United States of America.

The nice thing about football is that you have a scoreboard to show how you've done. In other things in life, you don't. At least, not one you can see.

CHUCK NOLL,
Pittsburgh Steelers coach (1969–91)

You love football—the roar of the crowd, the chill in the air, the smell of hot dogs wafting out of the concession stand. You love the sound of crunching shoulder pads, the thrill of a receiver dashing downfield, the joy of a victory for the home team. You love to see those big, strong men battling it out on the gridiron.

Football's a great game, with a fascinating story and a great cast of characters. Read *First and Ten* to relive some of the most exciting moments of football, learn the history of the sport, and meet many of the colorful personalities of the game. Read on, too, for an introduction to some of the many Christians who've made professional football their career. They're the guys who best understand Coach Noll's "unseen scoreboard"—*God's* scoreboard of life.

Be encouraged by the player testimonies from *Sports Spectrum,* the premier Christian sports magazine. Enjoy the facts and figures, the quips and quotes, the terms and timelines. *First and Ten* is a crash course in football fandom. Read on, then watch your favorite game with a whole new perspective!

Christian's Faith

Bob Christian could wallow in how frustrating his career has been. Instead, the Atlanta Falcons' fullback is enjoying having the turf as his mission field again—after being cut three times and missing the 1996 season with an injury.

This season Christian is sharing his faith and favorite Bible verse, Romans 8:28, in public service announcements (PSAs) filmed for an Atlanta television station and for use in the Georgia Dome. "During football games, if we make a good play, they can use it in the stadium on big screens," he says. "It's a way to get the gospel out to people who might not go to church."

Fans who see the PSAs may recognize Christian's favorite verse, "And we know that in all things God works for the good of those who love him, who have been called according to his purpose." The verse jumped out at him when he first accepted Jesus as Savior and started reading the Bible, he says. But it has meant even more during his career struggles.

"I can look back and see how every situation in my life has worked for my good, from injuries to getting cut to sitting at home trying to figure out what I'm going to do," he says.

The former Northwestern standout was cut by the Falcons in 1991 and by the London Monarchs of the WFL and San Diego in 1992. He made the practice squad with Chicago that year, playing in the last two games and two more seasons with the Bears. He became a Carolina Panther in 1995 and was signed by the Falcons as a free agent in 1997.

"The main reason God has me playing football in Atlanta is to be a witness for Him to the other guys on the team," says the five-foot-eleven-inch, 230-pound full-back. "They're bleeding and sweating alongside me in the battle. Those are the people I love dearly."

—by LORI WIECHMAN

Pro football is like nuclear warfare. There are no winners, only survivors.

FRANK GIFFORD,
announcer and former
New York Giants running back (1952–64)

I played football before they had headgear, and that's how I lost my mind.

CASEY STENGEL,
New York Yankees manager (1949–61)

A Pro Football Chronology

Part I

1869

- Rutgers and Princeton play the first ever college soccer-football game.
- Rugby gains favor over soccer in eastern schools. Modern football begins to develop from rugby.

1876

- The first rules for American football are written at the Massasoit Convention.
- Walter Camp, the father of American football, becomes involved with the game.

1892

- Football is a major attraction of Pittsburgh-area athletic clubs. The Allegheny Athletic Association (AAA) and the Pittsburgh Athletic Club (PAC) are rivals.
- Former Yale All-America guard Pudge Heffelfinger is paid $500 by the AAA to play in a game against the PAC. He is the first person to be paid to play football.

1893

- The Pittsburgh Athletic Club signs halfback Grant Dibert for all its games—the first pro football contract.

1896

- The Allegheny Athletic Association team fields the first completely professional team for its two-game season.

1897

- The Latrobe Athletic Association football team goes entirely professional—the first team to play a full professional season.

1898

- The value of a touchdown is changed from four points to five.

1899

- Chris O'Brien forms the Morgan Athletic Club on Chicago's south side. The team is later known as the Normals, the Racine Cardinals, the Chicago Cardinals, the St. Louis Cardinals, the Phoenix Cardinals, and, presently, the Arizona Cardinals. This team is the oldest continuing pro football organization.

1900

- William Temple takes responsibility for paying the Duquesne Country and Athletic Club—the first known individual club owner.

1902

- Baseball's Philadelphia Athletics and Philadelphia Phillies both form professional football teams. With the Pittsburgh Stars they attempt the first pro football league—the National Football League.
- The Athletics win the first night football game, 39–0 over Kanaweola AC at Elmira, New York.
- All three Pennsylvania teams claim the championship. The Stars are named champions by the league president.
- Hall of fame pitcher Christy Mathewson plays fullback for Pittsburgh.

- The first World Series of pro football—a five-team tournament—is played at New York's original Madison Square Garden. Here, New York and Syracuse play the first indoor football game. Syracuse, with Pop Warner at guard, wins 6–0 and eventually wins the tournament.

1903

- The Franklin (Penn.) Athletic Club wins the second (and last) World Series of pro football.
- Pro football is popularized in Ohio by the Massillon Tigers, who hire four Pittsburgh pros to play in the season's final game against Akron.

1904

- The value of a field goal is changed from five points to four.
- Ohio has seven pro teams.
- Massillon wins the Ohio Independent Championship, the current pro title.
- Halfback Charles Follis signs with the Shelby (Ohio) AC—the first African-American pro football player.

It's a very interesting game. They have big bears up front and little rabbits in the back. The idea is for the bears to protect the rabbits.

Viktor Tikhonov,
National Soviet hockey coach,
seeing American football for the first time

Gridiron Glossary

The Odd Language of Football
Part I

AUDIBLE: A play called by the quarterback at the line of scrimmage that changes the play that was previously called in the huddle; a change of plans in game play, just before the ball goes into play. Also called an automatic.

BALANCED LINE: A formation with an equal number of linemen on either side of the center.

BIRDCAGE: The face mask, donned by linemen, which has extra vertical and horizontal bars.

BLIND SIDE: The side opposite the side a player is looking toward.

BLITZ: An all-out run by linebackers and defensive backs, charging through the offensive line in an effort to sack the quarterback before he can hand off the ball or pass it. Also called red dogging.

BUTTONHOOK: A pass route in which the receiver heads straight downfield, then abruptly turns back toward the line of scrimmage.

CHAIN CREW: Three assistants to the officials whose job it is to handle the first down measuring chain and the down box.

CHEAP SHOT: A deliberate foul or other violent act against an unsuspecting player.

CHECK OFF: Calling an audible.

CLIPPING: Blocking an opponent from behind, typically at leg level. Clipping is a foul with a fifteen-yard penalty.

CLOTHESLINE: A foul. To clothesline is to strike another player across the face with one's extended arm.

COFFIN CORNER: One of the four corners of the field. A punter often tries to kick the ball out of bounds near a "coffin corner" to stop the other team from returning the ball and make them put the ball back into play close to their own goal line.

CONVERSION: A point after a touchdown.

CRACKBACK: A foul. Blocking by an offensive player who goes downfield, then turns back to the middle to block a player from the side.

CURL/CURL IN: A maneuver where the receiver runs downfield before turning back to run toward the line of scrimmage.

CUT: To suddenly change direction to lose a pursuing player. Also, to drop a prospective player from the team roster.

If you can count to eleven you'll have no trouble playing football. Count to twenty-two and you can play quarterback.

DARYLE LAMONICA,
Oakland quarterback (1963–74)

It's bad luck to be behind at the end of the game.

HUGH "DUFFY" DAUGHERTY

Stats

7+ Reception Games (1998)

GAMES	PLAYER	TEAM
7	Herman Moore	Detroit
6	Marshall Faulk	Indianapolis
6	O. J. McDuffie	Miami
5	Antonio Freeman	Green Bay
5	Keyshawn Johnson	New York Jets
5	Carl Pickens	Cincinnati
5	Frank Sanders	Arizona
5	Jimmy Smith	Jacksonville
5	Rod Smith	Denver
4	Tim Brown	Oakland
4	Ben Coates	New England
4	Terry Glenn	New England
4	Keenan McCardell	Jacksonville
4	Frank Wycheck	Tennessee
3	Kimble Anders	Kansas City
3	Cris Carter	Minnesota
3	Larry Centers	Arizona
3	Marvin Harrison	Indianapolis
3	Michael Irvin	Dallas
3	Tony Martin	Atlanta
3	Ed McCaffrey	Denver
3	Rob Moore	Arizona
3	Johnnie Morton	Detroit
3	Muhsin Muhammad	Carolina
3	Ricky Proehl	St. Louis
3	Jerry Rice	San Francisco
3	Duce Staley	Philadelphia
3	Cameron Cleeland	New Orleans
2	Isaac Bruce	St. Louis
2	Wayne Chrebet	New York Jets

GAMES	PLAYER	TEAM
2	Sean Dawkins	New Orleans
2	Joey Galloway	Seattle
2	Courtney Hawkins	Pittsburgh
2	Raghib Ismail	Carolina
2	Charles Johnson	Pittsburgh
2	Dorsey Levens	Green Bay
2	Terance Mathis	Atlanta
2	Mike Pritchard	Seattle
2	Andre Reed	Buffalo
2	Andre Rison	Kansas City
2	J.J. Stokes	San Francisco
2	Ricky Watters	Seattle
2	Michael Westbrook	Washington
2	Amp Lee	St. Louis
2	Randy Moss	Minnesota
2	Fred Taylor	Jacksonville
1	Derrick Alexander	Kansas City
1	Reidel Anthony	Tampa Bay
1	Tiki Barber	New York Giants
1	Chris Calloway	New York Giants
1	Albert Connell	Washington
1	Stephen Davis	Washington
1	Warrick Dunn	Tampa Bay
1	Quinn Early	Buffalo
1	Bert Emanuel	Tampa Bay
1	Bobby Engram	Chicago
1	Terrell Fletcher	San Diego
1	Oronde Gadsden	Miami
1	William Henderson	Green Bay
1	Ike Hilliard	New York Giants
1	Priest Holmes	Baltimore
1	Michael Jackson	Baltimore
1	Brian Mitchell	Washington

GAMES	PLAYER	TEAM
1	Eric Moulds	Buffalo
1	Terrell Owens	San Francisco
1	Bill Schroeder	Green Bay
1	Darnay Scott	Cincinnati
1	Leslie Shepherd	Washington
1	Torrance Small	Indianapolis
1	Bryan Still	San Diego
1	Yancey Thigpen	Tennessee
1	Wesley Walls	Carolina
1	Andrew Glover	Minnesota
1	Tony Gonzalez	Kansas City
1	Stephen Alexander	Washington
1	Jerome Pathon	Indianapolis
1	Floyd Turner	Baltimore

On the first day of rookie camp Floyd Peters came in and told the defensive linemen, "The number one rule is this—tackle the man with the ball." That immediately cleared things up.

BUBBA BAKER,
St. Louis defensive end (1980–88)

Bruce Matthews's Be-all, End-all

The careers of Tennessee Oilers' all-purpose offensive lineman Bruce Matthews and Denver's Hall of Fame-bound quarterback John Elway draw interesting parallels.

Matthews and Elway both broke into the NFL in 1983 as first-round draft choices. Both are Pac 10 products (Matthews played at Southern California; Elway at Stanford). Both have been named to just about every all-NFL team you can think of. And both have remained with the same club their entire professional careers.

But Matthews's and Elway's paths took a fork in the road last January as Elway finally captured a Super Bowl title. Getting fitted for a Super Bowl ring is certainly something that Matthews hopes will take place before he retires.

Although the Oilers failed to make the playoffs for four straight years (1994–1997), they're well acclimated to postseason pressure. With Matthews spearheading their offensive line—he's played all five positions in his career—the Oilers qualified for the playoffs seven straight seasons from 1987–1993. Unfortunately, Houston (now Tennessee) either bowed out in the wild-card game or never made it past the divisional playoffs.

Elway had a hand in ending Houston's season twice—in 1987 and 1991. Still, Matthews's respect for his long-time rival runs deep.

"I was glad to see that he got one [a Super Bowl ring]," says Matthews. "You can say it's not that big of a deal, but when you see somebody win it, it's special."

Matthews, who has been around for sixteen NFL campaigns, is well aware that the clock is winding down on his dream to play for the Lombardi Trophy. What if he falls short? Well, he'll be disappointed, but he'll never feel empty inside, thanks to his relationship with God through Jesus Christ—a relationship he began to develop during his rookie year.

Things couldn't have worked out better for Matthews that first season. He made the big time, but he also realized something was missing. A few of his Christian teammates encouraged Matthews to let Christ fill that void inside him.

"I was always spiritually inclined, but I never dedicated my life to the Lord," he says. "[I said] this [football] can't be the be-all, end-all. It became very apparent to me that God had a plan for my life.

"It doesn't matter what the situation is, winning or losing, as long as you're playing hard for the Lord and glorifying Him," says Matthews. "[Getting to] the Super Bowl would be a great honor, but I can be happy using the talents and abilities that God has blessed me with."

—by Mike Sandrolini

A Pro Football Chronology

Part 2

1905

- Canton AC (later, the Bulldogs) go professional. Massillon again wins the Ohio League championship.

1906

- The forward pass is legalized.
- George (Peggy) Parratt of Massillon throws a completion to Bullet Riley—the first pass completion in a pro game.
- Rivals Canton and Massillon vie for the championship. They play twice—Canton wins the first game, but Massillon wins the second and the Ohio League championship.
- A betting scandal combines with huge player salaries to cause a decline in interest in pro football in Ohio.

1909

- The value of a field goal drops from four points to three.

1912

- The value of a touchdown is increased from five points to six.
- Jack Cusack revives a pro team in Canton.

1913

- Jim Thorpe, double gold medal winner at the 1912 Olympics in Stockholm, plays for the Pine Village (Indiana) Pros.

1915

- Massillon fields a strong team. The rivalry with Canton is renewed.

- Jack Cusack signs Thorpe to play for Canton for $250 a game.

1916

- Thorpe and teammate Pete Calac lead Canton to a 9–0–1 season and the pro football championship.

1917

- Canton wins the Ohio League championship again.

1919

- Canton again wins the Ohio League championship.
- Earl (Curly) Lambeau and George Calhoun organize the Green Bay Packers when Lambeau's employer, the Indian Packing Company, provides $500 for equipment and the company field for practices. The team goes 10–1.

1920

- Akron Pros, Canton Bulldogs, Cleveland Indians, and Dayton Triangles hold an organizational meeting at the Jordan and Hupmobile auto showroom in Canton, Ohio, and form the American Professional Football Conference.
- A second organizational meeting is held in Canton. The league name is changed to the American Professional Football Association. Jim Thorpe is elected president of the league.

1921

- The 1920 season championship is awarded by the league to the Akron Pros. The league is reorganized, with Joe Carr as president. Carr moves the Association's headquarters to Columbus, drafts a league constitution and by-laws, and generally organizes the league.

- The Association is composed of twenty-two teams, including the Green Bay Packers.
- A.E. Staley turns the Decatur Staleys over to George Halas, who moves the team to Chicago.
- Player-coach Fritz Pollard of the Akron Pros is the first African-American head coach.
- The Staleys are the APFA champions with a 9–1–1 record—George Halas's first championship.

1922

- Bad weather and low attendance plague the Packers. Head coach and manager Curly Lambeau goes broke. Green Bay merchants arrange a $2,500 loan for the club and set up a public nonprofit corporation to operate the team.
- The American Professional Football Association changes its name to the National Football League on June 24. The Chicago Staleys are renamed the Chicago Bears.
- The NFL is composed of eighteen teams, including the new Oorang Indians of Marion, Ohio, an all-Indian team featuring Thorpe. The team is sponsored by the Oorang Dog Kennels.
- Canton finishes the season 10–0–2.

Pro football gave me a good sense of perspective to enter politics. I'd already been booed, cheered, cut, sold, traded, and hung in effigy.

JACK KEMP,
US Congressman and former quarterback (1957–62)

Gridiron Glossary

Part 2

DEAD BALL: A ball that is no longer in play, that is, a ball that is not held by a player or loose from a kick, fumble, or pass.

DELAY OF GAME: A delay caused by a team using or requesting excessive time-outs, resulting in a five-yard penalty.

DOWN AND IN: A maneuver where the receiver runs straight downfield, then suddenly cuts toward the middle of the field.

DOWN AND OUT: The opposite of the above maneuver. In a down and out, the receiver runs downfield then turns out, toward the sideline.

DOWN BOX (DOWN INDICATOR): A seven-foot metal rod, on the end of which are four cards (numbered one to four), used to keep track of the number of the down being played.

DRAFT: The selection of new players into the pro ranks from among the various top college players. Teams doing poorly are allowed to choose before those doing well.

ELIGIBLE: An offensive player who is able (by the rules) to catch a forward pass; "eligible" to receive the pass.

ENCROACH: Contacting an opposing player before the snap. Encroaching is illegal, with a five-yard penalty.

END LINE: The very end of the field in either direction. There are two end lines (one at each end of the field).

END ZONE: The area between the goal lines and the end lines; the last ten yards at either end of the field.

EXTRA POINT: After scoring a touchdown, a team can earn one more point by making a successful place-kick.

FAIR CATCH: When there is a punt and a receiver fielding the ball signals that he will not advance after catching it (by raising his hand), this is a fair catch. Opposing players may not tackle the receiver making the fair catch.

FLANKER: An offensive player on the right or left side of the formation. A flanker usually plays as a receiver.

FLAT: The field on either side of the formation.

FLOOD: An attempt to swamp the opposition or an area of the field with sheer numbers of players.

FREE AGENT: A professional athlete who is not constrained to deal with one team. Rather, a free agent may sign with any team he or she chooses.

FREE SAFETY: One of the two defensive backs deepest in the field who isn't assigned a particular area or player to cover and is thus free to follow the play anywhere it goes.

FREEZE: Holding on to the ball for a long time without scoring or attempting to score, to "freeze" the game.

FRONT FOUR: The defensive front line; made up of two ends and two tackles.

FULLBACK: A position used in college and high school football. A member of the offense whose job it is to run the ball, receive passes, and block for a teammate running the ball.

FUMBLE: A ball that is dropped while in play.

Tom Landry is a perfectionist. If he was married to Raquel Welch, he'd expect her to cook.

DON MEREDITH,
Dallas Cowboys quarterback (1960–68)

Stats

100-Yard Rushing Games (1998)

Games	Player	Team
12	Jamal Anderson	Atlanta
11	Terrell Davis	Denver
8	Curtis Martin	New York Jets
8	Barry Sanders	Detroit
7	Emmitt Smith	Dallas
6	Jerome Bettis	Pittsburgh
6	Gary Brown	New York Giants
6	Eddie George	Tennessee
6	Garrison Hearst	San Francisco
6	Fred Taylor	Jacksonville
5	Robert Smith	Minnesota
4	Corey Dillon	Cincinnati
4	Marshall Faulk	Indianapolis
4	Priest Holmes	Baltimore
4	Napoleon Kaufman	Oakland
4	Natrone Means	San Diego
4	Ricky Watters	Seattle
4	Robert Edwards	New England
3	Karim Abdul-Jabbar	Miami
3	Adrian Murrell	Arizona
3	Antowain Smith	Buffalo
2	Mike Alstott	Tampa Bay
2	Tim Biakabutuka	Carolina
2	Warrick Dunn	Tampa Bay
2	Terrell Fletcher	San Diego
2	Darick Holmes	Green Bay
2	Fred Lane	Carolina
2	James Stewart	Jacksonville
1	James Allen	Chicago
1	Donnell Bennett	Kansas City

Games	Player	Team
1	Charlie Garner	Philadelphia
1	Greg Hill	St. Louis
1	Dorsey Levens	Green Bay
1	Bam Morris	Kansas City
1	Lamar Smith	New Orleans
1	Duce Staley	Philadelphia
1	Kordell Stewart	Pittsburgh
1	Chris Warren	Dallas
1	Ahman Green	Seattle

Defensive backs. Nothing but reactions. You train 'em like seals.

Sam Baker,
Washington Redskins
fullback/kicker (1953–59)

In life, as in a football game, the principle to follow is: Hit the line hard.

Theodore Roosevelt,
twenty-sixth President of the United States

Trying to Find a Way to Give God the Glory

Arizona Cardinals all-pro cornerback Aeneas Williams spent his first two years at Southern University living the life of a model student-athlete.

Wanting to follow in the footsteps of his older brother Achilles—who was also attending Southern at the time—Williams got involved in student government, like his brother, and was on a fast track to graduation.

Williams held his own on the gridiron over that span, too—the intramural gridiron.

Aeneas had enjoyed a fine prep career at Fortier High School in New Orleans, which has produced a handful of NFL players, but he failed to land a football scholarship. Yet Williams wasn't heartbroken. He was content with completing his class requirements, playing intramural football, and looking up to his brother.

But things would change. Achilles Williams graduated from Southern in 1988, leaving his little brother to fend for himself. Aeneas seized the moment. "My brother graduating from college that particular year gave me an opportunity to find out who Aeneas was," he says.

And find out he did. That summer, Williams tried out for the other football program at Southern—the one that sports helmets and shoulder pads. Williams not only made the team; he went on to play three collegiate seasons and intercepted eleven passes his senior year alone. Over the years, Williams hasn't missed a beat, nor many opposing quarterbacks' errant passes, as a pro.

A Pro Bowl starter every year since 1994, Williams has been the NFL's co-leader in interceptions four times. Now the eight-year pro is setting his sights on helping the improved Cardinals get into the NFC playoffs with an eventual goal of making it to the Super Bowl.

"One of the things I've seen and [has] stuck in my mind is seeing [Green Bay's] Reggie White win it," says Williams. "It ignited something even more in me to get into the Super Bowl and win it. If I don't win a Super Bowl, the only question I want to ask myself is this: Did I do my best? I want to leave the game with no regrets."

From Williams's perspective, however, being a part of a Super Bowl-winning club in Arizona wouldn't be the highlight of his career. "I get the most fulfillment leading my teammates and friends throughout the league to the Lord and discipling them," he says. "I am still in awe of what the Lord has done in my life. My heart's desire is to disciple young believers and to give them the heart I've been given."

"A lot of times the interviewers [from the media] want me to give myself the credit," says Williams. "I'm always trying to find a way to give God the glory."

—by MIKE SANDROLINI

A Pro Football Chronology
Part 3

1923

- Jim Thorpe, playing for the Toledo Maroons, fumbles. The Bears' George Halas picks up the ball and returns it ninety-eight yards for a touchdown—a record that lasts until 1972.
- Canton has its second consecutive undefeated season, going 11–0–1 and winning the NFL title.

1924

- The league has eighteen franchises.
- League champion Canton is purchased by the owner of the Cleveland franchise, who takes the best players for the Cleveland Bulldogs.
- Cleveland wins the title with a 7–1–1 record.

1925

- Five new franchises are admitted to the NFL.
- The New York Giants are awarded to Tim Mara and Billy Gibson for $500.
- The NFL establishes its first player limit—sixteen.
- All-America halfback Harold (Red) Grange signs to play with the Chicago Bears.
- On Thanksgiving Day, a crowd of 36,000—the largest yet in pro football—sees Red Grange and the Bears play the Chicago Cardinals to a scoreless tie.
- The Chicago Cardinals, with the best record in the league, are named the 1925 champions.

1926

- Grange bolts the Bears over a salary/ownership dispute.

- Grange's manager starts the first American Football League. It lasts one season.
- A new rule prohibits any team from signing a player whose college class has not graduated.
- The NFL grows to twenty-two teams, including the Duluth Eskimos with All-America fullback Ernie Nevers of Stanford. "The Iron Men of the North" play twenty-nine exhibition and league games, twenty-eight on the road. Nevers plays in all but twenty-nine minutes of the season.
- Frankford (Pennsylvania) beats the Bears for the championship.

1927

- The NFL is reorganized into twelve teams.
- The league's center shifts from the Midwest to the cities of the East.
- The championship goes to the New York Giants, with ten shutouts in thirteen games.

1928

- Grange and Nevers retire from pro football.
- The NFL is reduced to ten teams.
- The Providence Steam Rollers win the championship in the Cycledrome, a ten thousand-seat oval built for bicycle races.

1929

- A fourth official, the field judge, is added.
- Grange and Nevers return to the NFL.
- Nevers scores six rushing touchdowns and four extra points for the Cardinals to beat Grange's Bears 40–6.
- Providence becomes the first NFL team to host a game at night under floodlights.

- The Packers, with back Johnny Blood (McNally), tackle Cal Hubbard, and guard Mike Michalske, win their first NFL championship.

1930

- Dayton, the last of the NFL's original franchises, is purchased, moved to Brooklyn, and renamed the Dodgers.
- The Packers edge the Giants for the title.
- George Halas retires as a player.
- Rookie All-America fullback-tackle Bronko Nagurski joins the Bears.
- The Giants defeat a team of former Notre Dame players coached by Knute Rockne 22–0 at the Polo Grounds. The proceeds go to help those suffering because of the Great Depression.

1931

- The Bears, Packers, and Portsmouth are each fined $1,000 for using players whose college classes had not graduated.
- The Packers win an unprecedented third consecutive title.

1932

- The Boston Braves join the league.
- NFL membership drops to eight teams, the lowest in history.
- Official statistics are kept for the first time.
- The Bears and the Spartans finish the season in the first tie for first place.
- The resulting first playoff game in NFL history is held indoors at Chicago Stadium because of bitter cold and heavy snow. The arena allows only an eighty-yard field so the rules are adjusted: The goal posts are moved from the end lines to the

goal lines, inbounds lines (hash marks) where the ball is put in play are drawn ten yards from the walls that butt against the sidelines.

- The Bears win 9–0.

1933

- The NFL makes significant changes from the college game for the first time.
- The adjustments from the 1932 championship game are adopted—hash marks and goal posts on the goal lines. The forward pass is legalized from anywhere behind the line of scrimmage.
- The NFL divides into two divisions. The winners are to meet in an annual championship game.
- New franchises join the league—the Pittsburgh Pirates, the Philadelphia Eagles, and the Cincinnati Reds.
- Halas becomes sole owner of the Bears and reinstates himself as head coach.
- The Boston Braves name is changed to the Redskins.
- In the first NFL Championship Game, the Western Division Bears defeat the Eastern Division Giants 23–21.

1934

- The Portsmouth Spartans move to Detroit and become the Lions.
- The Bears play the best college football players. The game ends in a scoreless tie before 79,432 at Soldier Field.
- Rookie Beattie Feathers of the Bears is the NFL's first 1,000-yard rusher, gaining 1,004 yards on 101 carries.

- Graham McNamee, announcer for NBC radio, calls the Thanksgiving Day game between the Bears and the Lions—the first NFL game broadcast nationally.
- The championship game occurs on an extremely cold and icy day at the Polo Grounds. The Giants trail the Bears 13–3 in the third quarter, change to basketball shoes for better footing, and win 30–13. The contest becomes known as the "Sneakers Game."
- The player waiver rule is adopted.

My parents sent me to Harvard to be a specialist. I don't think they were thinking of this.

Pat McInally,
Cincinnati Bengals punter (1976–85)

I remember one time when Bronko Nagurski was horsing around in a second-floor hotel room with a teammate, and Bronko fell out of the window. A crowd gathered and a policeman came up and said, "What happened?" "I don't know," said Nagurski. "I just got here myself."

Ronnie Gibbs,
former referee

Gridiron Glossary

Part 3

GAME BALL: The ball given to a winning team's player or coach considered to have made the most contribution to their win. (It is supposed to be the ball or a ball used in the game.)

GOAL LINE: The line over which the ball must pass to score a touchdown. There are two goal lines, one at each end of the field, ten yards from the ends of the field.

GOAL-LINE STAND: Making a tough defensive effort against the opposition at or near one's goal line.

GRIDIRON: A football field.

HAIL MARY: The quarterback throwing the ball up in the air without really targeting any particular receiver, hoping someone on his side catches it. Typically done when the quarterback's about to get sacked!

HALFBACK: A position in college and high school football. A member of the offense whose job it is to run the ball, receive passes, or block for another teammate running the ball.

HAND OFF: Quite literally what it says: to hand the ball off to a teammate.

HANG TIME: The time a punt remains in the air.

HASH MARKS: These marks divide the field into thirds. Whenever the ball becomes dead on or outside one of these marks, it is placed on its respective hash mark.

HITCH AND GO: A maneuver where a runner runs downfield to catch a pass, fakes a quick turn (as if to catch), then continues downfield for a deeper pass.

HOLDER: A player who holds the ball during a place kick.

HOLDING: Keeping another player from advancing by literally holding him back with one's hand(s). Usually illegal.

HOTDOG: A player who uses theatrics and "hams it up" for the camera.

HUDDLE: The action of the players grouping together to plan the next play(s). As a noun, the group itself.

ILLEGAL MOTION: Movement by an offensive player before the snap. Illegal motion is, obviously, illegal and yields a five-yard penalty.

ILLEGAL PROCEDURE: Used to indicate a number of infractions, including an illegal snap, having less than seven players on the offense's line of scrimmage, and taking more than two steps after making a fair catch.

INCOMPLETE: A forward pass that is not caught or intercepted.

INTENTIONAL GROUNDING: The quarterback purposefully throwing the ball out of bounds or into the ground to avoid throwing a bad pass (which might be intercepted). Intentional grounding can be difficult to call, but a referee may assign the offending team a five-yard penalty and the loss of a down.

KEY: Watching a player to try to determine the direction in which he is going to be moving. A player may make small movements, such as foot placement, that can give away his next move to an observant player who is "keying" him.

Everyone has some fear. A man without fear belongs in a mental institution. . .or on special teams, either one.

WALT MICHAELS,
Cleveland Browns linebacker (1951–63)

Stats

Multiple Interception Games (1998)

Games	Player	Team
2	Percy Ellsworth	New York Giants
2	Robert Griffith	Minnesota
2	Ty Law	New England
2	Sam Madison	Miami
1	Jay Bellamy	Seattle
1	Jeff Brady	Carolina
1	Zack Bronson	San Francisco
1	Terrell Buckley	Miami
1	LeRoy Butler	Green Bay
1	Mark Carrier	Detroit
1	Ray Crockett	Denver
1	Charles Dimry	San Diego
1	Cris Dishman	Washington
1	Darrien Gordon	Denver
1	Victor Green	New York Jets
1	Henry Jones	Buffalo
1	Robert Jones	Miami
1	Sammy Knight	New Orleans
1	Kwamie Lassiter	Arizona
1	Ray Lewis	Baltimore
1	John Lynch	Tampa Bay
1	Ronald McKinnon	Arizona
1	Lawyer Milloy	New England
1	Kurt Schulz	Buffalo
1	Phillippi Sparks	New York Giants
1	Shawn Springs	Seattle
1	Zach Thomas	Miami
1	Brian Walker	Miami
1	Darnell Walker	San Francisco
1	Dewayne Washington	Pittsburgh

Games	Player	Team
1	Darryl Williams	Seattle
1	Rod Woodson	Baltimore
1	Artrell Hawkins	Cincinnati
1	Fred Weary	New Orleans

The idea is to have a plan and still allow for the unforeseeable. I've been reading about Nelson's battle with the Franco-Spanish fleet at Trafalgar in 1805. He had twenty-five days to make his plan. He was outnumbered, but his plan worked. He had steps prepared for the contingencies, and the plan left a certain flexibility in the choices of his captains. That is the basis of football.

Bill Walsh,
San Francisco 49ers coach (1979–88)

Nobody in football should be called a genius. A genius is a guy like Norman Einstein.

Joe Theismann,
Washington Redskins quarterback (1974–85)

A Good Name and Loving Esteem

"If you must choose, take a good name rather than great riches; for to be held in loving esteem is better than silver and gold" (Proverbs 22:1 TLB).

King Solomon didn't have professional athletes in mind when he dispatched this scriptural morsel of wisdom—but it fits. In an age of continual fiscal selfishness and personal gratification, it has become common for pro sports figures to ignore this exhortation and choose silver and gold above a good name. So what happens when a player chooses both: to be held in loving esteem and obtain riches?

The answer can be found in the form of five-time Pro Bowl receiver Cris Carter—a player snatched by the Minnesota Vikings for a meager $100 when he was waived by the Philadelphia Eagles in 1990. Once in Minnesota, Carter became a Christian, and it showed both on and off the field. He has developed a "good name" and is held in "loving esteem" by fans, players, and coaches. Carter's good name, coupled with his great skills, has parlayed itself into great riches as he is in the midst of a substantial four-year contract.

With both proverbial components intact, one would

think Carter's career was complete. However, football-related fullness eludes him as he has yet to compete for a Super Bowl crown—an opportunity he contends would be an answer to prayer.

Now in his twelfth NFL season, Carter feels he has learned what it takes to realize his gridiron goal. "I've always wanted to make it, but I never really understood what it took to win it all," he says. Carter learned the value of experiencing rough times while watching former Eagle teammate and fellow believer Reggie White hoist the Lombardi Trophy after Super Bowl XXXI with the Green Bay Packers. "I've learned a lot from Reggie, and I realized that he had a lot of failures along the way. Regardless of whether he ever won a title, he's still had a tremendous career," Carter says.

Despite his arduous drive to claim the ultimate football prize, Carter, thirty-two, realizes that becoming a champion does not define him as a person. "Just because I am not in a Super Bowl doesn't make me a loser," he explains. "My life does not revolve around the Super Bowl."

The sure-handed receiver's professional ambition does less to define him than does his personal mission. Carter is unmistakably a preacher who contends that an NFL locker room is "not a place to preach Christianity; it is a place to live it. My number one job is to live a life that people would see me and know that there is something different," he says.

That difference is a name that will be recorded in the Book of Life long after any on-field accomplishments are forgotten and eternal riches that will outlast even the most lucrative contract.

—by Troy Pearson

A Pro Football Chronology

Part 4

1935

- An annual draft of college players is scheduled to begin in 1936.
- The inbounds line, or hash marks, are moved nearer the center of the field, fifteen yards from the sidelines.
- The Lions defeat the Giants 26–7 in the NFL Championship Game.

1936

- All NFL member teams play the same number of games.
- The Eagles sign University of Chicago halfback and Heisman Trophy winner Jay Berwanger—the first player ever selected in the NFL draft.
- A rival league, the American Football League, forms. The Boston Shamrocks are its champions.
- In the NFL Championship Game, Green Bay defeats the Redskins 21–6 on December 13.

1937

- A new Cleveland franchise is named the Rams.
- The Redskins move to Washington, D.C. and sign TCU All-America tailback Sammy Baugh.
- Baugh leads the Redskins to a 28–21 victory over the Bears in the NFL Championship Game.
- The 8–0 Los Angeles Bulldogs win the AFL title, but the league soon folds.

1938

- Hugh (Shorty) Ray becomes technical advisor on rules and officiating.
- A new rule is implemented: a fifteen-yard penalty for roughing the passer.
- Rookie Byron "Whizzer" White of the Pittsburgh

Pirates leads the NFL in rushing. White later becomes a justice of the U.S. Supreme Court.

- The Giants defeat the Packers 23–17 for the NFL title.
- The Pro Bowl game is established between the NFL champion and a team of pro all-stars.

1939

- The New York Giants defeat the Pro All-Stars 13–10 in the first Pro Bowl.
- NBC broadcasts the Brooklyn Dodgers–Philadelphia Eagles game from Ebbets Field to approximately 1,000 sets in New York—the first NFL game to be televised.
- Green Bay defeats New York 27–0 in the NFL Championship Game.
- For the first time, NFL attendance exceeds one million in a season—1,071,200.

1940

- A rival league, the third to call itself the American Football League, is formed with six teams. The Columbus Bullies are its champions.
- The Bears defeat the Redskins 73–0 in the NFL Championship Game—the most decisive victory in NFL history.
- This is the first championship to be carried on network radio, broadcast by Red Barber.

1941

- The league by-laws provide for playoffs in case of ties in division races and sudden-death overtimes in case a playoff game is tied after four quarters.
- An official NFL Record Manual is published for the first time.
- Columbus again wins the AFL championship—but the two-year-old league folds.
- The Bears and the Packers tie for the Western

Division championship. The Bears win the first divisional playoff game in league history, 33–14.
- The Bears defeat the Giants 37–9 for the NFL championship.

1942

- Players depart for service in World War II, depleting the rosters of NFL teams.
- With George Halas in the Navy, the Bears go 11–0 in the regular season.
- The Redskins defeat the Bears 14–6 in the NFL Championship Game.

1943

- The Cleveland Rams co-owners join the armed forces, and the team is granted permission to suspend operations for the season.
- The league adopts free substitution, makes the wearing of helmets mandatory, and approves a ten-game schedule for all teams.
- Philadelphia and Pittsburgh merge for one season.
- Sammy Baugh (league leader in passing, punting, and interceptions) leads the Redskins to a tie with the Giants for the Eastern Division title. The Redskins win the divisional playoff game, 28–0.
- The Bears beat the Redskins 41–21 in the championship game.

1944

- A new franchise in Boston is named the Yanks.
- The Brooklyn Dodgers change their name to the Tigers.
- Coaching from the bench is legalized.
- The Cardinals and the Steelers merge for one year under the name Card-Pitt.
- Green Bay defeats the New York Giants 14–7 in the NFL Championship.

1945

- The inbounds lines (hash marks) are moved from fifteen yards away from the sidelines to twenty yards from the sidelines.
- Brooklyn and Boston merge and become the Boston Yanks.
- Steve Van Buren of Philadelphia leads the NFL in rushing, kickoff returns, and scoring.
- World War II ends, with 638 NFL players having served in the war. Twenty-one died in action.
- Rookie quarterback Bob Waterfield leads Cleveland to a 15–14 victory over Washington in the NFL Championship Game.

1946

- The free substitution rule is withdrawn. Substitutions are limited to no more than three men at a time.
- The NFL champion Rams move to Los Angeles.
- The rival All-America Football Conference begins play with eight teams. The Cleveland Browns, coached by Paul Brown, win the AAFC's first championship.
- Giants players are questioned about an attempt to fix the championship game.
- Chicago beats New York for the championship, 24–14.

Gridiron Glossary

Part 4

LATERAL: As a forward pass, but not thrown in the direction of the opponents' goalpost. Rather, the ball is thrown in any direction other than toward the opponents' goal.

LINEBACKER: Defensive players placed behind the defensive linemen. Their job is to tackle runners and block or intercept passes. There are three or four linebackers.

LINE JUDGE: An official who keeps track of time and also watches for various violations, including the quarterback's position when passing (the quarterback isn't allowed to go past the line of scrimmage to pass).

LINE OF SCRIMMAGE: Before each play, a set of two imaginary lines are used to determine where the players will line up. These are the lines of scrimmage and pass through each tip of the ball, running parallel to the goal lines.

LIVE BALL: Opposite of a ball that is dead. A live ball is either loose as a result of a kick, fumble, or pass or is held by a player.

MAN IN MOTION: The player who turns and runs behind the line of scrimmage, parallel to it, as the signals are called. He then runs downfield just as the ball is snapped.

MAN-TO-MAN DEFENSE: Covering each member of the offense with a member of the defense. Also called player-to-player defense. See also "zone defense."

MIDDLE GUARD: The defensive lineman positioned between the tackles, opposite the offensive center. Also called the nose guard.

MOUSETRAP: A trap block.

MULTIPLE OFFENSE: Offense strategy using a number of formations.

NICKEL DEFENSE: A defensive formation involving five defensive backs, hence the name.

NOSE GUARD: The middle guard.

OFFENSE: The team with the ball; the offense attempts to run or pass the ball across the defense's goal line.

OFF SEASON: When football teams don't play; in the NFL, February through the middle of August.

OFFSIDE: When a player is over the line of scrimmage (on the opposing team's side) before the ball is snapped.

ONSIDE KICK: A short kick (though at least ten yards), with the plan being to recover the kick and thus regain possession.

OPTION PLAY: An offensive play wherein the player with the ball has the option of running or passing.

OUTSIDE: Toward the sideline.

Three hundred pounds of player and thirty-four pounds of equipment just teeing off.

DAVE BUTZ,
St. Louis Cardinals/Washington Redskins
lineman (1973–1988)

Super Bowl	MVP	Winner
XXXIII	John Elway	Denver 34
XXXII	Terrell Davis	Denver 31
XXXI	Desmond Howard	Green Bay 35
XXX	Larry Brown	Dallas 27
XXIX	Steve Young	San Francisco 49
XXVIII	Emmitt Smith	Dallas 30
XXVII	Troy Aikman	Dallas 52
XXVI	Mark Rypien	Washington 37
XXV	Ottis Anderson	NY Giants 20
XXIV	Joe Montana	San Francisco 55
XXIII	Jerry Rice	San Francisco 20
XXII	Doug Williams	Washington 42
XXI	Phil Simms	NY Giants 39
XX	Richard Dent	Chicago 46
XIX	Joe Montana	San Francisco 38
XVIII	Marcus Allen	L.A. Raiders 38
XVII	John Riggins	Washington 27
XVI	Joe Montana	San Francisco 26
XV	Jim Plunkett	Oakland 27
XIV	Terry Bradshaw	Pittsburgh 31
XIII	Terry Bradshaw	Pittsburgh 35
XII	Harvey Martin & Randy White	Dallas 27
XI	Fred Biletnikoff	Oakland 32
X	Lynn Swann	Pittsburgh 21
IX	Franco Harris	Pittsburgh 16
VIII	Larry Csonka	Miami 24
VII	Jake Scott	Miami 14
VI	Roger Staubach	Dallas 24
V	Chuck Howley	Baltimore 16
IV	Len Dawson	Kansas City 23
III	Joe Namath	NY Jets 16
II	Bart Starr	Green Bay 33
I	Bart Starr	Green Bay 35

—Winners and Losers

Loser	Location	Attendence	Date
Atlanta 19	Miami	74,803	1/31/99
Green Bay 24	San Diego	68,912	1/25/98
New England 21	New Orleans	72,301	1/26/97
Pittsburgh 17	Tempe	76,347	1/28/96
San Diego 26	Miami	74,107	1/29/95
Buffalo 13	Atlanta	72,817	1/30/94
Buffalo 17	Pasadena	98,374	1/31/93
Buffalo 24	Minneapolis	63,130	1/26/92
Buffalo 19	Tampa	73,813	1/27/91
Denver 10	New Orleans	72,919	1/28/90
Cincinnati 16	Miami	75,179	1/22/89
Denver 10	San Diego	73,302	1/31/88
Denver 20	Pasadena	101,063	1/25/87
New England 10	New Orleans	73,818	1/26/86
Miami 16	Stanford	84,059	1/20/85
Washington 9	Tampa	72,920	1/22/84
Miami 17	Pasadena	103,667	1/30/83
Cincinnati 21	Pontiac	81,270	1/24/82
Philadelphia 10	New Orleans	76,135	1/25/81
L.A. Rams 19	Pasadena	103,985	1/20/80
Dallas 31	Miami	79,484	1/21/79
Denver 10	New Orleans	75,583	1/15/78
Minnesota 14	Pasadena	103,438	1/9/77
Dallas 17	Miami	80,187	1/18/76
Minnesota 6	New Orleans	80,997	1/12/75
Minnesota 7	Houston	71,882	1/13/74
Washington 7	Los Angeles	90,182	1/14/73
Miami 3	New Orleans	81,023	1/16/72
Dallas 13	Miami	79,204	1/17/71
Minnesota 7	New Orleans	80,562	1/11/70
Baltimore 7	Miami	75,389	1/12/69
Oakland 14	Miami	75,546	1/14/68
Kansas City 10	Los Angeles	61,946	1/15/67

Those Trusty Placekickers

Part I

Muddy, sweaty, Behemoth-sized men. Guys so big they need two zip codes. Scale-tippers who run the forty-yard dash in 4.5 seconds. Men of extraordinary size, strength, speed, and endurance. These are football players!

Grown men who dent the scales at a mere 170. Former soccer stars. Men who carry little orange tools onto the field to assist them. Guys who don't even wear shoes that match. These are not football players!

Think again.

These are football players. Players of a different breed—these are placekickers.

While they obviously don't fit the stereotypical model of today's NFL star, kickers are just as important to the success of a team on a Sunday afternoon as any 300-pound lineman. Perhaps even more important.

If there's one player who gets stuck with the "hero" or the "goat" tag more than any other, it's the kicker. On a field full of muscled-up mortals it's these little giants who loom large. The guy who makes a living with a swift kick of his foot and tacks on three points at a time.

You know the scenario: The team is down by a point with seven ticks on the game clock. The two minute offense has just stalled at the thirty-three-yard-line. Who gets the call? It's the smallest guy in uniform, that's who. It's show time!

With the pressure of teammates, coaches, fans, and the media, it's the job of these little big men to come through.

Amid this pressure, more than a handful of the NFL's finest kickers find a peace that transcends the success/failure balance they often hang in. These strong-legged heroes have an inner peace they receive from only one place—their relationship with Jesus Christ.

Matt Stover of the Baltimore Ravens is one such kicker. Matt's world isn't wrapped up in a field goal. "I look at it like this: 'Okay this is an opportunity God's given me, and I'm gonna give it everything I've got.' When the failures happen, I look at them and say, 'Lord, help me through this. I know You can work this out for good.' I trust in that, and then I move on. Because life does go on. Football is not my life, it's not even my priority."

And Stover's not alone. Many of Matt's NFL kicking brethren also gain their strength and their focus from their personal relationship with Jesus.

Norm Johnson, a sixteen-year NFL veteran now with the Pittsburgh Steelers, says his faith in Christ is crucial to the mental aspect of kicking. It helps him focus and not get down on himself.

"In our job, things are up-and-down all of the time," explains Johnson. "Faith in Christ helps us get through the down times. It helps us deal with the fact that we lost a game or missed a kick. We know that not only our family still loves us, but so does Jesus. And when you know that, what's said about you in the newspapers or what fans yell at you has very little consequence. It doesn't affect you. If you don't have that kind of faith, a lot of those outside factors may get to you and overcome you."

(*to be continued*)

A Pro Football Chronology

Part 5

1947

- The NFL adds a fifth official, the back judge.
- The Cleveland Browns again win the AAFC title, defeating the New York Yankees 14–3.
- The Cardinals win the NFL Championship Game 28–21 over the Philadelphia Eagles.

1948

- Plastic helmets are prohibited. A flexible artificial tee is permitted at the kickoff. Officials other than the referee are equipped with whistles, not horns.
- Halfback Fred Gehrke of the Los Angeles Rams paints horns on the Rams' helmets—the first modern helmet emblems in pro football.
- The 14–0 Cleveland Browns win their third straight championship in the AAFC, defeating the Buffalo Bills 49–7.
- The Eagles defeat the Cardinals 7–0 in the championship game, which takes place in a blizzard.

1949

- The Boston Yanks become the New York Bulldogs.
- Free substitution is adopted for one year.
- For the first time the NFL has two 1,000-yard rushers in the same season—Steve Van Buren of Philadelphia and Tony Canadeo of Green Bay.
- AAFC franchises Cleveland, San Francisco, and Baltimore are scheduled to join the NFL in 1950.
- The Browns win their fourth consecutive AAFC title, defeating the 49ers 21–7.
- In a heavy rain, the Eagles defeat the Rams 14–0 in the NFL Championship Game.

1950

- Unlimited free substitution is restored, opening the era of two platoons and specialization.
- Curly Lambeau, founder of the franchise and Green Bay's head coach since 1921, resigns under fire.
- The American and National conferences are created to replace the Eastern and Western divisions.
- The Los Angeles Rams have all of their games televised—the first team to do so.
- In the first game of the season, former AAFC champion Cleveland defeats NFL champion Philadelphia 35–10.
- Deadlocks in both conferences occur for the first time. In the playoffs the Browns defeat the Giants in the American and the Rams defeat the Bears in the National.
- Cleveland defeats Los Angeles 30–28 in the NFL Championship Game.

1951

- The Pro Bowl game, dormant since 1942, is revived matching the all-stars of each conference. The American Conference defeats the National Conference 28–27.
- Rulesmakers decree that no tackle, guard, or center is eligible to catch a forward pass.
- The Rams reverse their television policy and televise only road games.
- The NFL Championship Game is televised coast-to-coast for the first time—the DuMont Network pays $75,000 for the rights to the game.
- The Rams defeat the Browns, 24–17, to become champions.

1952

- A new franchise in Dallas—the Texans—goes 1–11.

The owners turn the franchise back to the league in midseason. The commissioner's office operates the Texans as a road team. At the end of the season the franchise is canceled. This is the last time an NFL team will fail.

- The Detroit Lions win their first NFL championship in seventeen years, defeating the Browns 17–7.

1953

- The defunct Dallas organization becomes the Baltimore Colts.
- The names of the American and National conferences are changed to the Eastern and Western conferences.
- Jim Thorpe dies.
- The Lions defeat the Browns for the championship, 17–16.

1954

- Fullback Joe Perry of the 49ers is the first player in league history to gain 1,000 yards rushing in consecutive seasons.
- Cleveland defeats Detroit 56–10 in the NFL Championship Game.

1955

- The sudden-death overtime rule is used for the first time in a pre-season game. The Rams beat the Giants 23–17 three minutes into overtime.
- Rule change: The ball is immediately dead if the ball carrier touches the ground with any part of his body except his hands or feet while in the grasp of an opponent.
- The Baltimore Colts spend eighty cents on a phone call to Johnny Unitas and sign him as a free agent.

- Quarterback Otto Graham plays his last game as the Browns defeat the Rams 38–14 in the NFL Championship Game. Graham quarterbacked the Browns to ten championship game appearances in ten years.

1956

- The NFL Players Association is founded.
- New rules: Grabbing an opponent's face mask (other than the ball carrier's) is illegal. Using radio receivers to communicate with players on the field is prohibited. A natural leather ball with white end stripes replaces the white ball with black stripes for night games.
- George Halas retires as coach of the Bears.
- The Giants rout the Bears 47–7 in the championship game.

1957

- Pete Rozelle is named general manager of the Rams.
- Detroit defeats Cleveland 59–14 in the championship game.

1958

- Halas reinstates himself as coach of the Bears.
- Jim Brown of Cleveland gains 1,527 yards rushing—an NFL record.
- Baltimore, coached by Weeb Ewbank, defeats the Giants 23–17 in the first sudden-death overtime in an NFL Championship Game.

Gridiron Glossary

Part 5

PASS PATTERN: The specific route run by a receiver to catch a pass.

PASS RUSH: The rush by the defense to try to tackle the quarterback before he can complete a pass.

PENALTY: Punishment for a foul. Can consist of losing a down or even the ball, but usually sets back the penalized team five to fifteen yards.

PIGSKIN: Old term for a football.

PILING ON: Several players jumping on the player with the ball after he's been tackled. Also called "dogpiling." Piling on is illegal, with a fifteen-yard penalty.

PLACEKICK: A kick made while the ball is held in place on the ground (either with a tee or by another player).

PLAYBOOK: A notebook containing a team's terms, strategies, plays, etc., issued to each player.

PLAYMAKER: One skilled in helping their team score with winning strategy.

POCKET: The area where the quarterback sets up his pass. Guarded against the opposition to form a safe "pocket" for the quarterback.

POINT AFTER TOUCHDOWN: After scoring a touchdown, a team may score an extra point for a successful placekick through the opposition's goal post.

POINT SPREAD: The projected difference in scores between two teams about to play.

POST PATTERN: A pass pattern where the receiver runs ten to fifteen yards downfield before turning toward the middle of the field, but at a forty-five-degree angle (in the direction of the goal post).

POSTSEASON: The time when a tournament is played leading up to the Super Bowl. Also called the playoffs.

PRESEASON: The time during which teams play exhibition games and check out new talent, from August through Labor Day, when the regular season starts.

PRIMARY: The receiver who was chosen by the quarterback in the huddle to receive the ball.

PULLING: Leaving one's position to move elsewhere to block.

PUNT: A play in which the ball is dropped from the kicker's hands and kicked before hitting the ground.

QUARTER: A football game is divided into four quarters of fifteen minutes each (twelve minutes in high school football).

QUARTERBACK SNEAK: A play wherein the quarterback receives the ball after the snap and immediately runs forward through the opposition, with his own team blocking for him.

QUICK COUNT: When the quarterback calls the signals at the line of scrimmage very rapidly so as to throw off the other team.

QUICK KICK: A surprise punt.

I've got bruises all over my body from bumping into Dan around the kitchen or taking a gouge from him while he's asleep.

DIANE BIRDWELL,
wife of DAN BIRDWELL,
Oakland Raiders defensive end (1962–69)

The Big Bucks and Jerry Kramer,

Green Bay Packers offensive guard (1958–68)

In 1967, I had earned $27,500 for my regular season pay. In 1968, I negotiated a pretty unusual deal. I started with a salary of $26,000, but I also got a $2,500 bonus for signing and $3,500 for scouting, and that made my actual base pay $32,000. In addition, I was to get $500 extra for each field goal I kicked. . . , plus a $3,000 bonus if we won eight games, another $2,000 if we won ten games, and another $2,000 if we won our division. I thought I was a cinch to earn at least $43,000. I figured I had to kick at least fourteen field goals, an average of one a game, and I figured there was no way we could lose our division, no way we could win fewer than eight games. That meant $11,000 plus my $32,000 base. And if everything went well, I thought I had a reasonable chance of kicking eighteen field goals and the team had a reasonable chance of winning ten games. Including a potential $25,000 from the playoff and Super Bowl games, I calculated that my purely football income for the 1968 season could climb as high as $74,000, way up in the quarterback brackets.

If you'd ask me, what's the common religion among scouts, I'd have to say Hindu. They all believe in reincarnation. You're always hearing, "This guy's another Dick Butkus, this guy's another Willie Brown."

George Young

Those Trusty Placekickers

Part 2

For most kickers the game is as much mental as it is physical. There's no time for self-doubt or worry. No time to contemplate the magnitude of the upcoming attempt. A kicker is focused on one thing and one thing alone—kicking the football. They shut out the world around them and do their job.

"I can't hear the crowd," says New England Patriots placekicker Adam Vinatieri. "I'm focusing in on kicking the football. I don't even think of the game situation too much. I try to make every kick exactly the same and focus on the fundamentals, not on the consequences."

Norm Johnson takes it one step further.

"If I can get to the point where I'm not thinking of anything, that's the best situation for me to be in. You've done this motion so often that it becomes almost a reaction and a muscle reflex. Many times I'll come off the field, having just made a successful field goal, and I'll have to ask how everything went because it was almost blank."

Matt Stover adds, "Our game is so mental. You've got to relax back there and say, 'Hey, just kick it normal.'

You don't need to change anything, just continue to kick the same way and make sure you're mentally sharp."

Detroit Lions kicker Jason Hanson says he practices mentally. "I think kicking is seventy-five to ninety percent mental. So I mentally rehearse kicks. I'll sometimes do field goals without a ball."

A different breed of football player indeed. While the men in the trenches battle it out with brawn, the kicker wages war against his own mind.

Ryan Longwell of the Green Bay Packers credits his faith in Christ for his mental toughness.

"My faith keeps me at such an even keel," explains Longwell. "In what could be high-pressure situations, I'm usually the calmest guy on the field because I realize it's all in God's great plan."

While all of these kickers are quick to give God credit for their current position in the NFL, they don't use their faith as a crutch. They have a healthy balance of respect for God's sovereignty and for their responsibility to be good stewards of the exceptional physical and mental gifts He has given them.

"He's blessed me with a healthy leg and a great mind," explains Longwell. "But I think it's a two-way street. I've got to do my job working out and getting in shape to glorify Him by bringing the best I have to the table."

Stover says, "Prior to the game, I lift the game up [in prayer] to the Lord. But I don't send up too many prayers on the field. He's not going to kick the ball for me."

While you may never see our small wonders land a bone-jarring shot on an unsuspecting kick-returner, the placekickers of today are far from weak. They take their workout regimen seriously.

Stover uses a specifically designed workout put together by a kinesiologist.

Vinatieri does the same workout as the "little" guys

on his team. You can find Adam pumping iron with any New England teammate who isn't a lineman, a linebacker, or a tight end.

"You build team camaraderie when the guys see you working out," says Vinatieri. "And if you're in good shape, you have less chance of injury."

Longwell considers his workout routine as one of the keys to gaining the respect of his teammates.

"I know that if I was a big lineman or a quarterback getting beat up on every play and I saw some kid come in with a clean uniform and miss a kick, I'd be mad at him. So I'm in the weight room with the guys. I run with the guys. They see I'm putting in the effort to be successful and to help them win."

But try as they might, placekickers are still very different than the rest of their gridiron contemporaries. That's why there's such a strong bond among kickers across the league. Think about it—when was the last time you watched an NFL game when at its conclusion, one kicker didn't shake hands with the opposing team's kicker first? It's a fraternity!

But Vinatieri, Hanson, Stover, Longwell, and Johnson have a stronger, more important tie that binds them away from football. Their faith in Christ truly sets these men apart.

"Football is so temporary—the money, the fame—it's so temporary," says Hanson. "My life is centered around Jesus Christ. That's what life is about, not the football field!"

Vinatieri adds, "To God, I don't think the most important thing in our lives is to play football. It's about being a Christian, and being a disciple, and bringing other people to Him."

—by Rob Bentz

A Pro Football Chronology

Part 6

1959

- Vince Lombardi is named head coach of the Green Bay Packers.
- A second pro football league is organized and named the American Football League.
- The Colts again defeat the Giants in the NFL Championship Game.

1960

- Pete Rozelle is elected NFL Commissioner.
- The AFL adopts the two-point option on points after touchdown.
- The Boston Patriots defeat the Buffalo Bills 28–7 in the first AFL preseason game.
- The Denver Broncos defeat the Patriots 13–10 in the first AFL regular-season game.
- Philadelphia defeats Green Bay 17–13 in the NFL Championship Game.

1961

- The Houston Oilers defeat the Los Angeles Chargers 24–16 in the first AFL Championship Game.
- Canton, Ohio, where the league that became the NFL was formed in 1920, is chosen as the site of the Pro Football Hall of Fame.
- Houston defeats San Diego 10–3 for the AFL championship.
- Green Bay wins its first NFL championship since 1944, defeating the New York Giants 37–0.

1962

- Both leagues prohibit grabbing any player's face mask.

- The AFL makes the scoreboard clock the official timer of the game.
- The Dallas Texans defeat the Oilers 20–17 for the AFL championship. After 17 minutes, 54 seconds of overtime, the game lasted a record 77 minutes, 54 seconds.
- The Packers beat the Giants 16–7 for the NFL title.

1963

- Rozelle suspends indefinitely Green Bay halfback Paul Hornung and Detroit defensive tackle Alex Karras for placing bets on their own teams and on other NFL games.
- Paul Brown, head coach of the Browns since their inception, is fired.
- The Pro Football Hall of Fame is dedicated at Canton, Ohio.
- Jim Brown of Cleveland rushes for an NFL single-season record 1,863 yards.
- Boston defeats Buffalo 26–8 in the first divisional playoff game in AFL history.
- The Bears defeat the Giants 14–10 in the NFL Championship Game. This is the record sixth and last title for George Halas in his thirty-sixth season as the Bears' coach.

1964

- The Chargers defeat the Patriots 51–10 in the AFL Championship Game.
- Hornung and Karras are reinstated.
- Pete Gogolak of Cornell signs with Buffalo—the first soccer-style kicker in pro football.
- Buffalo defeats San Diego 20–7 in the AFL Championship Game.
- Cleveland defeats Baltimore 27–0 in the NFL Championship Game.

1965

- The NFL adds a sixth official, the line judge. The color of the officials' penalty flags is changed from white to bright gold.
- Field Judge Burl Toler is the first African-American official in NFL history.
- Green Bay defeats Baltimore 13–10 in sudden-death overtime in a Western Conference playoff game.
- The Packers defeat the Browns 23–12 in the NFL Championship Game.
- In the AFL Championship Game, the Bills again defeat the Chargers, 23–0.

1966

- Buddy Young is named Director of Player Relations—the first African-American to work in the league office.
- In the NFL, goal posts are offset from the goal line, painted bright yellow, with uprights twenty feet above the crossbar.
- The AFL–NFL merger is announced. Pete Rozelle is named Commissioner of the expanded league.

1967

- Green Bay defeats Dallas 34–27 in the NFL championship.
- Kansas City defeats Buffalo 31–7 in the AFL.
- The Packers defeat the Chiefs 35–10 in the first game ever between AFL and NFL teams.
- The "slingshot" goal post and a six-foot-wide border around the field are made standard in the NFL.
- Baltimore picks Bubba Smith, a Michigan State defensive lineman, as the first choice in the first combined AFL–NFL draft.
- Defensive back Emlen Tunnell of the New York

Giants is the first African-American player to enter the Pro Football Hall of Fame.

- Denver beats Detroit 13–7 in a preseason game—the first time an AFL team has defeat an NFL team.
- Green Bay defeats Dallas 21–17 for the NFL championship on a last-minute one-yard quarterback sneak by Bart Starr in thirteen-below-zero temperatures at Green Bay.
- Oakland defeats Houston 40–7 for the AFL championship.

1968

- Green Bay defeats Oakland 33–14 in Super Bowl II at Miami, January 14.
- Vince Lombardi resigns as head coach of the Packers, but remains as general manager.
- George Halas retires for the fourth and last time as head coach of the Bears.
- The Oilers play in the Astrodome—the first NFL team to play its home games in a domed stadium.
- NBC drops the last 1:05 of a Jets–Raiders game in order to begin the movie *Heidi* on time. The Raiders scored two touchdowns in the last forty-two seconds to win 43–32.
- Weeb Ewbank becomes the first coach to win titles in both the NFL and AFL—his Jets defeat the Raiders 27–23 for the AFL championship.
- Baltimore defeats Cleveland 34–0 in the NFL championship.

1969

- An AFL team wins the Super Bowl for the first time—the Jets defeat the Colts 16–7 in Super Bowl III.
- Monday Night Football is signed for 1970.

- The NFL marks its fiftieth year.

1970

- Kansas City defeats Minnesota 23–7 in Super Bowl IV.
- The merged twenty-six-team league adopts rules changes: names on the backs of players' jerseys, value of a point after touchdown worth one point, the scoreboard clock the official timing device of the game.
- Vince Lombardi dies of cancer at fifty-seven.
- Tom Dempsey of New Orleans kicks an NFL-record, game-winning, sixty-three-yard field goal against Detroit.

1971

- Baltimore defeats Dallas 16–13 on Jim O'Brien's thirty-two-yard field goal with five seconds to go in Super Bowl V.
- Miami defeats Kansas City 27-24 in sudden-death overtime in the AFC Divisional Playoff Game. After 22 minutes, 40 seconds of overtime, the game lasts 82 minutes, 40 seconds overall—the longest game in history.

This is a game for madmen.

VINCE LOMBARDI,
Green Bay Packers coach (1959–69)

Gridiron Glossary

Part 6

READY LIST: A list of several plays ready to be used in an upcoming game, tailored to an opposing team's strengths and weaknesses.

RECEIVER: A receiver, or pass receiver, is a member of the offense whose job it is to get into the open to catch a pass from the quarterback and then run with the ball. Additionally, in professional football, the end on the left is referred to as a "wide" receiver.

RECOVER: Grabbing a ball that has been fumbled (whether the recovering player's side initially had the ball or not).

RED DOG: A blitz.

REGULAR SEASON: A time period of seventeen weeks during which a team plays sixteen games to determine their ranking going into the postseason tournament.

RETURNER: A player who runs back kickoffs and punts.

REVERSE: A type of offensive play. In a reverse, the player with the ball runs in one direction, then hands off the ball to another player going the opposite direction, reversing the ball's direction of travel.

ROLL: The quarterback rolls when he moves left or right with the ball before throwing it.

ROSTER: A list of the members of a team.

ROUGHING: A personal foul with a fifteen-yard penalty. Called when a player illegally contacts another player, as in roughing the punter, when a player tackles the punter without touching the ball, or roughing the passer, where a defensive player attempts to tackle the quarterback after the ball has been thrown.

RUNBACK: Returning a kickoff, punt, or interception.

RUNNING BACK: Positioned behind the quarterback, there are two running backs, whose job it is to run with the ball, which is typically handed off by the quarterback. Part of the offensive backfield. In college and high school football, there are halfbacks and fullbacks in these positions, but in professional football they are simply the two running backs.

RUSH: To run from the scrimmage line with the ball.

SACK: Tackling the quarterback before he can throw a pass.

SAFETY: When a team forces the opposition to down the ball in their own end zone, the defense receives two points, called a safety. Also, the player position called safety is a defensive backfield position, the deepest in the backfield. There are two safeties.

SAFETY BLITZ: A charge by one or both safeties in an attempt to tackle the quarterback.

SAFETY VALVE: A short pass thrown to a running back when the wide receivers are covered.

SCRAMBLE: An unplanned offensive play in which a quarterback runs behind the line of scrimmage to elude tacklers.

SCRAMBLER: A quarterback who has earned a reputation for scrambling.

SCREEN PASS: A pass from behind the line of scrimmage in a play that allows the rushers to charge through as the offensive linemen fake blocking them, only to set up a wall for a receiver for the pass.

SCRIMMAGE: The action between two teams, starting when the ball is snapped.

SECONDARY: The defensive backfield, or second line of defense.

SHIFT: The movement of two (or more) offensive players between positions.

SIGNAL CALLER: The quarterback.

SIGNALS: The quarterback tells the other players, with signals, what the next play will be. Signals are also used at the line of scrimmage to tell the center when to snap the ball.

SLANT: Running, with the ball, at an angle.

Once, after a long gain, I was walking by the Eagles' huddle and I reached out and pinched Bill Bradley as hard as I could on the arm. He ran to the referee, screaming that I had pinched him and the ref told him they didn't have a penalty for that.

CONRAD DOBLER,
St. Louis Cardinals offensive guard
(1972–81)

Nothing devastates a football team like a selfish player. It's a cancer. The greatest back I ever had was Marion Motley. You know why? The only statistic he ever knew was whether we won or lost. The man was completely unselfish.

PAUL BROWN,
Cleveland Browns coach (1946–62)

Stats

300-Yard Passing Games (1998)

Games	Player	Team
7	Steve Young	San Francisco
4	Drew Bledsoe	New England
4	Randall Cunningham	Minnesota
4	Brett Favre	Green Bay
4	Dan Marino	Miami
4	Peyton Manning	Indianapolis
2	Mark Brunell	Jacksonville
2	Kerry Collins	New Orleans
2	John Elway	Denver
2	Trent Green	Washington
2	Jake Plummer	Arizona
2	Doug Flutie	Buffalo
1	Troy Aikman	Dallas
1	Jeff Blake	Cincinnati
1	Chris Chandler	Atlanta
1	Glenn Foley	New York Jets
1	Rich Gannon	Kansas City
1	Jeff George	Oakland
1	Brad Johnson	Minnesota
1	Erik Kramer	Chicago
1	Neil O'Donnell	Cincinnati
1	Steve Stenstrom	Chicago
1	Vinny Testaverde	New York Jets
1	Billy Joe Tolliver	New Orleans
1	Craig Whelihan	San Diego

Cunningham Alone Can't Do It

Randall Cunningham believes God has led him to the Twin Cities for a simple two-word reason: Super Bowl.

Cunningham's football career has been "born again." After a dozen seasons that saw him become the NFL's all-time leading rusher among quarterbacks, he scrambled completely out of the game, leaving the pocket to retire following the 1995 campaign. Cunningham, 35, contends that not taking a snap in '96 helped get him centered.

"My time away from football got me back in line with what God would have me to do," says Cunningham. "I had to sit back and think. I was really humbled as a person."

Admittedly, this fleet-footed player could no longer run from his Heavenly Pursuer. "Sometimes you get outside God's will, and you don't realize it," he says. "I look at things now as, 'What is God saying to me?' In the past I cared about what the world was saying." That gameless season allowed him to focus on a new strategy for his life and career.

With his personal priorities properly placed, Cunningham felt a fresh focus on football. This newfound perspective is evident as much on the field as off.

The one-time league MVP (1990) is staying in the pocket and using his teammates more than ever before. "I've learned that it's done as a team," he says. "There were times when I thought I could lead a team to a Super Bowl, but now I realize that one person can't do it."

Vikings coach Dennis Green echoes Cunningham's revolutionary realization. "We're not expecting Randall to be our savior. We've got other guys who have to play and hold up their end of the bargain. We're confident that Randall will do the same," says Green.

Cunningham is convinced that he was not ready to experience winning an NFL championship. . .until now. "As a non-Christian, I handled not winning a Super Bowl without a problem. But as a Christian, I believe that God has put me here to play football with a purpose," he explains. "I have to make sure that I stay in His will so He can allow me the time to do it [win a title]. I am just going to have to wait on it."

Does he think it is time for him to claim the NFL crown with the Vikings? "All I know is that it's God's will for me to be here," he says with a smile.

—by TROY PEARSON

The harder we work, the luckier we get.

VINCE LOMBARDI,
Green Bay Packers coach (1959–69)

A Pro Football Chronology

Part 7

1972

- Dallas defeats Miami 24–3 in Super Bowl VI.
- The inbounds lines (hash marks) are moved nearer the center of the field, twenty-three yards, one foot, nine inches from the sidelines.
- Franco Harris's "Immaculate Reception" gives the Steelers their first postseason win ever, 13–7 over the Raiders.

1973

- Miami defeats Washington 14–7 in Super Bowl VII, completing a 17–0 season, the first perfect-record regular-season and postseason mark in NFL history.
- The jersey numbering system is adopted.
- O. J. Simpson of Buffalo is the first player to rush for more than 2,000 yards in a season, gaining 2,003.

1974

- Miami defeats Minnesota 24–7 in Super Bowl VIII at Houston, the second consecutive Super Bowl championship for the Dolphins.
- Rules changes: one sudden-death overtime period added for preseason and regular-season games; the goal posts moved from the goal line to the end lines; kickoffs moved from the forty- to the thirty-five-yard line; after missed field goals from beyond the twenty, the ball to be returned to the line of scrimmage; restrictions placed on members of the punting team to open up return possibilities; roll-blocking and cutting of wide receivers eliminated;

the extent of downfield contact by a defender on an eligible receiver restricted; the penalties for offensive holding, illegal use of the hands, and tripping reduced from fifteen to ten yards; wide receivers blocking back toward the ball within three yards of the line of scrimmage prevented from blocking below the waist.

1975

- Pittsburgh defeats Minnesota 16–6 in Super Bowl IX—the Steelers' first championship since entering the NFL in 1933.
- Referees are equipped with wireless microphones for all games.

1976

- Pittsburgh defeats Dallas 21–17 in Super Bowl X. The Steelers, Green Bay, and Miami are the only teams to win two Super Bowls.
- New rule: adoption of two thirty-second clocks for all games, visible to both players and fans to note the official time between the ready-for-play signal and snap of the ball.

1977

- Oakland defeats Minnesota 32–14 in Super Bowl XI—the fifth consecutive victory for the AFC in the Super Bowl.
- Rules changes: defenders permitted to make contact with eligible receivers only once; the head slap outlawed; offensive linemen prohibited from thrusting their hands to an opponent's neck, face, or head; and wide receivers prohibited from clipping, even in the legal clipping zone.
- Chicago's Walter Payton sets a single-game rushing

record with 275 yards (on forty carries) against Minnesota, November 20.

1978

- Dallas defeats Denver 27–10 in Super Bowl XII—the first victory for the NFC in six years.
- A seventh official, the side judge, is added to the officiating crew.
- Rules changes permit a defender to maintain contact with a receiver within five yards of the line of scrimmage, but restrict contact beyond that point. The pass-blocking rule is interpreted to permit the extending of arms and open hands.
- A study on the use of instant replay as an officiating aid is made during seven nationally televised preseason games.

1979

- Pittsburgh defeats Dallas 35–31 in Super Bowl XIII—becoming the first team ever to win three Super Bowls.
- Rules changes prohibit players on the receiving team from blocking below the waist during kickoffs, punts, and field-goal attempts; prohibit the wearing of torn or altered equipment and exposed pads that could be hazardous; extend the zone in which there could be no crackback blocks; and instruct officials to quickly whistle a play dead when a quarterback is clearly in the grasp of a tackler.

1980

- Pittsburgh defeats the Los Angeles Rams 31–19 in Super Bowl XIV—becoming the first team to win four Super Bowls.

- Rules changes: restrictions on contact in the area of the head, neck, and face; players prohibited from directly striking, swinging, or clubbing on the head, neck, or face.

1981

- Oakland defeats Philadelphia 27–10 in Super Bowl XV—becoming the first wild-card team to win a Super Bowl.

1982

- San Francisco defeats Cincinnati 26–21 in Super Bowl XVI.
- The season is reduced from a sixteen-game schedule to nine as the result of a fifty-seven-day players' strike.

1983

- Because of the shortened season, the NFL adopts a format of sixteen teams in a Super Bowl Tournament for the 1982 playoffs. The NFC's number-one seed, Washington, defeated the AFC's number-two seed, Miami, 27–17 in Super Bowl XVII.
- George Halas, the owner of the Bears and the last surviving member of the NFL's second organizational meeting, dies at 88.

1984

- The Los Angeles Raiders defeat Washington 38–9 in Super Bowl XVIII.
- Many all-time records are set: Dan Marino of Miami passes for 5,084 yards and 48 touchdowns; Eric Dickerson of the Los Angeles Rams rushes for 2,105 yards; Art Monk of Washington catches 106

passes; and Walter Payton of Chicago breaks Jim Brown's career rushing mark, finishing the season with 13,309 yards.

I remember in one game, head down, charging like a bull, [Bronko] Nagurski blasted through two tacklers at the goal line as if they were a pair of old-time saloon doors, through the end zone, and full speed into the brick retaining wall behind it. The sickening thud reverberated throughout the stadium. "That last guy really gave me a good lick," he said to me when he got back to the sideline.

George Halas,
Chicago Bears founder,
owner, player, coach (1920–68)

Football is a game played with arms, legs, and shoulders; but mostly from the neck up.

Knute Rockne,
Notre Dame coach (1918–30)

Gridiron Glossary

Part 7

SLOT: A gap in the offensive line between a receiver and a tackle.

SNAP: The handing of the ball by the center, reaching back between his legs, to the quarterback or punter.

SPEARING: Contacting another player with one's head; a foul in college football.

SPECIAL TEAMS: A special group, or "platoon," of players specializing in one particular maneuver, such as punts or kick-offs. When the maneuver is about to be done, the coach will substitute the special team. Special teams give their all to their specialties and consequently suffer higher injury rates than the rest of the team. That's why they are also called bomb squads or suicide squads.

SPIRAL: The football's rotation, about its longitudinal axis, when it's thrown.

SPLIT END: A receiver who lines up several yards away from the next player along the line of scrimmage.

SQUARE IN/OUT: A pass route where the runner goes downfield, then turns "in" at a "square" or right angle to the center of the field or "out" to the sideline.

STRAIGHTARM: To defend against an opposing tackler by using the hand and arm.

STRONG SIDE: In an unbalanced line, the side with the most players.

STUNT: An unusual charge by the offensive linemen, sometimes in concert with the linebackers, in which they loop around each other during the charge instead of running straight ahead.

SUICIDE SQUAD: See "special teams."

SUBSTITUTION: Putting a player into the game as a

substitute for another. For example, a play requiring a very fast player may cause the coach to bring out one player and replace him with another, faster player.

SUPER BOWL: The National Football League's championship game.

I considered naming the team the Chicago Cubs. . . . But I noted football players are bigger than baseball players; so if baseball players are cubs, then certainly football players must be bears!

George Halas,
Chicago Bears founder, owner,
player, coach (1920–68)

"Trent Dilfer has been saved by Jesus Christ"

Trent Dilfer has just endured the day's first two hours of practice in the Florida sun. He's tired, the sun has scorched his head, and he misses his wife and two children, who are out of town. He doesn't complain. You won't hear him do that. His withered blue eyes tell the story.

He smiles and looks sheepishly at a reporter as they sit in the University of Tampa cafeteria. "Can we maybe do this tomorrow? I'm just really tired, and I'd like to collect my thoughts and do this right."

Dilfer, who in 1997 enjoyed his first Pro Bowl season with the Tampa Bay Buccaneers, realizes that just about every writer in the greater Tampa–St. Petersburg area, and many from across the country, wants to talk to him about the most-anticipated season in franchise history.

He offers to do part of the interview then and there, but continue the rest of it another day—when he's better rested and at a time when he promises he'll be a better interview.

The difference between Trent Dilfer and the average multimillion-dollar athlete is that he cares. He doesn't tell you he won't, he doesn't tell you he can't, and when something changes he asks, "Is that okay?" An unlikely response from a guy who makes more than $4 million a season and has the future of the NFL's most resurgent franchise at his fingertips.

"The interviews aren't that hard," he says about his life as a football star. "Dealing with the kids and the autographs is not that hard. What's difficult is dealing with the parents. The grown-ups are the people that really ruin it for us. They should understand what we're going through in our busyness and our lifestyle, yet they continue to criticize us for not giving all of our free time to be with them and sign their autographs."

Tired as he might be, Dilfer can still talk. And what he enjoys talking about most is his faith and the difference it makes in his life.

"Trent Dilfer has been saved by Jesus Christ," he says. "And all of that other stuff doesn't really matter. That's where my value comes from, and that's why I can handle being criticized in the media. That's why I can handle people calling radio shows and lying about me. That's why I can handle some of the adverse situations I face, and that's why I can handle success.

"Throwing an interception does not change where I stand with God—it's how I deal with the interception that counts. Winning a Super Bowl will not mean anything eternally—it's how I deal with winning the Super Bowl that will make me the kind of person I am."

It may sound as if Dilfer doesn't care what people think, but he does. He cares what people—especially children—think. He's already the center of attention, especially after last season's franchise record twenty-one touchdown passes, but being liked and accepted is something that's important to him. It has been ever since he was a youngster.

Just listen to his mother: "When he was in high school and was probably a much better basketball player than a football player, the first time he was named Player of the Game, when they turned on the TV lights, he was just like a natural," says Marcie Lynch, who suffered through a divorce from Trent's father, Doug, when Trent was just two years old. She married Frank Lynch three years later. "He's always liked the limelight," says Mom.

He grew up looking out for number one and would do anything to become more popular. Dilfer was restless, and although athletics brought him attention, he yearned for more. He was a self-described "show-off."

Trent says it was more about being liked than popular, but it's a different story today. As far as his Buccaneer teammates are concerned, he says, he wants to be respected. "I want to do whatever it takes for them to achieve what we're all trying to achieve, and that's a championship. I don't necessarily get caught up in whether they like me or not, because personalities conflict. But I want them to respect me and I want them to know I'm here for them. I really am. I will be selfless in order to win, if that's what it takes. I'll make the sacrifices, both personally and professionally, to ensure our success as a football team."

It's a different perspective from the one he had as a rookie.

When Dilfer came into the league in 1994, Coach Sam Wyche handed the Bucs' top draft pick (sixth overall) the starting quarterback job over Craig Erickson early in his first year. Yet Erickson still had something that Dilfer wanted—the support of his teammates. Erickson's demotion led to resentment in the locker room, not necessarily because Erickson was the better man for the job, but because the guys liked Erickson. Dilfer has decided that respect is a better way to impress his teammates.

Trent grew up in a Christian home and went to church, but although he played the game of being a Christian, he didn't allow matters of faith to influence his life until the summer before his sophomore year of college at Fresno State University. It was 1992, and Trent was at a Fellowship of Christian Athletes camp in Thousand Oaks, California, where he was a "huddle leader" for ten underprivileged children. Even the camp leaders thought he was a Christian. At the camp, Trent ended up being the pupil instead of the teacher.

As he observed the other counselors, he was impressed with their love for Jesus Christ. He knew he didn't have that love. "These guys just loved me to death," he says. "I saw Christ through them."

At that camp, where he had been brought in to be a counselor, Dilfer prayed a sincere prayer of faith, asking Jesus Christ to be his Savior. "I confessed everything to Him and made a decision to trust Him," he says.

He returned home and told his mother that he'd had a change in his life.

"He lay on the sofa in the family room and cried," says Lynch of her son. "He said he never really realized how much he had." Finally, he was experiencing real faith in Christ.

Trent's life changed in another way around that time as well. He had met and befriended Fresno State swimmer and classmate Cassandra Franzman before attending the FCA camp. Later, regular Bible study brought the couple together, and they were married in July 1993. They've since added to the flock with children Madeleine and Trevin.

"I want to raise kids that are blessings to God," says Trent. "That's the bottom line. That's our goal as parents—to raise children who are blessings to God, who know

Him personally, and who serve Him diligently throughout their life.

"The biggest people I want to be a witness to in my life are my kids. When they're asked about their dad they can say, 'Oh yeah, he played in the NFL, but I want them to say first, 'He loves Jesus.' That's a great, great challenge."

In the past, Trent and Cassandra's Christian lifestyle kept Dilfer from being "one of the guys," but now having the guys' respect and being a righteous man takes precedence.

He won't change. He won't go against his beliefs, but there's still a big part of Trent that wants to be embraced by his teammates. He so much wanted to be accepted that in his second season he went along with teammates to a handful of bars, but he found himself feeling like a fish out of water. His prayer life, studying God's Word, being discipled, and fellowship with other believers have helped him to achieve the consistency that is now so evident in his life.

"It's hard, but I want to be real," says Dilfer. "They all know where I stand and there are certain things I won't compromise, but at the same time I don't mind being real."

Football Fortunes

Since Trent was the son of a physical education teacher and coach, it would seem only natural that he would excel on the gridiron. As a preadolescent, he was a waterboy and ballboy for Aptos High School near Santa Cruz, California, where he understood the offense better than the quarterbacks.

"He was a student of every game he's been involved

in. He knew the offense better than my college quarterbacks," says Frank Lynch, Dilfer's mentor and stepfather, who coached for both Aptos High and Cabrillo College, a community college in Aptos. "He and I used to banter back and forth about what to do in certain situations when we were watching games. He enjoys the mental part of the game and the logistics and dissecting the game."

After a successful football career at Aptos High, where he was a two-time All-Conference selection in both basketball and football, Dilfer headed to one of the three schools that recruited him. Santa Clara and Northern Arizona also offered the four-sport letterman (golf, basketball, football, baseball) a scholarship, but Dilfer decided to play for the Bulldogs in the Western Athletic Conference.

At Fresno State, he got his first chance as a redshirt freshman when starting quarterback Mark Barsotti was injured. As expected, Dilfer was nervous, but he stepped in, started the final four games of the season, and helped his club to a berth in the California Raisin Bowl.

In Dilfer's sophomore year, Fresno State was playing at San Diego State for the right to go to the Freedom Bowl. Fresno State led in the fourth quarter, but SDSU scored and took the lead with just three minutes left in the game. Dilfer drove the Bulldogs the length of the field before facing a fourth-and-goal on the six-yard line with ten seconds left. The sophomore then promptly tossed a perfect fade to Tydus Winans in the corner of the end zone for the winning score.

Former Fresno State teammate and current Buccaneer teammate Lorenzo Neal says, "In that play, he showed some leadership, and he showed poise as a sophomore and in a game of that magnitude. I was like, 'Boy, this kid can play.' To do that in that type of game and that type of environment you just say, 'Hey, this guy's arrived.' "

From there, Dilfer truly typified the excellence of execution. In 1993, his junior and final year of college, Dilfer set an NCAA record by throwing 318 passes without an interception. In just his second full season starting, he drew the interest of pro scouts by running the Bulldogs' pro-style offense to perfection and throwing for twenty-eight touchdowns with just four interceptions.

Dilfer's first two years in the NFL weren't so glorious. Doubts began to surface among some experts about his ability to get the job done in the big time. But then along came Tony Dungy and the new "plan" the man brought to the team.

"We wanted to build from the ground up," Dungy says of his plan. "But there was a lot of foundation here. I just felt that if the guys believed in what we were trying to do, it would go well. We got some guys to believe that, and it's starting to come."

Dungy surprised Dilfer in their first year together by telling him that he would have to win the starting job in training camp, but that if he did, he was their guy. He was the one they would stick with, win or lose. Dilfer respected that, and he responded by recording career highs in passing yardage (2,859), completions (267), and attempts (482), even though the Bucs went 6–10.

Tampa Bay ended the 1996 season winning five of its last seven games, catapulting the Buccaneers and Dilfer into 1997, the most successful season in franchise history. The Bucs opened the season by winning their first five games, and the team went on to the playoffs for the first time in fifteen years. The end came in a disappointing 21–7 loss to the Green Bay Packers, but Tampa Bay showed it had arrived when a league-high eight players, including Dilfer, were named to the Pro Bowl.

The Pro Bowl selection followed a year that saw

Dilfer start every game for the third consecutive season, connect on 217 of 386 passes for a career-best 56.2 completion percentage, and throw a team-record 152 passes without an interception.

The numbers, accolades, and life he keeps in perspective.

"I've learned some very valuable lessons through football. I'm at the point now where I'm excited about how I'm going to grow spiritually," says Dilfer. "I'm excited because I know the Lord's going to make me richer spiritually. I don't know if it's going to be through failure, I don't know if He's going to do it through success—but I know I'm going to grow."

—by BUDDY SHACKLETTE

They say I teach brutal football, but the only thing brutal about football is losing.

PAUL "BEAR" BRYANT,
University of Alabama coach (1958–82)

A Pro Football Chronology

Part 8

1985

- San Francisco defeats Miami 38–16 in Super Bowl XIX.

1986

- Chicago defeats New England 46–10 in Super Bowl XX. The Patriots are the first wild card team to win three consecutive games on the road.
- Limited use of instant replay as an officiating aid is adopted.
- Players are prohibited from wearing or otherwise displaying equipment, apparel, or other items that carry commercial names, names of organizations, or personal messages of any type.
- Instant replay is used to reverse two plays in thirty-one preseason games. During the regular season, 374 plays are closely reviewed by replay officials, leading to 38 reversals in 224 games. Eighteen plays are closely reviewed by instant replay in ten postseason games with three reversals.

1987

- The New York Giants defeat Denver 39–20 in Super Bowl XXI—their first NFL title since 1956.
- The 1987 season is reduced from a sixteen-game season to fifteen as the result of a twenty-four-day players' strike.
- Instant replay is used to reverse eight plays in fifty-two preseason games. During the strike-shortened 210-game regular season, 490 plays are closely reviewed by replay officials, leading to fifty-seven

reversals. Eighteen plays are closely reviewed by instant replay in ten postseason games, with three reversals.

1988

- Washington defeats Denver 42–10 in Super Bowl XXII.
- The instant replay system is retained for the third consecutive season; the instant replay official is assigned to a regular seven-man, on-the-field crew. A forty-five-second clock is approved to replace the thirty-second clock. The interval between plays is changed to forty-five seconds from the time the ball is signaled dead until it is snapped on the succeeding play.
- Johnny Grier becomes the first African-American referee in NFL history.

1989

- San Francisco defeats Cincinnati 20–16 in Super Bowl XXIII.
- Commissioner Pete Rozelle announces his retirement.
- The instant replay system continues for the fourth straight season. The policy regarding anabolic steroids and masking agents is strengthened. NFL clubs called for strong disciplinary measures in cases of feigned injuries.
- Art Shell is named head coach of the Los Angeles Raiders, making him the NFL's first African-American head coach since Fritz Pollard coached the Akron Pros in 1921.
- Paul Tagliabue becomes the seventh chief executive of the NFL.

1990

- San Francisco defeats Denver 55–10 in Super Bowl XXIV—making the 49ers and Pittsburgh the only teams to win four Super Bowls.
- A limited system of instant replay is adopted.
- Dr. John Lombardo appointed as the league's Drug Advisor for Anabolic Steroids. Dr. Lawrence Brown named as the league's Advisor for Drugs of Abuse.
- For the first time since 1957, every NFL club won at least one of its first four games.

1991

- New York defeats Buffalo 20–19 in Super Bowl XXV—the Giants' second title in five years.
- Instant replay continues for the sixth consecutive year.
- Paul Brown, founder of the Cleveland Browns and Cincinnati Bengals, dies at age eighty-two.

1992

- Washington defeats the Buffalo Bills 37–24 in Super Bowl XXVI—the Redskins' third championship in ten years.
- The use of a limited system of instant replay is rejected.

1993

- Dallas defeats the Buffalo Bills 52–17 in Super Bowl XXVII—the Cowboys' first NFL title since 1978.
- Don Shula becomes the winningest coach in NFL history with 325 victories, one more than George Halas.

1994

- Dallas defeats the Buffalo Bills 30–13 in Super Bowl XXVIII—as the Cowboys become the fifth team to win back-to-back Super Bowl titles.
- Rules changes: modifications in line play, chucking rules, and the roughing-the-passer rule; adoption of the two-point conversion and moving the spot of the kickoff back to the thirty-yard line.
- The NFL celebrates its seventy-fifth anniversary.

1995

- The San Francisco 49ers become the first team to win five Super Bowls by defeating the San Diego Chargers 49–26 in Super Bowl XXIX.
- Rules changes adopted primarily relate to the use of the helmet against defenseless players.
- Many significant records and milestones are achieved: Miami's Dan Marino surpasses Pro Football Hall of Famer Fran Tarkenton in four major passing categories—attempts, completions, yards, and touchdowns—to become the NFL's all-time career leader. San Francisco's Jerry Rice becomes the all-time reception and receiving-yardage leader with career totals of 942 catches and 15,123 yards. Dallas's Emmitt Smith scores twenty-five touchdowns, breaking the season record of twenty-four set by Washington's John Riggins in 1983.

1996

- The Dallas Cowboys win their third Super Bowl title in four years by defeating the Pittsburgh Steelers 27–17 in Super Bowl XXX.
- Former NFL Commissioner Pete Rozelle dies.

Rozelle, regarded as the premiere commissioner in sports history, led the NFL for twenty-nine years, from 1960–1989.

1997

- The Green Bay Packers win their first NFL title in twenty-nine years by defeating the New England Patriots 35–21 in Super Bowl XXXI.
- The ten-thousandth regular-season game in NFL history is played when the Seattle Seahawks defeat the Tennessee Oilers 16–13 at the Kingdome in Seattle.

1998

- The Denver Broncos win their first Super Bowl by defeating the defending champion Green Bay Packers 31–24 in Super Bowl XXXII.

1999

- The Denver Broncos again win the Super Bowl, defeating Atlanta 34–19 in Super Bowl XXXIII.

I once asked [offensive lineman] Dave Herman how his wife enjoyed coming to the games. "All she looks for," he said, "is to see whether I get up or not."

PAUL ZIMMERMAN,
Sports Illustrated writer

Gridiron Glossary

Part 8

TACKLE: To bring down another player. For example, to sack the quarterback is to tackle him. Also an offensive position. There are two tackles, one outside each guard, whose job is to block the onrushing defensive line and open up holes for a runner.

TAILBACK: A member of the offensive backfield whose job is to run with the ball. Also called a running back or halfback.

THREE-POINT STANCE: The position players at the line of scrimmage take before the snap, leaning forward on one hand with their feet spread.

TIME: In professional and college football, the game is limited to sixty minutes (forty-eight minutes in high school football). This is divided into two thirty-minute halves, each of which is divided into two fifteen-minute quarters, or "periods." In between the two halves is halftime, which lasts fifteen minutes. If the teams are tied at the end of the time limit, the game goes into overtime, continuing until one of the teams pulls ahead.

TOUCHBACK: A touchback occurs when the defensive team gains possession of the ball in their own end zone on the same play in which the offensive team caused the ball to cross the goal line.

TOUCHDOWN: Carrying the ball into or catching the ball in the opposition's end zone. Worth six points.

TRAP BLOCK: When a player is allowed through the enemy line only to be blocked by surprise from another player behind the line. Also called a mousetrap.

TURN IN/OUT: A pass route where the player runs

downfield, then turns in toward the middle of the field or out toward the sidelines.

TURNOVER: Losing possession of the ball, typically by error.

UNBALANCED LINE: A formation with more players on one side of the center than the other.

UPRIGHTS: Vertical posts supporting the crossbar in the goalpost.

WEAK SIDE: The side of an unbalanced line with the least players.

ZONE DEFENSE: A defense strategy where each player has an area, or "zone," of the field to defend. See also "man-to-man defense."

When we had the head slap, that's when they had some real football. Blood and stuff trickling down your legs. You don't hardly see no snaggle-toothed linemen anymore. Everything's changed. All of 'em got teeth.

CHARLIE JOHNSON,
San Francisco 49ers noseguard (1966–68)

Boom Town Eisenhauer

Larry Eisenhauer was the defensive end for the Patriots in the old AFL. One afternoon a San Diego Charger public relations man stopped by and handed the Boston players a bunch of "Charley Charger" coloring books. The Patriots took them over to poolside, and the rumor that night was the Eisenhauer had spent the rest of his day coloring his Charley Charger book.

"It's a lie," he said later. "I wasn't coloring the thing. I was just reading it."

Before games Eisenhauer was one of the noted dressing room maniacs. He'd attack walls, lockers, anything that got in his way. On the field he played with a wild intensity seldom seen today. Boston used to have a daytime kiddie show in those days called "Boom Town," featuring Rex Trailer and his sidekick, Pablo. One day they decided to film a show at Fenway Park, and the action would center around the Patriots football team. Pablo would grab the ball and run for a TD, with all the Patriots chasing him. Eisenhauer was picked to be one of the chasers.

Once the action started, though, a hidden bell clanged and all the 6′5″, 250-pounder saw was an enemy player running for a touchdown, a guy who had to be stopped. So he stopped him.

"I'm kind of ashamed of it now," he said later. "Pablo was only about 5′3″, and he was slow, so it wasn't any trick catching him. I didn't really hurt him; I just sort of jumped on his back. Why give the guy a free touchdown?"

Stats

100-Yard Receiving Games (1998)

GAMES	PLAYER	TEAM
6	Antonio Freeman	Green Bay
5	Wayne Chrebet	New York Jets
5	Tony Martin	Atlanta
5	Frank Sanders	Arizona
5	Jimmy Smith	Jacksonville
4	Joey Galloway	Seattle
4	Terry Glenn	New England
4	Keyshawn Johnson	New York Jets
4	Ed McCaffrey	Denver
4	Herman Moore	Detroit
4	Eric Moulds	Buffalo
4	Rod Smith	Denver
4	Michael Westbrook	Washington
4	Randy Moss	Minnesota
3	Tim Brown	Oakland
3	Cris Carter	Minnesota
3	Sean Dawkins	New Orleans
3	Bobby Engram	Chicago
3	Marshall Faulk	Indianapolis
3	Michael Irvin	Dallas
3	Raghib Ismail	Carolina
3	Terance Mathis	Atlanta
3	O. J. McDuffie	Miami
3	Johnnie Morton	Detroit
3	Muhsin Muhammad	Carolina
3	Jerry Rice	San Francisco
2	Derrick Alexander	Kansas City
2	Isaac Bruce	St. Louis
2	Marvin Harrison	Indianapolis
2	Garrison Hearst	San Francisco

Games	Player	Team
2	Shawn Jefferson	New England
2	James Jett	Oakland
2	Jermaine Lewis	Baltimore
2	Keenan McCardell	Jacksonville
2	Rob Moore	Arizona
2	Terrell Owens	San Francisco
2	Carl Pickens	Cincinnati
2	Darnay Scott	Cincinnati
2	Torrance Small	Indianapolis
2	Bryan Still	San Diego
2	J.J. Stokes	San Francisco
2	Floyd Turner	Baltimore
1	Reidel Anthony	Tampa Bay
1	Brett Bech	New Orleans
1	Brandon Bennett	Cincinnati
1	Ben Coates	New England
1	Albert Connell	Washington
1	Stephen Davis	Washington
1	Rickey Dudley	Oakland
1	Bert Emanuel	Tampa Bay
1	Oronde Gadsden	Miami
1	Andre Hastings	New Orleans
1	Courtney Hawkins	Pittsburgh
1	Ike Hilliard	New York Giants
1	Charles Johnson	Pittsburgh
1	James McKnight	Seattle
1	Ernie Mills	Dallas
1	Keith Poole	New Orleans
1	Ricky Proehl	St. Louis
1	Andre Reed	Buffalo
1	Jake Reed	Minnesota
1	Chris Sanders	Tennessee
1	Bill Schroeder	Green Bay

Games	Player	Team
1	Leslie Shepherd	Washington
1	Yancey Thigpen	Tennessee
1	Lamar Thomas	Miami
1	Chris Penn	Chicago
1	Mark Carrier	Carolina
1	Cameron Cleeland	New Orleans
1	Tony Simmons	New England

Question to Norm Van Brocklin, Los Angeles Rams quarterback (1949–60): What's your favorite play?
Answer: "Our Town" by Thornton Wilder.

I've compared offensive linemen to the story of Paul Revere. After Paul Revere rode through town everybody said what a great job he did. But no one ever talked about the horse. I know how Paul Revere's horse felt.

Gene Upshaw,
Oakland Raiders offensive guard
(1967–81)

References

Christian's Faith—from *Sports Spectrum,* December 1998.

Pro Football Chronology—adapted from *NFL Record & Fact Book,* http://www.nfl.com

Gridiron Glossary—adapted from *Football Dictionary,* http://www.football.com.

The Stats—compiled from http://www.nfl.com.

Bruce Matthews' Be-all, End-all—from *Sports Spectrum,* January/February 1999.

Trying to Find a Way to Give God the Glory—from *Sports Spectrum,* January/February 1999.

A Good Name and Loving Esteem—from *Sports Spectrum,* January/February 1999.

Those Trusty Placekickers—from *Sports Spectrum,* November 1998.

The Big Bucks and Jerry Kramer—from *Farewell to Football* by Jerry Kramer. World Publishing, 1969.

Cunningham Alone Can't Do It—from *Sports Spectrum,* January/February 1999.

Trent Dilfer has been saved by Jesus Christ—from *Sports Spectrum,* November 1998.

Boom Town Eisenhauer—from *The Fireside Book of Pro Football,* Richard Whittingham, ed. Simon and Schuster, 1989.

SPORTS
Chad Curtis and Friends
SPORTS
David Robinson
The Admiral
Talks about his family, his faith, and Dennis Rodman
Chad
Curtis
SPURS
50
SPORTS
Tom Lehman?
A Special Report
Mark Brunell
Also
ESPN
Harold Reynolds
Racer
Terry MacDonald
Paul Henderson